Lieberman's
Day

Stuart Kaminsky

Lieberman's Day

WHEELER
PUBLISHING, INC.

★ AN AMERICAN COMPANY ★

Copyright © 1994 by Stuart Kaminsky.

Published in Large Print by arrangement with Henry
Holt and Company, Inc.
in the United States and Canada.

Wheeler Large Print Book Series.

Set in 16 pt. Plantin.

Library of Congress Cataloging-in-Publication Data

Kaminsky, Stuart M.
    Lieberman's day / Stuart Kaminsky.
        p.   cm.
    ISBN 1-56896-115-9 : $23.95
    1. Large type books.   2. Lieberman, Abe (Fictitious character)—
Fiction.   3. Police—Illinois—Chicago—Fiction.   4. Chicago
(Ill.)—Fiction.   I. Title.
    [PS3561.A43L495   1994b]
    813'.54—dc20   94-12987
                                                              CIP

To Jim and Margaret Taylor,
who know well the city of which
you now shall read

In such a state, my friends, one cannot
be moderate and restrained nor pious either.
Evil is all around me, evil
is what I am compelled to practice.

—Sophocles, Electra

Two Minutes Past Midnight
on a Winter's Night
in Chicago

Cold.

The frozen-fingered wind goes mad and howls, beating the lid of the overflowing green dumpster in a metal-against-metal tattoo. Ba-bom, *boom-boom*.

Through the narrow slit between the concrete of the two high-rise buildings, Lake Michigan, not quite frozen at the shore, throws dirty ice chunks onto the narrow beach and retreats with a warning roar.

"It is cold, man. I tell you. I don't care what you say. I don't care how you say. It is cold."

George DuPelee, his huge body shivering, his shiny black face contorted and taut, shifted from booted foot to booted foot. George wore a knit hat pulled down over his ears and an oversized olive drab military overcoat draped down to his ankles. He was hugging himself with unmatched wool gloves, one red and white, the other solid purple.

Boom-boom.

George grabbed the frigid rusting metal of the dumpster lid and pushed it down on the frozen plastic sacks of garbage inside it. The angry wind

1

rattled the lid in his hand and it broke free. Boom-boom-boom-boom.

"What are you doing?" Raymond whispered irritably, adjusting his glasses.

"Goddamn noise driving me nuts," George whispered back. "I don't like none of this none. I don't like this cold."

George certainly looked cold to Raymond Carrou, who stood beside him in the nook behind the massive garbage cans. Raymond was lean, not an ounce of fat to protect him under his Eddie Bauer jacket, and he, too, was cold; not as cold as George DuPelee, but cold.

It was December in Chicago. It was supposed to be cold. People like George and Raymond didn't come here from Trinidad to enjoy the warm days and cool nights. People came to the States to make a dollar or to get away from something.

George DuPelee was a complainer. Raymond had known George for only a few days and he was now deciding that, however this business turned out, after tonight he would deal no more with the whining giant whose teeth rattled loudly as the two men waited for an acceptable victim to come out of the apartment building.

By the dim light of the mist-shrouded street-lamp, George watched the cars no more than twenty yards away on Sheridan Road lug through the slush, sending sprays of filthy ice over the sidewalk. Sheridan Road at this point north of Lawrence was a canyon of high-rise condominiums through which the wind yowled at the cars that passed through on the way to Evanston going north or downtown going south.

"Tell me you ain't cold," George challenged. "Tell me. Skinny thing like you. Got no fat. Wind go through your bones and you no more used of this than me." George concluded with a grunt of limited satisfaction, pulling his hat more tightly over his ears and continuing his steady foot-to-foot shuffle.

"Cold never bothered me much," said Raymond, watching as the door to the building opened and an old couple came out already leaning into the night as the blast of icy air ran frozen across their faces and down their backs.

"Them, they old, rich, no trouble, no bubble," said George, his bulky body nudging Raymond toward the light beyond the shadows of the buildings and the dumpster.

Raymond watched the old couple struggle against the cold wind. The old man almost toppled over, but caught his balance just in time and moved cautiously forward, gasping through the wind, reaching behind him to pull the old woman with him.

"No," said Raymond, stepping back into the shadow so the old couple wouldn't see him.

"No," moaned George, turning completely around in a circle like a frustrated child. "No. Man, what we come all the way down here for? Places closer. Over back there on Chestnut, you know? Look at those old olds. They got money, rings, stuff. Just take it, throw them old people in the air and let the wind take them."

"Up," said Raymond, his eyes back on the entrance to the high-rise condo building.

"Up?"

"Up," said Raymond. "We came uptown, north, not downtown."

George stopped turning and looked as if he was going to cry.

"Up, down, what's the difference here? I got no watch. I got no need. I got no job like you got."

Raymond ignored him and looked up one-two-three-four-five-six floors to a lighted window covered with frost. A shape, a woman, stood in the window.

"Carol?"

Carol turned away from the window and faced Charlotte Flynn.

"Carol, are you all right?" Charlotte said. "You look . . ."

"Fine," said Carol, touching the older woman's hand and giving her a small, pained smile. "Just tired."

"God," said Charlotte looking at her watch. "I . . . It's past midnight. Poor thing. You must be exhausted."

Carol shrugged.

Charlotte was a sleek, elegant woman in a simple black dress. Charlotte was plastic-surgery taut with a cap of perfect silver hair. Charlotte

4

had been the wife of a television station manager for more years than Carol had been on earth. And Charlotte's husband was, for another month, the boss of Carol's husband, David. In one month, David was being transferred by the network to New York City where he would be program manager. Not exactly higher in rank or salary than Bernie Flynn, the jobs were not parallel, but certainly equal to Bernie with the promise, no, the likelihood, that David would one day be Bernie's boss if Bernie did not retire or move on.

And so, the evening had been, as Carol knew it would be, awkward. Awkward and long. Carol wondered at least five times, through poached salmon she could barely touch and conversation that had an edge sharp enough to cut a throat, whether she could keep from screaming.

"I think David should get you home," Charlotte said gently, taking Carol's hand. "Your hands are freezing."

"Circulation," said Carol. "Doctor says its normal."

"I don't remember," Charlotte said. "My last, youngest, Megan, is thirty-four. I have a vague sense of being pregnant for two or three years and suffering two hours of something white and loud that must have been pain."

Carol nodded.

"Oh, God," Charlotte said, closing her eyes and shaking her head. "That was a stupid thing for me to say."

5

"It's all right," Carol said. "Really. I think we should go."

"Sit down," Charlotte said. "I'll get David and your coat."

The older woman strode confidently through the thick-gray-carpeted living room / dining room furnished in contemporary Scandinavian white wood, the look broken up only by the out-of-place yet tasteful eighteenth-century English oak sideboard that Bernie Flynn had brought back from England a decade ago when he covered a summit meeting in London. The sideboard had been converted to a bar. Bernie had converted to Republican conservatism, and Charlotte had converted to three drinks in the afternoon and Catholicism. At least that was what David told Carol, and the conversation had tended to support his observations.

Carol folded her hands, which felt cold even to her, as Bernie and David entered the room. Bernie was tall, workout lean, and winter tan. His hair was full and white. He looked every bit as camera-ready as he had for almost ten years before becoming an affiliate executive. The sleeves of Bernie's red sweater were pulled back. The collar of his shirt was open. His arm was around David, who was almost six inches shorter and ten pounds heavier.

"Carol," Bernie said, moving to her side with a show of large white teeth that were, indeed, his own. "I'm sorry. All my fault. We were talking business and . . ."

"We were talking replacements," said David seriously.

Carol's eyes met her husband's. She saw concern and question.

"What's wrong, Carol?"

"Just tired," she said. "We should go."

"Got your coats right here," said Charlotte, hurrying back into the room.

"Might be a good idea to check in with your doctor in the morning," Bernie said, helping her on with her fur coat. "You look . . ."

". . . very pregnant," David said, pulling on his Eddie Bauer jacket.

"I think I *will* call the doctor in the morning," Carol said.

David reached for her arm, but she took a quick step forward to hug Charlotte. They all moved to the apartment door and went into the hallway where the women moved ahead toward the elevator.

"None of my business," Bernie whispered, "but Carol doesn't look well."

"*Rosemary's Baby* syndrome," David whispered back. "She's a little ambivalent. Doctor says it's natural."

"And I say it's natural," Bernie said softly. "Charlotte came close to not having our last. Between you, me, and the one-too-many double Scotches I just had, she almost decided on an abortion, long before they were politically correct."

Ahead of them Charlotte was supporting Carol

and whispering to her. Probably, David thought, revealing some small, confidential sin of her husband's. It had been an awkward evening. An evening of ambivalence with Bernie shifting from proud mentor to comically envious rival to potential underling.

David hadn't wanted to come. He had given Carol a list of last-minute excuses, the best of which was Carol's sixth month of pregnancy and a night of cheek-freezing cold. But Carol had insisted on going, had been willing, it seemed, to even fight about it when he insisted.

"It's the last time," she had said. "It's the right thing to do."

"You hate them," David had reminded her as they got ready to leave that evening.

"I dislike them," Carol had corrected, hands trembling.

"Look at you," David had insisted.

"Look at yourself," Carol had answered shrilly.

And then she regretted it. David had let himself go, though he was less than forty. He had a little belly and his father's heavy, sad dark face.

"Let's hope the baby doesn't look like me," David had said bitterly.

Carol had laughed.

"What's so funny?"

She had taken to laughing, crying at odd times for no reason that made sense to David. And it had gotten worse as Carol grew more and more obviously pregnant. David's mother had assured

8

him that this was not abnormal. His aunt Esther had assured him. Doctor Saper had assured him, but it made David feel no better.

The elevator eased to a halt and the doors opened.

"We had a great time," David said, shaking Bernie's hand. "I won't forget all you've done for me and taught me."

"And I know you'll make me proud of you," Bernie said.

"Come on, guys," Charlotte said. "The lady's tired."

David joined his wife in the elevator, faced forward with a smile, and watched the doors close on Charlotte and Bernie, whose arm was around his wife's shoulder, hugging her close to him.

"What a man," David said. "Everyone knows he's *shtupping* Betty the receptionist, who's young enough to be his granddaughter. And there he stands. Big-city Gothic."

"Maybe he needs to be appreciated as a man," Carol said.

"Carol. Wrong is wrong. Family is family."

"Bertrand Russell, Immanuel Kant?" Carol said.

"You O.K., Carol?" David asked, taking his wife's arm as she tottered backward a step as the elevator dropped.

"I'll be fine," she said as the elevator bounced to a stop and the doors opened to the lobby.

"We don't need stoicism here, honey," David said, holding her. "The baby . . ."

9

"The baby will be fine, David," she said. "The baby will be fine."

Raymond had known from the start that George was stupid. He was beginning to think that George might actually be feeble-minded like Jack-Jack Shorely's sister back on the island. She babble-babbled like George, sounded like she was making sense from a distance, but if you listened long enough you could start getting feeble-minded like her.

"Quiet," said Raymond.

"Got to keep everything working, mouth, feets, knees, neck or it gonna freeze," whined George. "Cold gonna kill me dead. Cold is no good for a big man. You ever see any fat Eskeemos?"

"I never see any Eskimos," said Raymond.

Inside the building he was watching, beyond the frosted windows, the doorman stood up and moved to the inside door. Two shapes inside, another couple.

"Eskimos look like Chinese," said George, squinting. "Like this. Only not."

The doorman opened the inner door and the couple stepped into the outer lobby, little more than a glassed-in square with a desk and phone for the doorman.

"Them," said Raymond.

George stopped shuffling and stepped to Raymond's side.

The couple was in their thirties, maybe. The

man was not big, but he was bigger than the old man they had let pass and a lot younger.

"Why?" asked George.

"Look like he has got money," said Raymond, letting himself slide into the Islands patois he had struggled to lose. He wondered why he was doing it. To make George more comfortable? To make himself more comfortable with what he was about to do. "I know these things. Look at those coats. That's a fur she's wearing. You want to stand here all night? Maybe no one else come out for hours."

"No," said George, rocking as the doorman opened the outer door for the couple.

Raymond and George could hear the couple thanking the doorman as a gasp of driving air hit the man and woman and pushed at the open door. The doorman put his shoulder to the door from the inside and closed it as the couple moved past the empty stone fountain in the circular driveway.

Boom-boom-boom. The gray-green dumpster clanged next to George's ears. Behind him waves hurled grating ice chunks and rage.

"Let's go," said Raymond.

Happy to be moving, thinking of someplace, anyplace warm, George almost knocked Raymond over as they stepped out of the rattling protective shadows of the dumpster.

Raymond looked back at the condo lobby. The doorman was sitting at his desk, a magazine open in front of him, one leg folded over the other.

11

"Slow," whispered Raymond. "Slow."

"I remember," George grunted.

The couple talked, but the two men could not hear what they were saying. The man said something and held the woman's hand. The woman sounded nervous. The man wore a jacket much like Raymond's, but this Eddie Bauer was new, clean, not a hand-me-down from who-knows-where. The jacket was nice, but it was the man's hat, one of those Russian fur hats, that fascinated George. The woman's head was uncovered except for fuzzy white earmuffs. In the blue-white streetlights and the cold gray of the building windows, her hair looked like silver frost.

George looked down the street in both directions as Raymond held him back with a hand on his sleeve, giving the couple a twenty-yard lead. Raymond checked the doorman again. He was still looking at his magazine.

No one on the street now but the four of them and a slow sea of cars, see-no-evil cars moving past through the river of slush.

"They gettin' away," George whispered, trying to move ahead.

Raymond held the bigger man's sleeve.

"They goin' for their car, looks like," he said.

The couple, still talking, moved ahead slowly, the man's arm supporting the woman. The distance between the couple and the two men narrowed.

"Now, now, now," Raymond suddenly urged, and both men hurried forward.

George almost fell. He reached for the chill branches of a bare bush next to the building and kept himself erect.

Now the couple was next to the black metal gate of a fence around an old gray house, a holdout family home in the forest of high-rises. A brass plaque against the house identified it as the offices of J.W.R. Ranpur, M.D., Cardiologist. There were no lights on in the home and office of Dr. Ranpur. Raymond had checked this only half an hour earlier. He had also checked to be sure the metal gate was open.

"Stop," Raymond said, stepping in front of the couple.

As he had been told to do, George moved close behind the man and woman, hovering over them.

The couple stopped.

Now Raymond, by the hazy light of the nearby streetlamp, could see the faces of his victims. The woman was pale, pretty, with a round, frightened face whose cheeks were chilled pink. The man, who seemed curious but not frightened, was short, a bit on the pudgy side. He wore glasses that were partly frosted along the upper rim.

"In here," said Raymond, opening the gate, watching to be sure no cars stopped.

It would, he hoped, look like nothing more than four people chatting in front of a house.

"What's going on?" asked the man.

Raymond removed his hand from his pocket and showed the pudgy man his gun, a gun he had bought only the day before for fifteen dollars and which he was not at all sure would fire.

"Step in there, man," he said, nodding through the gate. "You lose a few dollars and you and the lady go on."

"I don't . . ." the man started.

"Come on, come on here," George said, pulling out his own gun and shoving it into the back of the man with the Russian fur hat. George wanted that hat. But more than the hat he wanted to be out of there.

"David," the woman said, "do it. Give them your wallet."

"Not out here," Raymond hissed, looking back over his shoulder. "Get through the gate, man."

With George following close behind, the woman pulled at the arm of the man with the hat, and they edged through the gate.

Frozen grass crunched under George's feet as he pushed the man and woman toward the shadows of Dr. Ranpur's house.

"I'll give it to you," said David. "Let's not panic here."

"No one is panicking, man," said Raymond, looking toward the house and then the street. "Just don't give trouble."

"Come on, come on," George said, reaching up to remove his hat and shoving it in his pocket before yanking the man's hat from his head and putting it on his own. The hat was just a little too small and gave him an instant headache. But it was warm.

Without a hat the white man in front of him looked younger than George had thought him, even though the man's hair was getting thin. He reminded George of some actor.

"Take what you want," David said, holding one hand protectively in front of Carol and reaching into the pocket under his jacket with the other. "Just don't touch her. She's going to . . ."

"Touch . . . ? What you think we are?" asked George indignantly. "You think we gonna rape your woman out here like on an iceberg? What you think we are?"

Raymond took the wallet from David and shoved it into the frayed pocket of his blue ski jacket.

"Shut up," he said.

Carol let out a small sound like an island dove and her bareheaded husband took her in his arms.

"David," she said softly. "Please . . ."

"Don't you be saying that in front of these people," said George, facing Raymond. "Don't you be putting me down like you some kind of boss man."

"Fur," said Raymond, pointing his gun at the woman.

"She'll . . ." David began.

"Then you just give her your Eddie Bauer," said Raymond. "Better yet: I give her my Eddie Bauer and take yours."

Carol was whimpering now as she pulled away from David and began to take off the fur.

"No," said David.

George stepped forward, pushed David back, and pulled the fur coat to his chest the instant Carol had taken it off. Soft, cool fur brushed gently against his cheek.

"We got no time for this," said Raymond.

David took a step toward his wife, lost his footing, and crashed into the front steps of the office-home of J.W.R. Ranpur. His knee hit wood with a chill thump and crack.

Carol screamed. Without her fur, she looked pitiful, not cold, in a blue-and-white dress that hung on her like one of George's mother's shifts.

"Shit," said George. "She gonna have a baby."

And then, as David pulled himself up from the steps, George heard the snap of a hammer against rock. Carol screamed again as David staggered back and sat spread-legged on the stairs.

Cars rushed by. Lake waves battered the shore behind the house. George thought he heard the clang-boom of the rusting green dumpster and then the sound of hammer and rock again. The man called David was sprawled on the steps now, his Eddie Bauer stained with black splotches, and George understood. Raymond had shot the man.

George felt a rush of warm imagined air from the beach of his childhood and the pain of the hat's tightness on his head. His eyes met Raymond's, and George was afraid of what he saw.

"Let's go," said Raymond. "George, you hear, let's go."

George didn't move. He turned to the woman,

whose eyes were wide with terror. Her mouth was open and she couldn't catch her breath. The way she looked at him. Oh, the way she looked. She would haunt him. He knew that. She would haunt them both.

Raymond pulled at the big man's sleeve.

"Let's go," he commanded.

George looked at the man sprawled on the steps and then at the crying woman in the blue dress, her head moving from side to side with fear in the winter chill. He could not live with that look.

George was not fully aware of what he did next. His body, his arms, his hands did what they were commanded, but the orders came from something slithering beneath his skin in the bloodred caverns of his skull.

George fired at the accusing woman. His gun was bigger than Raymond's, much bigger. He fired only once, but it sat the woman down, open-mouthed, surprised. She looked up, not at George who had shot her, but at Raymond, who turned suddenly on George, his gun leveled at the bigger man's chest.

"You crazy bastard," Raymond screamed. "The baby."

The two men stood over the bodies in the chill of Dr. Ranpur's ice-covered yard, their weapons raised at each other's chest for heartbeats upon heartbeats. And then Raymond pocketed his gun, looked at the woman, and took a step toward her, gun leveled in her direction. He let out a small, tortured cry as her bloody hands reached toward him and she spoke. Raymond turned and leaped over the black iron gate, almost losing his glasses. George didn't want to look back, but he couldn't stop himself. A light went on in the house, a light that seemed to drench the front yard. And George saw clearly what they had done. The man called David, looking bewildered, wisps of yellow-white hair quivering in the night wind, sat there, dead. The woman just sat looking up at him in her blue-and-white dress.

Perhaps she screamed or spoke, but George could hear nothing but the senseless steel-drum sound of the winter night. Hugging the fur to his face, he pushed open the gate and ran after Raymond, who was a gray running ghost far ahead of him in the mist.

Six Minutes Past One A.M.

Abraham Lieberman placed his sandwich—radish, sliced chicken, and cholesterol-free, fat-free Kraft salad dressing on white bread—carefully on the folded paper towel on his knees. This had been his favorite comfort sandwich as a kid on the West Side. Now, at best, it captured only a hint of the satisfaction at that first bite.

The only light in the living room came from the hall just outside Abe and Bess's bedroom. Bess, when she caught him, insisted that Abe turn on a light in the living room when he was watching television.

It did Lieberman little good to point out to his wife that one of the few working parts of his frail sixty-two-year-old anatomy that seemed to be working at a reasonable level, well above rapid deterioration, were his eyes. Granted, Abe wore glasses, but only to read. Besides, there was something comforting about watching television in the dark with a white-bread sandwich on his lap, just as he had done back when he came home from night school and watched *Rocky King, Detective*, with Roscoe Karnes, who used to make up his own lines, or Jim Moran's Courtesy Motors variety show in his parents' living room in the apartment on Troy Street.

Abe balanced the sandwich in his hand as he rose and padded quietly to the television, turned it on with the volume low, and found the American Movie Channel. His thin, underweight, bloodhound face smiled in the white glow of *Mildred Pierce*. It was the scene in which Joan Crawford bakes a cake for an ungrateful Ann Blyth.

Abe's blue cotton robe billowed against his narrow body as he went barefoot to the armchair and sat back down again. Abe Lieberman standing, or in any position of repose, was not an impressive figure. Slightly shy of 145 pounds and slowly shrinking from five seven, his sad and baggy eyes, little white mustache, and curly gray hair made him look a good five years older than he was.

Early-early-morning television viewing was one of Abe's responses to chronic insomnia. *New York Times* crossword puzzle books done in the bathtub were another, and finally, so were novels. He had already done a crossword, as always in ink, making two or three mistakes and growing impatient before he could finish. He had read a chapter from a novel by Joyce Carol Oates, Bess's favorite author. Sleep, or the hint of it, had not come, so Abe had made himself the sandwich, poured himself a large glass of decaffeinated iced coffee from the thermos in the refrigerator, and headed for the living room, hoping that a Joan Crawford movie or anything with John Garfield would be on.

Prayers were sometimes answered.

Things had gotten better for Abe in the last month since it had become clear that his daughter, Lisa, and his grandchildren, Barry and Melisa, were not extended weekend guests but semipermanent inhabitants of the house on Birchwood Avenue. The realization had resulted in Lisa's old room upstairs being reshuffled with beds for Barry and Melisa, and the small guest room across from it, which had been used by Bess and Abe for storage, being converted into a bedroom for Lisa.

This acceptance of long-term occupation had liberated the living room, where Barry and Melisa had camped for more than a month while Lisa

20

and her husband, Todd, did battle over life, love, commitment, responsibility, freedom, and custody of the 1989 Chevy, the house in Evanston, several hundred books that neither of them really cared about, and the crucial question of who would pay the outstanding bills for Barry's braces.

Lisa and Todd each lived under the illusion that Abe was on their side. The illusion was fostered by the fact that he was a good listener. No, he was a great listener. He had been a cop for more than thirty-five years and had learned two lessons: First, no one wants advice; second, if you shut up and listen, eventually anyone will confess to something. He had also learned that it was pointless to try to pass these valuable truths on to others.

Son-in-law Todd Cresswell—a *goyisha* name that made Abe sigh whenever he realized that his grandchildren would bear it and his grandson would pass it on—had told Abe of Cassandra. He had told Abe more than once of Cassandra, for Todd was an associate professor of classics at Northwestern and given to frequent quotations from dead Greeks. Abe now had, as birthday and Hanukkah gifts over the years from Todd, the complete Ancient Greek tragedies. On sleepless nights when he felt that nothing could be worse, he read of people whose lives were infinitely worse.

But Cassandra was Abe's favorite. Cassandra,

like Abe, was given the gift of prophecy and the curse of never being believed.

Zachary Scott was being unctuous on the nineteen-inch screen across the room. He showed teeth. He wore a smoking jacket. He smoked too much. Anyone in his right mind would know better than to trust Zachary Scott, but even if he had been in the room with them Abe would have known better than to tell that to Joan Crawford.

Abe curled his toes into the carpet and considered turning up the heat as he took another bite of his sandwich, knowing that telltale crumbs would give him away in the morning. Outside, the wind wailed down the corridor of small 1950s houses and Abe tried not to think about whether it was snowing again and whether he would be able to start his car. Lisa's car was in the garage, protected, so she could be certain of transportation for Barry and Melisa and herself. Abe's car was parked on the street, huddled angry and sullen, probably deciding whether or not it would start after being sufficiently pampered or coaxed.

That could wait until morning. For now there was a radish-and-chicken sandwich and Ann Blyth already acting like a spoiled kid who bore, Abe suddenly realized, an uncanny and uncomfortable resemblance to his own daughter, who was sleeping almost directly over his head.

"Who's that?"

The voice came from the bottom of the stairs next to the kitchen.

"Jack Carson," Lieberman said, looking at his grandson, who blinked and scratched his groin.

"I gotta pee," said Barry.

"Sounds reasonable," said Abe.

"Bad."

"You got evil pee? Waste no more time. Exorcise the cursed body fluid."

"You sound like my dad," said Barry.

"Use my bathroom. Be my guest."

Barry staggered into the bathroom and closed the door.

Above the clanging of dishes in Mildred Pierce's restaurant, Abe could hear a faint tinkle from the bathroom followed by the flushing of the toilet and the running of the faucet in the sink.

He took another bite from the sandwich and turned his attention to the screen as the bathroom door opened. The toilet was still filling with water. Abe would probably have to get up, take the porcelain top off the tank, and jiggle the rubber ball until it decided to fall into place and cover the hole.

"What are you watching?" Barry whispered, taking a step toward his grandfather.

"*Mildred Pierce*," said Abe. "You want some sandwich?"

"What kind?" asked Barry, advancing toward his grandfather's chair, his eyes on the television set.

Barry's two-piece pajamas, about a size too large, were white and covered with Chicago Cubs logos. His braces glittered in the pale light from the television screen.

"Chicken and radish," said Lieberman as Barry sat on the sofa.

"Guess so," said the boy with a shrug.

"I'm not torturing you into a commitment here," said Abe.

"I'll have some if it's cut off the part where you ate."

"Here's a half, clean. Unmarred by your grandfather's tainted teeth."

Barry took the half-sandwich solemnly, examined it, turned it over, and took a small bite.

He looked like his father. No doubt. He didn't look like a Lieberman. And he didn't look like Bess's family, the Zelakovskys, which wouldn't have been so bad. No, Barry looked like a Cresswell.

"How old are you?" asked Lieberman.

"Grandpa," Barry said with a sigh and a mouthful of sandwich. "You know."

"Twelve," said Lieberman. "I know. It's a rhetorical question. An opener."

"Like you ask a stoolie?" asked Barry.

"Belcher," Lieberman corrected. "You've been watching *Little Caesar* too many times."

Barry nodded and took another bite of his sandwich. Lieberman watched the movie, trying to remember the name of the actor talking to Joan Crawford.

"Grandpa?"

"Yeah."

"You think my father is an asshole?"

Lieberman looked at his grandson, considered the question, and scratched his chin. He was quite clean shaven. He had taken care of that in his bath less than half an hour earlier.

"No," said Lieberman. "Who said he was?"

Barry shrugged.

"You heard your mother tell someone on the phone."

Barry nodded.

"Your father is not an asshole. Nor is your mother. They are both stubborn, confused, directionless, and selfdestructive. That is the human condition. Watch this part here. Joan Crawford's eyes. The way they go up."

"Which one is Joan Crawford?" asked Barry, whose half-sandwich was almost gone.

"The one with the hair piled up," said Lieberman.

Barry nodded seriously, finishing his sandwich with a final bite.

"Can I ask you a question?"

"Ask me a question," said Lieberman, turning his head toward his grandson.

"You ever really shoot anybody? I mean, I know you tell me and Melisa you shot hundreds of bad guys, but really."

"Yes," said Lieberman.

"Really?"

"Really, yes."

"How many?"

25

"Three, an average of one every eleven years," said Lieberman.

"Did any of them die?"

"One."

"Should I shut up?" Barry said.

"Maybe for a few years," said Lieberman.

"My friend Alex, the one who came over last week . . ."

"I remember. Looks like a parrot."

"He doesn't believe you're a policeman. He says you don't look like a policeman."

"Alex the Parrot is right."

"But you are a policeman."

"I don't look like one."

"You're an anomaly," said Barry seriously, with his father's face.

"Let's say I am in a perpetual disguise."

"You like my father?"

"I like your father."

"My mother?"

"I love your mother."

Barry got up and ambled across the room in front of the television.

"I'm sorry. I can't talk anymore. I've got to get some sleep and get up for school."

"I'm not offended," said Lieberman.

"You look sad, Grandpa."

"I always look sad. The family curse. I look a little better in the late spring when the Cubs come back from Arizona."

"Good night. Coffee's no good for you."

"Good night, Barry. This isn't real coffee."

Lieberman listened to the sound of his grandson's feet going up the creaking stairs, heard the bedroom door open and close, and followed the faint sound of the boy as he crossed the bedroom and bounced into bed.

Lieberman knew the phone would ring soon. It was not a sudden feeling, just a sense within him. He was rising when the first ring came. In spite of his stiff, arthritic knees he was across the room as the ring was dying. He entered the kitchen and reached for the phone as it began its second ring, which he cut off before it could reach through the doors and wake Bess.

"Hello," he said.

"Rabbi," came Bill Hanrahan's voice.

Lieberman imagined the handsome, flat, pink-cheeked Irish face of his burly partner, imagined it reflecting the strange sadness he heard in the wavering tenor. Hanrahan had been more than reasonably sober for more than four months, but there was something of the grape or mash in his voice tonight.

"You all right, Father Murphy?"

"Abraham, it's a homicide."

Lieberman waited.

"Abe, it's your nephew, Davey."

The sound stayed inside Lieberman, but he felt it explode in his stomach and order him to vomit. He fought it back.

"You there, Abe?"

"I'm here, Bill. What happened?"

"There's more, Abe—his wife. She was shot

too. She's alive, emergency room, Edgewater Hospital."

Lieberman couldn't see. His eyes were wet and the familiar kitchen an unfamiliar blur.

"The baby," said Lieberman, softly, slowly. "She's pregnant."

"Touch and go, Rabbi. Touch and go. I'm on Devon and Western. You want, I'll pick you up in fifteen minutes, God and traffic willing."

"No, I'll drive. Does my brother know?"

"Hospital called him. He's on the way there."

"Fifteen minutes."

"Fifteen," Hanrahan confirmed, and hung up.

Lieberman looked at the phone, afraid that if he hung it up he'd convince himself that it was a dream, late-night radishes. But it was no dream. The telephone clicked and bleated, a long insistent bleat. He hung it up, looked at his trembling hands, and, as his father and his father before him and their fathers before them back to the beginning of recorded history had done, Abe Lieberman gripped the open flap of his favorite robe and pulled until the cotton tore.

He stood for a beat in his torn robe, rocking slightly, his bare feet aware of the cool kitchen linoleum. And he remembered a night in 1944 or '45. He and his brother, Maish, had been working for Uncle Murray, who had a small deli-grocery for the summer tourists in Union Pier, Michigan. Uncle Murray had sent them home after two weeks—the sad-faced brothers had driven customers away—but Maish, who had by then acquired the nickname Nothing-Bothers Maish, had declared to Abe on the bus back to Chicago that he would someday have his own deli.

It seemed a modest-enough ambition and Maish had achieved it, but now Abe Lieberman stood in his own kitchen and imagined not his brother as he was now, but as a sour-faced, chubby little boy who would have to be told that his own son had died.

Lieberman stopped rocking, took a deep breath, and walked quickly and as quietly as he could back to his bedroom. He took forever to open the door and enter, listening for Bess's even breathing. There was no light and he wanted none. He made his way around the foot of the bed, past the pink chair, and away from the highboy that had been a wedding gift from Bess's brother. He dressed carefully, knowing that if Bess awoke he would have to tell her. It wasn't that he was afraid that she could not cope. No, she would probably cope far better than he was doing, but he saw no reason to wake her when her strength would be needed in the morning and who knew how far beyond.

Lieberman succeeded and, using the key that he wore on a chain around his neck even when he slept, opened the drawer in the night table on his side of the bed, removed the pistol, put it in his holster, and closed the drawer.

Bess slept on, not quite snoring, but asleep.

He closed the door gently and walked to the kitchen, where he left a note saying he would call her. He didn't think the note would be necessary. He would try to call her a little after seven with the news. Who could know where he might be at the hour when the red-eyed alarm clock woke his wife?

The note done, Lieberman looked around the room and for an instant forgot where he was going and why. But the moment was gone in an instant and he went into the living room, got his coat, hat, scarf, and boots out of the closet, dressed for the howling wind and cold, and headed out the front door and into the early-morning darkness where his car sat frigid in the street.

One-Fifteen
in the Morning

Detective William Hanrahan sat in a low, straight-backed chair in a line of five such chairs directly outside the intensive-care unit of Edgewater Hospital.

He sat alone, a four-month-old *McCall's* magazine in his lap, looking at the pale green wall of the long corridor. He shifted his weight for the fortieth or fiftieth time since he had taken up residence on the chair, which was built, he was sure, for someone like the pretty, finger-thin model who grinned large and white-toothed from the cover of the magazine before him.

Bill Hanrahan was coming perilously close to his fifty-first year and his two hundred and twentieth pound. He wore a blue flannel shirt, heavy slacks, and a deeply pensive look.

Hanrahan had dozed, and in his doze he had dreamed, dreamed that he was at Guadio and Stanton's Bar on Fullerton drinking whiskey after whiskey with a beer to kick it down. In the dream he had felt no joy in the drinking, just the need to keep going, methodically, knowing with each drink that there was no stopping and no going back. It was a nightmare of faces behind the bar and surrounding him, watching intently, seriously.

Hanrahan had awakened when the magazine fell to the floor and he almost toppled from the little chair.

He had not had a drink in four months and nine days, but there wasn't a day that he didn't want something, anything, and, at the same time, didn't want it, was repulsed to near nausea at the thought of even a cold beer.

He had shared his nightmares and fears with no one, not Abe nor Iris, who would have been willing to listen. He and Iris had been talking seriously about marriage for about three weeks and even Iris's father, a wispy Chinese who spoke little English, seemed to think it not necessarily a terrible idea. Hanrahan, however, was not so sure. It would mean finding Maureen and asking her for a divorce. Though it was Maureen who had left him, she was the good Catholic who went to church and didn't want to face that particular sin.

The hospital smell was seeping into Hanrahan's consciousness. He fought it, but its pull was strong. He had spent two weeks in a hospital not many months ago with a bullet in his head and drugged dreams that went on for days until he was sure that the dreams themselves were death.

Hanrahan stood, fighting a small, rough ball of panic in his gut, looking for something to distract him. The perfect girl on the cover of the magazine beckoned to him. He picked her up and set her gently on the chair.

And Lieberman appeared. Hanrahan hadn't heard the elevator down the corridor rise nor the door open, but there was the thin, pale man striding toward him, coat, hat, and scarf draped over one arm, boots sloshing with each step.

"Looks like she's going to make it," said Hanrahan.

Lieberman stopped and the two men stood awkwardly, a few feet apart.

"The baby?" asked Lieberman.

"Doc says touch-go, nip-tuck, who knows. How pregnant is she?"

"I don't know," said Lieberman. "Four, five months, maybe more, maybe less. We don't see them much and Maish is never straight on things like that. When can we see her?"

Hanrahan shrugged. "Who knows? Doc says he'll let us know."

"David."

It wasn't a question, but Hanrahan nodded, knowing what his partner wanted. He turned and started down the corridor, Lieberman sloshing hurriedly to catch up. They went down one flight, turned, and headed toward the emergency room. Abe Lieberman had spent hours in every emergency room of every hospital in Chicago. He had stories to tell, but none like this.

"Here," said Hanrahan as they came to a dull, ivory-colored swing door. "Behind the curtain on the left. You want me to . . ."

Lieberman shook his head no and went through the door alone. There were starched-curtained cubicles on both sides of him, three cubicles on each side. The fluorescent lights hummed and beamed white and shadowless. He pushed back the curtain on his left and stepped in.

His nephew David lay on a cart, eyes closed, wearing a suit and open tie. The blood had dried on his chest and drained from his face. He looked nothing like a Lieberman. He looked like his mother's side of the family, which was fortunate.

Lieberman stepped to the side of his dead nephew and looked at his face, at the wounds. He didn't touch the flesh. He had touched dead flesh many times and he didn't want to remember David this way.

David looked troubled, puzzled, his full, dead-purple lips tight, as if someone had asked him

33

one of those questions about trains traveling in different directions at different speeds.

Lieberman muttered a few words of the Kaddish, the prayer for the dead in Hebrew, a language he did not understand. He did not know all of the prayer, knew very little, but he felt the need to try.

Then he turned, went through the curtain and out the swing door to where Hanrahan stood.

"You all right, Rabbi?"

"No."

"Don't see how you could be. Nurse just came down. Doc says we can see Carol for a minute or two. Doesn't look like Maish is here yet."

When they got back upstairs in front of the intensive-care unit, a young surgeon in a blue operating-room uniform was standing in front of the row of chairs where Hanrahan had spent more than an hour. The surgeon looked tired and ill and young and a little like Alan Alda. He was certainly no older than Lieberman's dead nephew

"Detective Lieberman?" he asked, holding out his hand.

The grip was firm, the look of sympathy sincere. Lieberman nodded.

"I'm Jason Lorie. I'm sorry about your nephew."

Lieberman nodded and looked into the young doctor's eyes and saw that he meant what he was saying.

"Carol?" asked Lieberman.

"I think she'll be fine," Lorie said, rubbing

his eyes. "If there aren't any complications, she should be fine. The bullet didn't hit an organ. Broken rib and muscle damage."

"And . . . ?" Lieberman said, leaving unfinished the question they both understood.

"I don't know about the baby," said Lorie. "The bullet didn't hit the fetus, but it did sever blood vessels and scraped part of the umbilical cord. Vital signs are very good. We keep the mother strong and the baby should be fine. We're watching. I'm trying to track down her obstetrician. If we have to remove the baby, we will, but I doubt if that will be necessary. It looks like a seven-, possibly eight-month fetus, so the chances are . . ."

"Can we talk to her?"

"I'm not sure she'll make a lot of sense. She's heavily sedated and just went through some rough surgery. If you can wait till morning . . ."

"By morning whoever did this could be halfway to California or Little Rock," said Hanrahan.

Doc Lorie held open his hands in resignation and led the two policemen to and through the doors of the ICU.

The unit was dark with a round nurses' station in the center. Facing the circle of the nursing station were glassed-in rooms with large windows. Green lights flickered beyond each window.

A white-haired nurse with her glasses perched precariously on her nose looked up at them, saw the doctor, and returned to a chart before her.

"There," said the doctor. "Room Three-sixteen. Two minutes. No more and possibly less. We're monitoring vital signs out here."

"We'll be fast," Hanrahan assured the doctor, softly, as Lieberman moved toward the door.

They could see Carol through the window before they entered. She was turned toward the door, her eyes closed, her face bloodless pale, her light blond hair over her face.

Lieberman approached the bed while Hanrahan stayed waiting at the door. Then Lieberman stood for perhaps a minute, his thighs touching the clean blanket that covered Carol, and looked down at her, saying nothing. She stirred, sensing a presence, moaned, and struggled to open her eyes.

"It's me, Abe, David's uncle," he said softly.

"David," she groaned.

"Yes."

Carol's dark brown eyes opened and fought to keep from closing. Her hand fluttered and Abe took it.

"They killed David," she said.

"Yes," said Lieberman.

"And me, they shot me. Why?"

"I don't know," said Lieberman.

"The baby. Someone, a doctor, someone said the baby was all right. Is he all right?"

"Yes," said Lieberman.

Carol sighed, gripped his hand tightly for an instant, and then closed her eyes.

"We can only stay a minute, Carol,"

Lieberman whispered. "What can you tell us about the people who did this?"

"People?"

"Who shot you and David. You said 'they.'"

"Yes. Two men. One skinny with a twisted face, one huge, like him," she said, nodding with closing eyes in Hanrahan's direction.

"Did they use names, say anything?"

"Black, they were black with accents."

"Accents?"

"Not Africa, not the South; Jamaica, Haiti. I don't know."

"Good," said Lieberman, patting her hand gently.

"They have one of those things in the back of my hand," she said, so low he almost missed it.

"Yes."

"It hurts. Thirsty."

"I'll tell the nurse. Can you remember anything else about the two men?"

Carol slowly shook her head no, started to drift into drugged sleep, and muttered something very softly.

"What did she say?" Hanrahan whispered.

"David's hat," Lieberman answered.

The doctor was gone when they stepped out of Carol's room and closed the door. The white-haired nurse with the slipping glasses looked up again.

"Thank you," said Hanrahan, and the nurse nodded.

The two men said nothing as they left the soft

darkness of the ICU and went down the corridor to the elevators. It wasn't until they were standing in the empty main lobby of the hospital, before an erect and quite gray fern, that Lieberman spoke.

"What do we have?"

"They went to dinner at the apartment of David's boss, left about midnight, maybe a little later. Not many people out. They were found in the front yard of a doctor, Doctor Ranpur, cardiologist. He's the one who called nine-one-one."

Lieberman nodded. "He see anything?"

Hanrahan shrugged. "That's all I've got, Rabbi. Evidence guys are probably there."

Lieberman looked over his partner's shoulder at the rattling, frosted windows of the hospital lobby.

"Kearney?"

"I called him," said Hanrahan. "Told him who it was. Told him we'd want the case."

"And . . . ?"

"We've got it. None of that stuff about being too close to it. Hughes wouldn't have let us take it, but . . . you O.K., Abraham?"

"There's O.K. and there's O.K. I'm O.K. We've got to move. I'm gonna have to call Maish."

"I know."

"See if they have a bag on David here and find out if Evidence took anything," said Lieberman.

"Got it," said Hanrahan. "Looking for something particular?"

"David's hat," said Lieberman, moving past his partner with a deep sigh and heading for the phone booths against the white wall next to a large, cheerful painting of a very red flower.

Three-Fifteen in the Morning

Dr. J. W. Rashish Ranpur's house was hot. Not just warm, hot. The heat hit the two policemen when the small, ancient man opened the door after being assured that they were, indeed, the police.

"I have great respect for the police," Ranpur said, ushering in Lieberman and Hanrahan, "but one must use caution in this neighborhood, in this world, in this very yard given what happened earlier in such proximity. Do not worry about your shoes and boots. All the floors are tile or wood."

They passed through a porchlike entry that ran across the front of the house and contained half a dozen dark chairs and several low, equally dark tables neatly covered with magazines, lined up against the stone wall of the house. The porch looked like and was a waiting room, Ranpur explained, ushering them through the door leading inside the house. The temperature rose even more.

"I have been unable to get back to sleep since the horror," the doctor said, shaking his head.

Dr. Ranpur hit a wall switch and overhead light bulbs in a small glass chandelier came on. The little man stood there, fully dressed in a brown suit and tie, looking decidedly nervous.

"On the left, my office. On the right," he indicated with an open hand, "my sitting room. Upstairs," he said with a shrug, "memories. My wife passed on many years ago. My children are scattered across six continents. I live alone with my work."

"Office," Lieberman said. He had stepped in a low snowbank while searching in the small front yard and on the street for David's hat. He hadn't found the hat, but he had managed to soak his socks.

Ranpur nodded his head as if to confirm that a move to his office was the proper and intelligent decision. He opened a door to his left, reached in, and turned on the light.

Both Hanrahan and Lieberman had unbuttoned their coats. Now they removed them as they stepped into the large room. There was a heavy wooden desk in one corner behind which stood a tall wooden cabinet. A round, dark table sat in the center of the room with four matching chairs around it, and a colorful madras-covered sofa with two matching armchairs facing it.

"I have tea or coffee ready if you . . ."

"No, thank you," said Hanrahan, looking at

Lieberman, who seemed far away from the moment. "I don't think this will take too long."

Ranpur nodded again and motioned the two men toward the table.

"My manners, my manners, forgive me, let me take your coats."

They handed the coats to Ranpur, who almost toppled from the weight but gamely staggered to a coatrack near the door, where he managed to hook the coats precariously. Then he returned to the two detectives, who were now seated at the table, and sat facing them, his thin, dark hands folded, a pair of rimless glasses now perched on his nose.

"What kind of practice do you have, doctor?" Hanrahan asked, looking around the room. There were eight certificates, degrees or diplomas, framed and mounted neatly on the wall behind the desk near the heavy wooden case, but they were too far for Hanrahan to read. Lieberman seemed to have little interest.

"I am by training a cardiologist. But I now limit my treatment to nutrition, holistic health, the same thing I practiced as a young man in Bombay and London when it had no name. Prevention through diet for those who are at risk. I get many referrals from other physicians, nutritionists. Surprisingly more work than I need to sustain my frail but healthy body. Would you like to venture a guess at my age?"

Hanrahan looked at Lieberman, who blinked his eyes with no hint of curiosity.

"Seventy," guessed Hanrahan.

"Eighty and six," Dr. Ranpur said with a satisfied smile, showing very white teeth. "I play the trombone and, weather permitting, walk five miles each and every day."

"Admirable," said Hanrahan, with a smile he hoped conveyed admiration and awe.

"Legumes and Dixieland," said Ranpur, looking at both men. "They sustain me physically and esthetically. Do you find it too warm in here?"

"A bit," admitted Hanrahan.

"I am sorry. By the time I turn it down and it comes into effect, you will probably have long left. You have questions other than the ones asked by the young man and woman in uniform?"

Lieberman tried to focus on the little man across from him, tried to pay close attention, but the memory of the telephone conversation he'd had with his brother, Maish, haunted him. They were in the car on the way to see Dr. Ranpur when the hospital had tracked Maish down outside the emergency room. Maish had not screamed, wailed, or cried.

"Maish, you there?"

"I'm here," Maish had answered, his voice flat, the voice of a man who expects the worst. "Carol and the baby are alive."

Maish had said he would get Yetta up and they would stay at the hospital for a while. Rabbi Wass was going to join them there.

"I'll meet you at the hospital later," said Abe.

"It may kill her, Abe."

"The doctor says . . ." Lieberman began.

"No, not Carol, Yetta. She's not a well woman. I don't know what to say to her. She's sitting out there. I can see her. I don't know what to tell myself. I don't know what to tell her. God help me, Abe. I hate my wife for having a baby that would grow up and get killed."

"Maish . . ."

"It's all right, Abe," Maish said with a sigh. "I'm just talking. I know it's not Yetta's fault. I'm just talking. You know how it is."

Abe Lieberman had no words for his brother. The sigh on the other end of the line had been enormous.

"Abe, David is dead."

And then Abe had heard the horrible wail and he knew that his sister-in-law, Yetta, was walking toward Maish, heard her husband's words. Abe imagined Yetta, a bulk of a creature, arms wobbling, staggering across the room in the first dress she had found in her closet, the bulky blue coat swishing as she moved.

"Abe," his brother had said in confusion, and the line had gone dead.

"He didn't pick up the hat, Abe," came Bill Hanrahan's voice; Lieberman returned to the hot room in which he was having trouble keeping his eyes open.

Both men were looking expectantly across the table at Lieberman.

"The hat?" Lieberman said, trying not to imagine the sad, resigned face of his brother.

"Dr. Ranpur didn't see a hat," explained Hanrahan with a look of concern that Abe tried to dispel by joining the conversation.

"May I presume," Ranpur said softly, "to prescribe something organic which may cause you some alleviation of your distress."

"The man who got shot was his nephew," Hanrahan explained.

"Ah," said Ranpur, sitting up straight, "that explains much. My offer of the alleviation remains."

"Thank you," said Lieberman. "Maybe I'll take you up on that. Why don't you just tell us what you saw tonight, what you heard, what you did?"

Ranpur nodded, looked at the two men, and told his story while Hanrahan took notes.

"I shall endeavor to speak slowly," he said. Hanrahan nodded in appreciation, though he had no intention of writing much of what the old man said. Other, younger, detectives and even some of the old-timers used little pocket tape recorders. Both Lieberman and Hanrahan had tried them and decided that they were too much work. You had to go back and listen to the whole thing again and take notes anyway. The tapes weren't admissible as evidence and they made a lot of witnesses uneasy about talking.

"I was soundly asleep upstairs," said Ranpur, actually pointing upward. "I could use the room

44

in the back as a bedroom so I would not have to climb stairs, but the climbing is good for me. I am a deep sleeper, but aware of approaches, changes in my environment, more a sense than a sound, you understand?"

Lieberman nodded.

"There have been four attempts in the past two years to break into the house, to rob me. All were thwarted by the alarm system, very noisy, lights, very upsetting to neighbors in the nearby apartments, but very effective."

"So," Hanrahan guided, "you thought you were about to be burgled."

"Precisely, and I came awake. There were voices, a woman's voice and weeping, and I came down in darkness to determine if this was taking place inside or beyond my fence. Before I could get to the bottom of the stairs, there was the firing of bullets."

"How many?" asked Lieberman.

"At first, two, three, four. I don't know. Then a pause and another shot and the woman shouted to her husband as I reached the bottom of the stairs. I turned on the lights and walked onto the porch. There was no one there but the poor young man and the stricken woman. I called the nine-one-one number, put on my coat, and attempted to minister to them."

"Did you see anyone else?" asked Hanrahan.

"No."

"Did the woman or the wounded man say anything else?"

45

"No. He was quite dead when I came to him and she was decidedly unconscious."

"You said she called to her husband after the first round of shots," said Lieberman. "How do you know?"

"She called him by name. 'George,' she called."

Hanrahan looked at his partner, but Abe was awake now and focused on the doctor.

"You sure she said 'George'?"

"Oh, yes. My hearing is outstanding. I may have a bit of difficulty with discernment of range, but . . ."

"You sure it was the woman who said 'George'?" asked Lieberman.

Ranpur considered the question seriously as he examined his hands and pursed his lips.

"The voice was high, but so was the wind. Perhaps it was not the voice of the woman. The name was called in horror and I assumed . . . but, perhaps not, perhaps it was one of the assailants."

"Perhaps it was," said Lieberman, getting up. "Thank you for your time."

"Wait," said Ranpur, rising and hurrying to the wooden case behind his desk as the detectives moved to their coats and began to put them on. Ranpur pulled a key from his pocket, opened the case, and retrieved a plastic vial of tablets, which jiggled as he hurried back across the room and handed the vial to Lieberman.

"Three times a day after meals," said Ranpur, as Lieberman put the vial into his coat pocket.

"Thanks," said Lieberman.

"You are, perhaps, wondering why it is that an old man like me lives and a young man is murdered," said Ranpur, touching Lieberman's sleeve.

"No," said Lieberman. "Maybe later when I have time I'll think of all kinds of things to torture myself, but . . ."

"Well then, perhaps, I was thinking it," said Ranpur. "I see from your eyes. You sleep badly. The pills should help you. If you need more, please come back. There will be no charge."

"Thanks," said Lieberman, as the old man escorted them back to the porch and out into the predawn cold.

On the sidewalk Lieberman, hands plunged deeply in his pockets, said, "What've we got?"

"Not much," said Hanrahan, enjoying the cold after the soporific heat of the house. "Pair of perpetrators, both black, Caribbean maybe, one maybe named George, and maybe they ran off with your nephew's hat. Not much, Rabbi."

"Have faith, Father Murphy," said Lieberman, starting to feel the cold again. "We'll see what the computer and some friends can come up with."

"Not gonna find much at this hour," said Hanrahan. "Want me to come home with you or back to the hospital?"

"No. I'll meet you at the station at eight."

"It's Thursday, Rabbi."

"So?" said Lieberman.

"The sting at Montrose House at nine-thirty. We can call it off or postpone it."

"We might lose them," said Lieberman, shaking his head. "O.K. I'll meet you there at nine."

"Nine," agreed Hanrahan. It would give him enough time to get back to his house in Ravenswood, no more than fifteen minutes away, take a hot bath with his eyes closed, get a few hours of sleep. "Want to come to my place?"

"Got to get home and tell Bess," said Lieberman as they moved to the car parked alone on Sheridan Road.

"It's gonna be a hard day, Rabbi."

"It's already a hard day, Father Murphy. It's also getting to be one hell of a hard rest of our lives."

"We'll find them," said Hanrahan.

"We'll find them," Lieberman agreed, opening the car door. "Now, get in before you get hit by a drunk."

Four-Ten in
the Morning

The Rogers Park police station on Clark Street just north of Devon was flanked by a Wendy's to the south and on the north by a long, five-story brick building with apartments on top of used-furniture shops, bars, and small groceries where Spanish was the language of choice. In one of the apartments, not long ago, Frankie Kraylaw had lived with his wife, Jeanine, and his son, Charlie.

Now Frankie sat patiently in the window of a reupholstery shop across the street watching the dark-stone police station with its lights always on behind thick opaque windows. The station had been considered modern and efficient when it was built in 1966 and opened with a ceremony featuring his honor Mayor Richard J. Daley himself. Now the building looked like a forgotten outpost of a besieged inner-city community college.

On warmer nights, prodded by the taunts of their friends, a young boy or girl might sneak up to the station to the sound of distant giggling and encouraging words in Spanish from shadowed doorways. The brave one would spray paint his girlfriend's initials or even her first name or a few words on the concrete walkway or even on the building itself.

Most of what was painted was in Spanish. Almost all of what was painted was hostile and obscene.

Frankie Kraylaw, who had an open smile of white, even teeth and a head of straight hair that tended to fall over his right eye, sat watching the entrance to the police station, waiting for the big Irish policeman who, along with the little Jew, had driven him from the city only months ago, driven him as Pharaoh had driven Moses from

49

the land of Egypt, and like Moses, Frankie Kraylaw had returned to do the Lord's justice, had broken into the reupholstery shop from the rear and taken up his vigil in the window, waiting for the one called Hanrahan or the little Jew who liked to threaten.

Now it might come to pass, Frankie told himself, that neither of them would come in today or that they had been transferred or were on vacation or that the old one had retired. It might come to pass, but Frankie would find them. With the help of the Lord, he would find them. He would sit there until just before dawn and then nurse a coffee at Wendy's, with a view of the police station, for as long as he could.

He would find them. He would kill them.

Frankie Kraylaw had never killed anyone, though he had come close on many occasions. Generally, his potential victims had very little or no idea about what caused his sudden bursts of fury and violent explosions. It was not always terribly clear to Frankie either, but he knew it had to do with offenses to the Lord, offenses that Frankie was keenly aware of and found difficult to put into words.

But God did speak to Frankie Kraylaw, though the voice might be distant and muted like a bad connection from Edgewater to Uncle Saul back in Tennessee, and sometimes the God in Frankie Kraylaw's head did not use words. It would have been nice if the Lord could have been just a little bit clearer, the way he had been to Frankie's father before his father lost the channel to Heaven by losing first his soul and then his liver and life to drink. Amen. Amen and always Amen. Goddamn it. The ways of the Lord are many, mysterious, and not to be questioned.

Frankie shifted in the chair. There was no heat in the store, and the wool sweater and Mackinaw jacket he had picked up at the Goodwill couldn't keep out the cold. The gospel station on the pickup truck radio had said it was ten degrees with a below-zero wind chill. Couldn't be more than twenty degrees in the shop.

So be it. A trial by the Lord. A test of the will of Francis Jackson Kraylaw. So be it. He would meet the test and then some. Nothing he could not do if the Lord just kept speaking to him.

The two policemen had forced him out of the city of sin on a Greyhound bus, making him leave behind his wife and son. They had warned him never to return. Well, the Lord had told Frankie that he should return and reclaim his family, and the only way to do that and be safe was to smite the policemen.

Frankie was ready. He had gone back to Tennessee, and there had frightened his family— brother Carl, sisters Beth and Luann, three aunts, an uncle, and even some cousins—into giving him enough money to buy Roy Willett's 1984 Honda pickup and still have enough left over for gas and living for maybe a week.

They had all thought Frankie's going back to Chicago for Jeanine and Charlie a good idea.

They had encouraged him, told him he should get his family back and go someplace safe. They all assured him, every man, woman, and Pastor Griggs, that Codgetown would not be a safe place to bring his family. No, they said, in their own ways or together, the police would find him easily in Codgetown. Take some sandwiches, the cash, and a tankful of gas, and go with their blessing. Send a card, maybe, when it felt right, but go. And he had gone back to the cold and that which must be finished.

Cars came by, more as daylight neared. Policemen, never the right ones, came and went, sometimes in uniform, sometimes not, heads down against the cold and wind, holding on to their hats and holsters. A runaway aluminum garbage can came cling-clanging down Clark Street, caroming off parked cars, heading south out of sight.

Patience.

His plan was simple. When one of them came in and went out again by himself, Frankie would follow him in the Honda pickup, come on him when he was alone, with the old double-barrel shotgun his daddy had bought right after he came back from Korea, a shotgun Frankie had used to hunt with for years. Frankie would tell the sinner before him to tell him where Jeanine and Charlie were and then he would shoot him after he let the son of Satan pray. And if he didn't speak, if neither of them told where his family was, then Frankie would shoot them dead anyway, and be able to search the city for them without fear of the two policemen. Satan would probably make them watch from Hell while Frankie tracked his wife and son and made them understand their sins and come with him.

If Jeanine and Charlie didn't want to come, well, Frankie had beaten them before and it had put the fear of husband and God in them and he would beat them again and again and again and again . . .

Frankie was pounding his fists against his own chilled legs, pounding them so hard that the pain got through his reverie and made him stop.

And then although he thought he was saying it to himself, he muttered aloud, "Are you washed in the blood of the lamb?"

And far down Clark Street out of sight the aluminum garbage can running amok answered him by crashing through the window of a television repair shop.

As Frankie Kraylaw sat looking out of the window of the Sanchez Brothers' Reupholstery and Used Furniture Shop, Bill Hanrahan turned off the bubbling whirlpool machine that hung precariously over the edge of the old claw-foot bathtub. Then he hoisted himself up, the water cascading off him, and, holding on to the towel rack behind him, he tested first one knee and then the other. The results could have been better.

William "Hardrock" Hanrahan had been the fastest lineman on his Chicago Vocational High

53

School football team, one of the fastest high school linemen in the whole state of Illinois, probably in the Midwest. In his senior year, Hanrahan had twisted his knee in a practice. The speed went; not overnight but in an instant. He had still gone on to a football scholarship at Southern Illinois, though he had been hoping for Notre Dame or Illinois; but even with a good knee a top-twenty school had been only an outside possibility. He had lasted two years at Southern, a journeyman lineman who lost his nickname and stopped finding the game a hell of a lot of fun. He had left Carbondale, left school, and come back to Chicago to join his father as a cop, as his father had joined his father before him.

More than twenty-five years after his last football game the knee still locked on him, went numb when it had a mind to, referred a longing ache to his other knee, and made walking a chore; but Hanrahan covered up the problem to his satisfaction.

He stood wet and aching, a hairy hulk of a man, wondering what his ex-wife Maureen was doing and with whom. He stepped carefully out of the tub onto the bath mat and dried himself. Jeanine had done the laundry. The towels were clean. But they didn't smell as good as when Bill did them. Jeanine had cleaned the floor and, he had to admit, done a good job, but not as good as Bill did.

Stepping into the clean jockey shorts he had laid out on the clothes hamper, Hanrahan considered, as he had done many times in the last month, what he was going to do about Jeanine and Charlie Kraylaw, who were now soundly asleep in the bedrooms upstairs.

He had taken in the pair when he and Lieberman had ridden Frankie Kraylaw out of town. There had been no doubt in either of their minds that Frankie, who had torn up the store of a man who felt sorry for Frankie's wife and son, was on the verge of doing something very crazy and very violent to his family. In the name of Jesus, Frankie had given signs of losing what little control he had been floating on.

They were quiet, the young mother and son, too quiet and too anxious to please. Jeanine had found work at the McDonald's on Western Avenue near Granville, gotten Charlie back in school, and begun to look like the pretty young woman she was instead of the frightened sheep who had come into the house Bill had once shared with Maureen.

Hanrahan pulled on his pants, listening to the jingle of his change and feeling the heft of his wallet in the back pocket.

Jeanine had said twice that she owed her and Charlie's lives to Bill Hanrahan. She had even made it clear that she would, if he wanted, share Bill's bed. Hanrahan had made it just as clear that he wanted no payment other than for her to work her way up to a job that would allow her to move into an apartment with her son. And so

Jeanine stayed, saved a little money each week, and made Hanrahan extremely uncomfortable.

He put on his blue button-down shirt and looked at himself in the mirror over the bathroom sink. He saw a strong Irish face with a hint of the rose in his cheek and nose from the years of his friendship with the bottle. He saw the flat features of his father and grandfather, tempered just a bit by the warmer heart of his mother. All in all not a bad face to have.

Jeanine, he thought, sitting on the edge of the tub and putting on his socks, was a good kid, but not a very bright one. Conversation tended to be brief unless he could bring himself to listen to her recounting her day with the fillet-o-fish and Big Mac. Charlie seldom spoke. The few times they had gotten him together with Lieberman's grandchildren, Charlie had dutifully done what they had engaged him in and had soberly said "thank you" and announced in a whisper in the car that he had had a good time.

Truth was, Hanrahan admitted, turning off the light and moving into his bedroom, Jeanine and Charlie were innocent, gentle, and none too smart. They reminded him, in contrast, of the arguments, jokes, banter, and business that had filled this very house when Maureen had lived in it and the boys had grown up in it bringing home friends, battling, and leaving lights and television sets on all over the place.

The house now had the stillness of an Amtrak station at midnight. All creaks and howling wind, the lone sound of the television filling only a narrow band of cold space.

Hanrahan turned out all the lights but the one on the night stand and looked at the small television in the bedroom which showed him the silent scene of some distant war on CNN. He lay back on the bed, feeling the familiar indentation of his body on the mattress.

He had kept the house clean, perfect, neat, better even than Maureen had kept it, even when he had been on the needle edge of the worst of his sessions with the bottle. He had kept it for the moment that Maureen might drop in or one of the boys might pay an unexpected visit and find not that Hanrahan had gone the way of the slovenly bachelor but had and could make a commitment.

The first time she had seen it Iris had marveled at the house, at the shine on the polished hardwood floors, the nap of the area rugs, the lack of dust. Iris, her pretty, ageless Chinese face surveying the rooms politely as they spoke, had trodden carefully, lightly, as if in a museum. Which was what it was.

He and Iris had never made love. Neither wanted to, and the few nights she had stayed over she had spent in the room in which Jeanine Kraylaw was now asleep.

The knees felt better on the oversized pillow on which he had rested them. He closed his eyes, put his right arm over his face to block out the light, and sensed the flicker of changing images as the wind shook the bedroom windows and CNN careened around the world in thirty minutes with no one in the room watching.

George DuPelee, clinging to the dead man's fur hat as if it was a teddy bear, lay on his back on the battered sofa, snoring gently. Raymond Carrou sat at the table in the corner of the room in the dim light of the television on the table in front of him, considering whether or not he should beat George to death as he slept or let him live so Raymond could make him suffer.

Nothing had gone right, nothing. And now he sat in this small, cold room over a hardware store on Grand Avenue listening to George snore, watching the news, changing stations to see if their crime would make the television, and wondering if they were safe.

It was cold in the room, which he had been renting for almost two years. Not cold like outside, but cold enough. And Raymond had been afraid to get a space heater. Just one block away a whole Vietnamese family had died because of one of those space heaters. Raymond wasn't sure what it was about the space heater that had made them die, but he had seen it on the television and walked past the very building.

It was never cold like this in Trinidad. In La Brea he had been respected, not just another black face with an accent. He had been a shift boss at the Pitch Lake natural asphalt mine, one of the wonders of the world. Tourists had come

58

to watch them work and marvel. But asphalt production declined in the 1980s. When he had started as a boy in 1970 they had produced 128,000 tons of asphalt in a single year, asphalt prized around the world and used for domestic roads and construction throughout the island and on Tobago. By 1985 asphalt production dropped to 21,000 tons and Raymond had been working few shifts and spending more time looking into the blue-green waters of the Gulf of Paria, picking up lonely older tourist women from England and the United States and wondering whether he should go inland in search of an oil job or take a boat over to Venezuela for whatever he could find.

In the end, he had spent all of his savings on bribing a U.S. immigration official to move him to the very top of the list for a work visa. He had made his way to New York City and then to Chicago in pursuit of a distant cousin who presumably lived there and owned a trio of music shops. He had found neither cousin nor work that suited him, and so he had taken the low-paying job in the sundries shop of the Stowell Building on Randolph Street.

Like his father and grandfather before him, Raymond was straight-backed, chocolate-skinned, handsome. He liked women and had little trouble drawing them to him.

And it was his woman, the woman he called Lilly because she reminded him of the flower. He had met her at work more than a year ago and in that year she had encouraged his ambition. He had begun by taking a night course at the downtown campus of Loyola University to show Lilly that he could become something. He would walk to the school from work even in a snowstorm and catch the subway a few blocks away after class. He had done well in that first class and in the next two, English and algebra, the following semester. He had begun to think he had a chance somewhere in the future to become a lawyer. He had told her of his plans and she had encouraged him while they lay in his bed trying to keep warm, and they had talked and planned for the future.

But life had changed so quickly.

And working in a matchbox shop in an office-building lobby paid little.

And people like George DuPelee were so easy to find.

And one was tempted to take a chance.

It would have gone perfectly had not George panicked and shot the woman. Raymond had no criminal record. He had a job. He was going to school. But, now . . .

Now what? Now where? In front of Raymond Carrou, gray-white in the light from the television, lay the money he had taken from the dead man, one hundred and eighty-seven dollars. The jewelry, worthless. To sell it would mean risking discovery by the police.

Raymond rubbed his forehead and looked at George.

Maybe there was still something to be done.

Maybe the woman was not dead. Maybe the baby inside her was still alive. He was sure the man he had shot was dead. No doubt about it. But the woman. George had shot her once. Maybe, maybe . . .

He tried to think. Could someone have seen them get into the car when they had run from the crime? Could someone in a window have seen them, be able to identify them? Not likely. Two black men bundled in the cold. But the car, a distinctive wreck. It was parked now behind the building in the space reserved for the Ace hardware store's customers. He would have to move it in a few hours. The Haitian family that ran the hardware store wouldn't give him a hard time. They were afraid of the lean, handsome man from Trinidad who smiled knowingly at their women and hinted at a violence his eyes confirmed.

Now he should sleep. When the sun came up he would drink strong coffee and make a plan. He was much calmer now as he turned off the television set. He had possibilities to work with, the first jagged pieces of a plan that might allow him to survive or maybe even come out of this with what he had planned for, more than the sad pile of bills he now folded and shoved into his pocket.

The floor was cold even through Raymond's socks. He moved to the bed, not bothering to undress, and climbed in, curling over on one side, covering his exposed ear with a pillow to mute the sound of George's snoring.

When the sun came up, Raymond would have his plan.

When the sun came up.

Six-Twenty in the Morning

Abe was sure even before he had fully opened the door that his wife and daughter knew about David and Carol.

Across the living room, sitting at the dining room table, dressed in a no-nonsense gray suit with a white blouse, her dark hair tied severely back, was his daughter, Lisa. It was too early for Lisa to be dressed. It was too early for Lisa to be up unless they knew.

He closed the door and looked across the room at his daughter, who shivered at the chill he had brought in.

"Your mother?" asked Lieberman, taking off his rubbers.

"With Aunt Yetta," said Lisa, pale, composed.

"And Maish?" Lieberman added, removing his coat and hat.

"Aunt Yetta says Uncle Maish walked out of the hospital without saying where he was going."

"Was he dressed warm? Did they say?"

"I don't know," said Lisa.

In more than thirty years of dealing with

sudden, violent, and unexpected death, Abe had seen a range of reactions from complete denial of reality to protective glee at the freeing of the soul of the victim from the troubles of the imperfect world. He had seen an old man and woman take each others' hands when informed of the death of their only grandchild and walk out of the front door of their apartment never to be seen again. One young wife, a black woman with an astonishingly beautiful Egyptian face, who had been told that her cab driver husband had been murdered for eighteen dollars by a big, white, red-headed man, had walked the streets with a gun until she encountered a man vaguely fitting the description and shot him in the face. The black woman had been a lawyer. The red-headed victim had been a Red Cross worker.

"Bess is angry with you," Lisa said as her father padded across the carpeted living room.

"I didn't want to wake her," said Lieberman, standing over his daughter. "David is dead. Your mother needed rest so she could help with the living."

"That should be her choice," said Lisa seriously. Lisa had always been serious, even as a child, seldom smiling. Biochemistry suited her. And though he had not thought so at first, Todd Cresswell suited her, too. Todd, tall, blond, brooding, saw in his wife the tragic bearing of the Greek tragedies he knew, taught, and loved. The sense of tragedy was there. What Todd had failed to see was the fire, which was not Greek but Semitic.

"How are you doing?" he asked.

Lisa shrugged and tapped her red fingernails on the polished dark tabletop.

"David is . . . really . . ." she said, looking up at him.

Her eyes were wide and brown, moist but not crying, a glint of light on her contact lenses.

Lieberman nodded his head yes and Lisa stopped tapping, stood up, and faced him. He held his arms open and she stepped forward to hug him. Lisa was not a world-class hugger. She held back, always held back, but this was better than most other times and she let Abe hold on for almost ten seconds before she stepped back. Her eyes were no longer moist.

"You? How are you?" she asked.

"The truth?"

"No, a lie," she said.

"The question was rhetorical," Abe said with a sad smile.

"Really," Lisa answered with her own sad smile. "How are you, Abe?"

"Tired, cold, especially my feet, wondering why I'm not angrier than I am, wondering what I'm going to say to your mother and how long she'll stay angry and hurt, readying myself to get dressed again and be with Maish for an hour or two, anxious to find the people who killed my nephew, my brother's son, to find them, get in their faces and repeat 'why, why, why' for hours or days till they sink to the floor crying the way Yetta and Maish must be crying. Am I making sense here or am I just rambling like a . . ."

"Classics professor," said Lisa, moving toward the kitchen. "Coffee's hot."

Lieberman followed his daughter knowing what she knew, that he wouldn't go back to bed or even rest, that he would look at the *Tribune* if it had been delivered yet, have a couple of cups of coffee, and be out the door again.

"Kids know?" he asked, moving to the table and sitting on the red-leatherette and chrome chair.

"No," said Lisa. "I'll tell them when they get up. I think I should let them go to school."

"Yeah," agreed Lieberman, accepting the hot cup his daughter handed him.

"I feel guilty," Lisa said, still standing, her arms folded over her breasts. "I'm feeling guilty that I'm not feeling more. You know if Carol will . . . ?"

"Doctor thinks so," said Lieberman.

"The baby?"

"Looks good," he said, after taking a long sip. "No promises."

The phone rang suddenly, piercingly. Father and daughter looked at it without reaction for two rings and then Lisa stepped to the wall and answered.

"For you," she said, holding out the phone.

The long cord reached to the table, but the receiver had to be held firmly or it would, as it had more than a dozen times, go skittering and crashing back toward the wall as if it were tied by a thick rubber band.

"Hello," he said.

"Abe?"

The voice was familiar. A man.

"Syd Levan here. Say, I'm sorry to call you at home, a morning like this. Let me say how sincerely sorry I am for your family's loss."

"Thank you, Syd."

Syd was one of the morning crowd of old men with nothing more to do with their lives than hang around Maish's T&L Deli on Devon. The group, known in the neighborhood as the Alter Cockers, consisted of Jews, with the exception of Howie Chen, whose family had owned the Peking Lantern Chinese Restaurant one block down just off California. Howie and his wife were the last of their clan in the neighborhood. Two sons and a daughter had all moved to California, where they were all engineers.

Syd had been the one who had dubbed Abe's brother Nothing-Bothers Maish back when they were kids on the West Side. That name had preceded the founding of the Alter Cockers, had gone back to the days in the '40s when Syd had been a classmate of Maish's back at Marshall High School.

"We're at the T and L," said Syd. "Maish is here. And he's acting, if I can say it, a little *meshugah*. He's got a right, considering. He's got a right, but we're . . ."

"I understand, Syd," said Abe, watching Lisa pour herself a cup of orange juice.

"Well, that's it," Syd whispered. "He's acting maybe not quite *meshugah*, but . . . He's acting like it's a day like any day, you know? And this is not a day like any other day."

"I'll be there in ten minutes," said Abe.

Lisa reached over to take the phone and crossed the room to hang it up as Abe drained his cup and stood up with a sigh.

"I gotta go," he said.

"Uncle Maish went to work?"

Lieberman nodded and walked toward the kitchen door, his feet not yet fully warmed in his thick white socks.

"If I got murdered on the street, would you go to work?" she asked.

"If something happened to you," Lieberman said, with a shudder he hoped did not show, "I'd find my own way to go crazy with grief. You tell Todd about David?" he asked, stepping past her.

"He has other interests," she said. "Other distractions."

Lieberman stopped and looked at his daughter, who turned from him and sat in the chair he had just vacated.

"Other interests?"

"A woman," Lisa said. "A new faculty member. Alice Stephens told me."

"Ah," said Lieberman.

"Ah," repeated Lisa, raising her eyebrows. "I walk out on him with the kids, tell him I want a new life. He chases me, pleads, begs, humiliates himself for five whole weeks, and then goes out and . . .''

Lieberman resisted the urge to check his watch.

"You think I'm being selfish," she said.

"No," said Lieberman.

"I don't want him, but I don't want anyone else to have him, at least not till I have someone first, if I wanted someone, which I do not."

"So you're not going to tell him," said Lieberman.

"You think he should know? He should know. He liked David. At least he said he liked David. I don't think they met more than two or three times, but . . . Can you tell him, Abe?"

"In my spare time," Lieberman said.

"I'll leave a message for him at his office," she said. "I'm not going to work today. I'll help Bess with Aunt Yetta, things."

"I'll tell Todd," said Lieberman.

Lisa looked down. "I can't stop thinking about myself," she said.

"Someone close dies," he said. "Sometimes you think about the time you've got and what you're going to do with it."

Lisa smiled. "You've been reading philosophy?"

"No, Mike Royko. I gotta go, Lisa. Tell Barry and Melisa I'll bring them something tonight."

"Are they going to have to go see David's body?" she whispered, so softly that he barely heard her.

"No," he said.

She nodded and drank her coffee, knowing that there was no point in asking the next question, that she would have to go.

Lieberman thought he heard the first faint stirrings of his grandchildren in the room above him as he shuffled to the closet, put on his still-chilled overcoat, and slipped into his shoes and wet boots.

The day was just starting.

"Get up."

George was aware of something, some presence, a voice, angry like his mother when he got up late for work back in Trinidad.

"Mmbunnn," he mumbled, pushing away the hand that rocked him by the shoulder.

"Get up," Raymond repeated.

George tried to open his eyes. He tried very hard and then made a special effort, spewing air from his puffed-out cheeks.

His eyes did not want to open, did not want to see, did not want to start a new day that would make him remember something he did not want to remember.

Raymond shoved him now, poked him with a long, thin finger.

"Get up. We've got work."

"Work?"

There was something different about Raymond this morning. George had only known him for about a week and Raymond had seemed like other people he knew from the Islands, even if he did have a look in his eyes and did always have a book with him. But there was something since last night, a look George did not like, and yes, Raymond was talking differently, talking like a white American.

Now George did open his eyes.

"It's morning. What we gonna do in the morning?"

Raymond was dressed as he had been during the night. He was cleaning his glasses with a wad of toilet paper and staring at George, who suddenly remembered, remembered and reached for his forehead as he sat up with a start, his head buzzing painfully from an ache and the memory. Yes, atop his head was a soft reminder of warm fur.

"Oh, my God. We killed them. Raymond, we killed them both dead."

"She may not be dead. The baby may not be dead," said Raymond.

"Pregnant . . . Oh God, yes. I remember. She be having a baby," said George.

Raymond looked angry. Raymond looked disgusted. But why should Raymond be angry? He had shot the man with the hat before George had shot the woman. He had shot the man with the hat when there had been no reason to shoot the man. George had simply lost his mind, his senses, but Raymond had . . .

"What are you thinking?" asked Raymond, looking down at his temporary partner.

"Nothin'," said George, planting his bare feet on the chilled floor and rubbing his face.

George needed a shave. He needed coffee. He needed food. He needed Raymond to tell him that they were safe, but Raymond had said something about working. How could they hide and work?

The sun was just coming up, gray through the dirty curtained windows. George wanted to sleep.

"What kind of work?" he asked.

"We need money. We need money to get out of here, get as far from here as we can, back to the Islands," Raymond said, walking to the wall and putting his forehead against it as he clenched his fists. "I called in to my job, left a message I'm sick."

"I don't know, man," George said, blinking his eyes.

"No, you don't know," Raymond agreed. "We're going down Sedgwick, over near Division. You know where that is?"

George nodded that he knew, but he had no idea what area of the city Raymond was talking about. George had been in Chicago for a few months and knew almost no streets or landmarks.

"We're going to rob three, four places fast, in-out, cash places that have morning money, Dunkin' Donuts, McDonald's. We've got nothing to lose if we get caught. What can they get on us worse than killing a white guy and his pregnant wife?"

71

Raymond turned from the wall to look at George like the sorry fool he was.

"That's what put us on Channel 5 this morning and maybe put us on the front pages," said Raymond. "They're going to have descriptions, maybe fingerprints, who knows. We've got to get money and get out of here fast."

"To the Islands?" asked George, stepping toward Raymond and looking ridiculous as he stood shirtless with a Russian fur hat clamped down to the top of his eyes.

"If we get enough," said Raymond. Then he moved on to his lie. "Now here's how we're going to do this. They got a good description of me, maybe from the woman you shot."

"Shot? She not dead?" asked George, stepping in front of Raymond, towering over him, shutting out the gray dawning light from the window. "Why didn't you start with that, man?"

Raymond strode past the giant and found a bag of pretzels on the cluttered table. He pulled out a handful, popped them in his mouth, and talked as he crunched with his back turned to George to be sure his face wouldn't betray him.

"I drive up to the place, keep the motor running. You run in, gun out, put it in the manager's face, have him . . ."

"Sometimes women run those . . ."

"Him, her, what difference does it make? You run in, gun up someone's nose, clean out the drawer into the bag I'm going to give you, and then you tear ass back to the car and we're on the way to the next Dunkin' Donuts before the cops even know we're still out there."

"I go in with the gun," George said, pointing to himself. "And you stay in the car?"

"You've got it," said Raymond, reaching for another handful of pretzels. He didn't even like pretzels, but it gave him something to do, something to concentrate on. "It's better if no one sees my face, puts two and two together. One black man robs, not two. The black man doing the robbing doesn't fit the description on TV. You hear what I'm saying?"

"I hear," said George, scratching his stomach.

Something about this didn't sit right with George, but he didn't know quite what and even if he knew quite what he wasn't sure he could raise it with Raymond. George was afraid of Raymond. No lie, though he wasn't about to tell anyone. It wouldn't pay to cross Raymond. Didn't seem to pay much being on his side either, but maybe that was changing.

"When we goin'?"

"Get your coat on," said Raymond.

"I gotta eat somethin'," said George.

Raymond nodded. "I'll get you a peanut butter sandwich," he said, moving toward the small, rattling refrigerator in the corner.

Then, Raymond thought but didn't say, we'll see what we can do about going out and getting you killed.

They weren't coming, at least not on this shift. Frankie Kraylaw knew that before the first sunlight tried to get through the slow, fat, dark clouds.

Frankie gathered his rubbish, put it carefully into the plastic bag he had brought with him, and went to the back door of the reupholstery shop. He hadn't broken the lock, only forced it, and the door was such a banged-up mess anyway that he doubted anyone would notice. Besides, people who lived next door to or ran businesses across the street from police stations didn't think they had to be careful.

That was wrong. Frankie knew that was wrong. The Lord had told him, well, not exactly told him but let him feel, that he wanted Frankie to be careful, because Frankie had God's work to do. Not that everyone didn't have God's work to do. Thank the Lord Jesus. It's just that there were those chosen few like Frankie who could feel the truth, know it without talking or thinking. It was the way our Redeemer wanted it.

The alley behind the shop was clear. Cold and clear. No cars parked across the way in the small lot behind a 7-Eleven. Frankie closed the door quickly, made sure it clicked locked, and then hurried, didn't run but hurried into the alley where he pitched his plastic bag of garbage into an open trash can, sending a rat scurrying.

Hat over his face, hands plunged deeply into his pockets, Frankie felt the jingle of pocket change as he headed around the corner where the alley turned and made his way toward Wendy's. A hot coffee and vigilance. He stopped in front of the pickup truck, opened the door, and checked in all directions to be sure he wasn't being followed. He pulled the old Colt shotgun out from under his jacket and shoved it under the driver's seat. He locked the door, checked the street again, and hurried across the street toward the early-morning lights of the fast food restaurant.

They had to come sometime. They had to come.

Seven Thirty-Six in the Morning

Abe Lieberman considered ramming into the wooden chair with the big white card on it. The chair was protecting the space that Kim the Korean, who owned the Devon Television/VCR Repair Shop, had dug out of the ice and snow. PARKING FOR TELEVISION REPAIR ONLY!!!!!!! the sign read in bold blue crayon.

It was early. Abe inched forward past Discount Toys, Devon Animal World, and Rogers Park Fruits and Vegetables, all of which had illegally reserved public parking spaces they had dug out. Abe settled for the space in front of the fireplug near the corner by the barbershop, flipped up his ON DUTY sign, and stepped out, trying to avoid the ruts of snow lined with treacherous ice.

Abe entered the T&L to the familiar smell of coffee, corned beef, and warm bagels and bialys, and the unfamiliar sound of silence.

Manuel, the short-order cook, had learned his craft while serving as a busboy at The Bagel two blocks away. The Bagel was the biggest Jewish-style restaurant on the North Side and in the suburbs. It was a matter of pride to Maish that he had a chef who had apprenticed at The Bagel itself, even if the chef was a Mexican Catholic. Manuel looked through the food passageway from the kitchen as Abe entered. There was a plea in his dark face. Manuel's eyes moved to the left toward the silent, lumpish figure of Maish, his back turned to the door, his apron tied around his waist. Maish was carefully making up a list of the day's specials on the sheet of clear plastic over white board that hung above the counter near the cash register.

There were eight seats at the counter. All empty. It was still a little early for the on-the-way-to-work crowd, the once-in-a-whilers and the regulars, the working women like Gert Bloombach, Melody Rosen, and Sylvie Chen who came by to get their usuals and ignore their fathers at the Alter Cocker table. Too early for the regulars. Too early for the Alter Cockers, too, but some of them were there: Syd Levan, the golfer, stoop-shouldered, tan from the lamp, hair whiter than the sands on the beaches down in Sarasota where he would soon be headed with his wife to their time-share; Howie Chen, always ready to smile and take a joke, short, hefty, one eye ignoring any and all instructions from the brain; and the unelected but accepted leader of the group, Herschel Rosen himself, antiquated, wearing his blue woolen hat and a smile and a drooping, unlit cigar. Herschel was the group comic, and the Alter Cockers were his willing audience—but not today. Conversation was nonexistent. Herschel, Howie, and Syd looked up at Abe hopefully as the heavy door with the little bell closed behind him.

"Hey, look who's here," Herschel tried. "The sheriff of West Rogers Park himself, Ricochet Lieberman. Howdy, pardner."

Abe waved to the table of old men and moved to the counter, where he took a stool. Maish didn't move. Abe didn't speak.

"*Lo siento, viejo,*" said Manuel from the grill.

"*Entiendo, gracias,* Manuel," Lieberman answered.

"*Su hermano es . . .*" Manuel started.

"*Si, no tiene miedo.*"

Maish finished his sign, held it up, turned to show it to his brother.

"Fine," said Abe. "Perfect. Frame it. Brisket six-fifty, a thing of beauty."

Maish nodded and placed the sign on the hook near the counter. He poured a cup of coffee from the pot of regular and brought it to his brother. Their eyes met.

"You should be with Yetta, Maish," Abe said softly, lifting his cup.

"You should be out finding David's killer," said Maish even more softly, unblinking.

"I finish my coffee, I go out and find them," said Abe, holding up his cup.

"Good," said Maish. "You got a reason to work, not to think. I got no reason but I've got to work or . . ."

He was an overweight bulldog of a man who at sixty-seven carried the family curse of looking older than his years.

"I understand," said Abe.

"Bess's with Yetta," said Maish, turning his back on his brother and lumbering toward the sink, wiping his hands on his apron. "I'm there and we just make each other worse. Yetta'll be busy cooking for the *minyon*. Bernard will be in, weather permitting, at noon. Rabbi Wass will . . . Yetta's better off without me there making her feel worse, making her feel she has to take care of me, worrying about me, asking me about my heart, my liver, my pancreas, my who-the-hell-knows."

Maish never swore. Maish never even said "hell." Abe sipped his coffee, let it burn the roof of his mouth. The coffee was bitter this morning. This morning it was right that the coffee should be bitter.

"You've got a *minyon*?" Abe asked, surprised

that his brother had already gathered a contingent of the ten Jewish men required for prayer, in this case prayer for the dead.

"The Cockers, you, me. They'll tell me. Right now I want to be a little left alone, a little crazy. You know? I can use it. Humor me."

"I'll humor you," said Abe, looking at Manuel, who retreated behind the partition to the heat of his grill.

And, thought Lieberman, I won't tell you that there will have to be an autopsy, soon maybe, but maybe not until late in the day, maybe even the afternoon or night. They would have to sit *Shiva*, mourn the loss of the loved one in the house of Maish and Yetta with the mirrors covered and turned to the wall while someone in the medical examiner's office on Polk Street behind Cook County Hospital opened flaps on the body of David Lieberman in an effort to find something that would help locate the people who killed him.

"Carol's going to be fine," said Maish. "We couldn't talk to her, but the doctor, he said . . . And the baby, a boy, he's going to be fine. Yetta's going to ask Carol to call him David. Not often a Jewish kid can be named for his father. Not often the father's dead so he can be."

Maish was making himself busy, cleaning the clean cream-colored countertop with a wet rag, his jowls rumbling.

"How's it look?" he said, stepping back.

Abe finished the coffee and stood up.

"Almost as clean as when you started," he said.

Maish nodded.

"I'll find them," said Abe.

"Then what?" asked his brother, rubbing his eyes.

"Then . . . we go on living."

"And if I ask you to shoot them down, make them beg for their lives and shoot them on their knees, would that be something you could do?" asked Maish.

"Would that make you feel better, Maish?"

"Yes, I think so."

"Maish, when did you ever hit anyone? In your whole life, when have you hurt anyone physically?"

"Never," Maish said intently. "Never, and my reward is that my son who never hurt anyone is murdered."

"The two aren't connected."

"Everything is connected in here," said Maish, pointing to his chest.

"We'll have four specials," called Herschel Rosen.

"It's seven-thirty in the morning," answered Maish, his eyes still fixed on his brother. "You want brisket seven-thirty in the morning?"

"You got it ready seven-thirty in the morning?" asked Howie Chen.

"Manny's got it ready," Maish said aloud, and then whispered to his brother, "It's in here, Avrum. My heart. Like a, I don't know, a heavy thing. If I know whoever did it is dead, maybe . . . Forget I said anything."

"Then we'll eat brisket at seven-thirty in the morning," said Syd Levan showing clean, false white teeth through the tan.

"Four early-morning briskets, Manny," Maish said, lost in thought.

"Leftover brisket in the morning," said Abe. "Remember when there was any left we ate it cold in the morning with Kraft's Miracle Whip on Wonder Bread?"

Maish was recleaning the countertop.

"That's probably why I look like this," said Maish. "But you, you eat like a garbage truck and you never gain weight."

"Go ask God," said Abe.

"I have, as recently as this morning," said Maish, inspecting a problematic shadow near the sugar dispenser. "He had nothing to say on the subject. It's a good ploy. He don't answer, he can't be wrong."

"I'll see you later, Maish," said Abe.

"Wait," said Maish.

Lieberman paused in front of the counter as Maish reached down and brought up a brown bag with grease stains.

"Mostly bialys, onions, poppies, and some cream cheese with chives. Jimmy just dropped by from the bakery. Maybe you could drop it off at the house. People'll be coming. Yetta'll need it."

Lieberman took the still-warm package in his arms.

"Sure, Maish."

"I'll go home in a little while," Maish said,

shaking his head and turning his back again. "Find them, Avrum," he said. "Find them. I can't . . . The idea of them walking around, free, while David . . . Find them. Do your work."

"Save a piece of brisket for me, Maish," Lieberman said, moving to the door and buttoning his coat.

"Marshall Earp," called Herschel Rosen, motioning to Lieberman. "Come over and share a few fingers of Folger's with the bunkhouse crew."

Lieberman moved to the table and Herschel motioned him to lean over. He did, and smelled the dry cigar and aftershave.

"We'll keep an eye," whispered Herschel.

"Some of us will be here all day," said Syd.

"Eating brisket," chimed in Howie Chen.

"And Izzy's on the way. You know the way Izzy makes Maish laugh," whispered Syd.

Lieberman nodded. Izzy Zedel couldn't make the town idiot laugh.

"Thanks," said Abe, knowing that each man he was facing had in his long life lost a wife, brother, sister, child, friend. Abe and Maish had been in their homes, apartments, paying condolences, weeping with them.

"*Adios,*" said Herschel, as Abe went to the door.

"*Hasta luego,*" answered Abe, waving at Manny, who was lining up the brisket breakfasts.

Manny nodded and went on working.

While the Alter Cockers were eating brisket, Bill Hanrahan, clean shaven, dressed in shirt, somber tie, and jacket, in keeping with his coming impersonation, sat down at his kitchen table for a breakfast of moo shu pork and eggs. Iris, slender, delicate, beautiful, and early, had appeared at the door with a bag full of Chinese morning treats, including almond cookies for Charlie.

They had all eaten with Jeanine, talking about her coworkers at McDonald's and her plans to take Charlie to Santa Fe, where Hanrahan knew a retired cop named Shea who would hire her as a waitress in his Tex-Mex restaurant. Charlie didn't talk. Hanrahan didn't talk. Iris didn't talk. Jeanine didn't notice. She thought that what she was saying was as interesting to the others as it was to her, and Hanrahan had no intention of dispelling her illusion. The girl had been through enough and back again for more. He marveled that after the hell Frankie Kraylaw had put her and her son through she could be this full of enthusiasm.

It had been more than a week since she had last said anything about Frankie and her fear that he would come back to find her and Charlie.

Hanrahan smiled and tried to listen, picking up enough, a cop trick, to be able to nod in the right places.

He reached for another moo shu crepe, put it on his plate, spooned the filling on it, and poured some thick plum sauce over the filling.

A horn blew.

"Myrna," Jeanine said, getting up. "Let's go, Charlie."

Charlie rose without comment and wiped his mouth with a paper napkin.

"I'm sorry I can't stay to clean up," Jeanine said to Iris. "But Mr. Hanrahan won't let me, anyway. Thank you for the delicious food. What do you say, Charlie?"

"Thank you for the delicious food," the boy echoed soberly.

"You are both welcome," said Iris. "Have a good day. Stay warm."

And then Iris and Bill were alone. He considered one more filled crepe. It would be his fifth. He decided against it. His appetite had grown enormously since he had stopped drinking. He tended to control it, but when someone placed a meal before him his stomach and the memory of his father's voice told him to eat until there was nothing left, eat as if there was no tomorrow; because for a policeman, there might be no tomorrow.

"A good cop enjoys every moment of life," his father had told him when he had decided to make a career of it. "He savors every moment, laughs at every joke, tries to put things right on the spot. The devil eats fast and leaves no leftovers."

"It was very good," said Hanrahan, pushing away his plate and standing up. "But you didn't have to come out this early in this weather to . . ."

"I did," said Iris.

Hanrahan had begun to remove the dishes one by one, to clean them off into the fresh plastic bag in the garbage can. He never nested the plates nor piled them.

"Why did you have to come?" asked Hanrahan.

"To observe you in the morning with the young woman," she said, with her hands on the table.

Hanrahan paused, dirty dish in hand, to look at her with a smile.

"You're not jealous?" he asked.

"Yes," she said calmly. "I am. And I have reason. She is a lovely young girl, very grateful to you. You are a man. To not respond would not be human. I know you to be human."

Hanrahan put down the dish, rubbed the side of his nose, and moved to the table to sit next to Iris, who watched him, her eyes never leaving his.

"I consider the possibility from time to time and reject it before it takes heart or form," he said. "Jeanine is a child of misfortune and not the brightest of God's creatures. I neither need nor want what such a thing might mean and I know she doesn't need such a thing. My goal is to get her money saved and ship her and the boy to Danny Shea in Santa Fe."

"I will contribute one thousand dollars," said Iris.

Hanrahan laughed.

"I am serious," Iris said.

"I know you are, darling," he said, realizing he was echoing the words his father often spoke to his mother. "Maybe we can each give her five hundred and send her on her way to warmth and happiness and leave me in frequent nightly solitude."

"I would be pleased if this were to happen," she said.

"Good, settled," he said. "When Jeanine and Charlie are gone, maybe we can do some serious talking about where we . . ."

Iris was shaking her head now, almost imperceptibly, but shaking it nonetheless.

"What?" he asked.

"It will take more than money to send out from this house the presence of your wife," she said.

"Maureen isn't coming back to me," he said.

"But you would not be unhappy if she did," said Iris. "I am not trying to make you uncomfortable. I'm trying to see what is true."

"Look . . ."

"This house," she said, looking around. "Even the way you do the dishes. You await the day she may return."

"If she walked in here tomorrow," he said, "she'd see I can take care of myself."

"She would see that you have kept a shrine," Iris countered gently.

Hanrahan rose slowly. "You been taking night classes in psychology?" he asked, with a hint of the smile still in his voice.

"No," she said. "I have been thinking. William, do you know how old I am?"

Hanrahan was decidedly uncomfortable. "I don't think . . ."

"No," she said. "That is true. Often you do not think. I am fifty-seven years old. I am more than seven years older than you are. I can have no children. I was content or resigned to what I was and what I had till you came into our restaurant. Now you have asked me to live with uncertainty and affection. I find it difficult."

"You want to stop seeing me?"

"No, I want you to give up the past or embrace it."

"Iris, my dear, this is heavy duty on a heavy morning after a heavy breakfast. Give me some time to think this through."

"Yes," she said. "Now, if you agree, I would very much like to have you make love to me."

She rose and faced him. She was lovely and he felt oafish, bloated, held together by his tight suit. She had never offered before and he had never pushed.

There was no way he could or would or wanted to reject her.

"I would consider that an honor I do not deserve," he said.

"Do you joke?"

"Not in the least," he said. "I'm being nervous and childish."

"No more nervous than I," she said, stepping toward him.

He took her in his arms and smelled her. He kissed her open lips and tasted distant mint.

"Only one request, one demand really," she whispered when their mouths were no longer touching.

"Yes," he said.

"We do not make love in the bed you shared with Maureen."

"I understand," he said.

"No, I do not think you do. I do not wish to overcome your past and erase your memories. I wish to be your present and future."

"And so say all of us," he said, picking Iris up and cradling her in his arms. She weighed so little. He felt he could fling her in the air and when she came down it would be floating and laughing.

She put her arms around his neck, lay her head against his shoulder, and said something that must have been in Chinese. Something told him to check the clock, reminded him that he had someplace to be. He did not ignore that something. He simply decided that it was not one tenth as important as that which he was about to do.

The old car was rattling, steam hissed from the cap. It shivered and shrieked for mercy, but Raymond Carrou tortured it onward with George DuPelee at his side. So far the plan was working just fine. George had entered the McDonald's on Clark, gun in hand, while Raymond waited outside. No more than two minutes later George had come out with two bags, one filled with money from the register, the other filled with Egg McMuffins.

The man was definitely a walking fool. And he looked a fool, the little dead man's hat on his head, a hopeful grin on his face, a mouthful of egg, bacon, and bread.

"How much you think we got?"

"Not enough, mostly singles," said Raymond, moving carefully down a narrow, slippery side street. "I'd say a couple of hundred maybe."

George's smile slipped and he stopped chewing, though his mouth was full.

"How much you say we need?"

Raymond shrugged, feeling his hands tremble.

"At least a thousand, maybe more. Don't worry. Next place I picked out should have all we need."

"What you say? You want one of these sandwiches?"

Raymond took a sandwich, unwrapped it awkwardly, and ate as he drove, spinning George a tale to lull him into fantasies of modest wealth and escape.

"Before we hit the Burger King up near Montrose," Raymond said, "we're going to do the same game we just played at a place I hear makes collections from hot-dog carts, ice-cream carts, things like that."

"Uh huh," said George. "But no hot-dog carts, ice-cream carts such like out in the cold. They're not gonna have much money."

Raymond hit the steering wheel with the heels of his gloved hands and said, "No, of course not, not outside. In the winter, those places go inside, office lobbies, factories. They're out all night. Taxi places. You know where they send the cabs out. Those guys come in hungry. You know Jason?"

"Cabo Jason?"

"No, man. Bass Jason, cab driver from Guayaguayare back home. He says there are money piles in this place we're going. We're going where they drop the money, all cash, every morning. Be no one in there but a couple of old men counting. Might be more than you can carry. Maybe you can use one of their bags."

They slid across Sedgwick, almost kissing the side of a slow-moving semi. Sandwiches and change went flying. Raymond straightened the car out on its nearly bald tires and moved slowly northwest.

"I don't know," said George, gathering money and meat in both hands and shoveling them into the brown McDonald's carryout bags. "I think I'd rather maybe be doin' another McDonald's."

"We just did one," Raymond said, easing the car past old red-stone factories and warehouses and across a bridge over railway tracks. "They'll be waiting, all alert if we do another one."

"Maybe so."

"We need money. Remember. You shot that woman with the baby. We've got to get out of here."

"But it's you she pictured, not me," George said, firmly adjusting David Lieberman's hat on his head. "Remember, you said she saw you good, not me."

"Right," Raymond said. "We're in this together. There, right there, doorway next to the restaurant."

George looked out the window while Raymond came to a stop. A deep horn blasted somewhere not too far away. The restaurant wasn't much of a restaurant, more of a small, old, one-story carryout diner wedged in between a railroad embankment and a three-story block-long warehouse.

"You sure?" said George, fishing for his pistol in his coat pocket. "I don't see no carts."

"Must all be gone by now," said Raymond, not meeting George's eyes. "Doesn't look like there's many people in the place. You see the door? Go in. I hear it's down the back. Just push open the door, bring up the gun, and tell the old man to give you the money. I'll pull the car around out of sight, back there by that fence. You come out slow or running and I'll be there. You hear? That clear?"

George nodded, opened the door, reached in the bag for an Egg McMuffin, and hurried across the street, steam puffing from his nose and mouth.

This was the careful time. No one really knew his connection to George DuPelee. They had met in a bar, struck up talk about the Islands, and got together. Raymond had to be sure no one saw the car.

91

When the Russian drug dealers in the office behind the diner shot George full of holes and dumped him and his gun in the river or in a dumpster, the police would find him, place the gun as the one that shot the woman, and maybe be satisfied. In any case, there would then be only one person who could connect him to the murder of David Lieberman, and that was fine with Raymond Carrou.

Raymond turned the car around, trying not to notice the grinding sound beneath him as he made the U-turn and headed back toward the fence. He opened the window a crack. It was cold in the car, but this made it much worse. There was no choice. He had to hear the shots, be sure George was dead. Besides, the inside of the car was beginning to smell of eggs and bacon grease and it was making Raymond quite sick to his stomach.

He kept the noisy motor running after he had pulled much farther down the street than he had said he would. His one fear was that after the Russians killed George they'd come running out looking for a getaway car, see him, and be crazy enough to start shooting. Those Russians were crazy men. That was what he was counting on, but he didn't want to take any chances on just how crazy they might be.

That was all the thinking Raymond had time for. There, running out of the door next to the diner, was George, gun in one hand, small pink plastic pail in the other. He was panting, running, tripping, and looking back over his shoulder at the doorway.

"Shit," said Raymond aloud, hitting the steering wheel again with the palms of his hands.

Turn and run leaving George there and hope they came out and finished him off, chased him down? What if they didn't? What if George came looking for Raymond? What the hell had happened?

George was lunging toward him down the middle of the street, the Russian hat tilted to one side. George fell to his knees, picked himself up, and came on.

Raymond drove slowly toward the running man and twenty yards from him made another slow U-turn. George caught up with him, opened the door with his gun hand, collapsed inside holding his stomach, and gasped, "Go, go."

Raymond went. The door next to George caught the wind and slammed shut. In the rear-view mirror Raymond watched for pursuers. There were none.

"Why . . . you . . . so . . . far?" George said, holding his stomach.

"You shot?"

"No . . . exhausted, man. Why . . . you . . . ?"

"Police came by. I couldn't have them put two and two together. You know. Be parked across the street asking me what I'm doing there just when you come running out with a gun in your hand. You understand what I'm saying? I saved your ass."

"Thanks," George said, sitting up, putting the gun in his pocket and straightening the fur cap on his head. He sat panting and clutching the plastic bucket.

"What happened?" asked Raymond, taking the first left turn he could.

"Like you said," panted George. "Go down this little hall. Go through this door. Two guys sitting there. Not old. Tough looking. You know. They be sitting there with some plastic barrels of some brown shit and piles of money. I dump the shit on the floor holding the gun on them and tell 'em till fill it with money. They be talking something. German, who knows, but they get the idea. They had guns, Raymond. I took 'em, dumped 'em in the snow when I came out after I shove them in a closet and lock the door. Still got the key."

He held up the key, opened the window, and threw it out.

"Let's see," said Raymond, now taking a right turn into decidedly unfamiliar and white-faced territory.

George tilted the plastic bucket so Raymond could look at the money. Then George lifted out some bills. Twenties, tens.

"Here's a fifty. Must be a couple of thousand dollars," George said with a grin and a cough. "We're on our way."

Raymond didn't know what had been in the buckets, but whatever it was, it was worth a hell of a lot more than the few thousand dollars

George had picked up. The Russians must have thought he was some stupid local dumb-shit nigger passing up who knows how much in shit for a few bills.

They'd come looking for him. If they couldn't speak much English, maybe they hadn't caught George's accent. But they had seen his face, the hat. They'd come looking for him. They'd have to make the effort or have the word out with every trigger-happy, knife-carrying punk that the Russians were good for a few thousand easy ones.

George sat there smiling, clutching the bucket. He was even more of a liability now for Raymond than he had been twenty minutes ago. And he deserved to die, to die for what he had done. Raymond seriously considered taking out his gun, shooting George in the face, and kicking his carcass out of the car, money and all. But he rejected the idea. First, he didn't know where they were, didn't know if he could get away safely. Second, there might be a way to link this fool to him. Raymond didn't know how, but there might be. No, it would be better to get things together, tie up all the ends, be packed and ready to move, and then kill George outside the city.

"Looking like good times now, Raymond," George said, patting him on the back.

"Yes," said Raymond, knowing that he had let in the devil's own fool two nights ago and the fool had not only ruined the plan but was sure to get Raymond caught or killed if he did not get things moving fast.

Eight Minutes After
Nine A.M.

Hanrahan was dizzy as he sat up in the pull-out bed in the living room. He couldn't remember how many years it had been since he'd last opened it. Eight, nine? Longer. When he had snored fiercely during the worst of his drinking, Maureen had kicked him out and told him to sleep in the living room.

He sat at the edge of the bed, looked at his suit crumpled on the chair, and wondered if he had dreamed the whole thing, if he had gotten up in the middle of the night, gotten drunk, and imagined the morning. Iris had been more than fine; willing, giving, gentle, satisfied, soft. Reserved though she was with her clothes on and in the sight of others, in bed she had been all passion and plumage, and he feared for an instant that if it weren't a dream, he might not be able to keep up with the Iris who had exhausted him.

Iris had gone. She had kissed his nose, placed his right hand between her legs for an instant, and then disappeared. He had closed his eyes, arm over his face for what felt like a moment, and then came awake seconds ago, dizzy.

He reached for his watch, found it on the table where he seemed to remember leaving it, and realized he was late. There would be no time to finish the dishes, no time to make up the pull-out bed.

The fleeting thought of Maureen coming through the door, seeing the unmade bed in the living room, finding the dishes on the table in the kitchen, gave him a moment of near panic. He considered trying to reach Lieberman, telling him he would be a few minutes late. Claim illness, an emergency.

Then he stood up and grew calm.

If he called, Lieberman might think he had been drinking. Lieberman's nephew had been murdered hours ago and Lieberman was still going to go ahead with the sting. Could Hanrahan miss the whole four-week setup to clean house?

"Hell with it," Hanrahan muttered, and he frantically began to put on his now-rumpled suit.

Frankie Kraylaw was nearing panic too, but for a very different reason.

Nothing wrong with his plan. Sit, let the Lord enter his mind, sip the hot drink, ignore stupidity, blasphemy, remember the greater goal given him, the test for which he had been commanded to return from distant lands to redeem his family. And yet they sat where he could not avoid them, not if he was to be able to see the entrance to the Clark Street police station.

Two women, little more than girls, painted, tight dresses under their open coats. And a man. They ate, they drank coffee, and though he could not see beneath the table he was sure that the man was reaching over, touching the young women where he should not, making them laugh the laugh of the demons. And words would come, the sick words of the city, of corruption. *Cunt, fuck, asshole, prick.* Frankie could not cut the words out with prayer. Could not move to avoid them, could not keep himself from glancing at them, praying for a bolt of lightning that would crack the window, launching shards of glass to tear them to pieces.

"You," came the voice of the man.

Frankie kept his eyes on the window.

"You, kid, you with the pink titty cheeks," the voice of the man came again.

"Leave him alone, J.J.," said one of the women. "Don't start no shit here. Come on. Cops are right over there."

"What am I doin' that's so bad?" said J.J. "I wanna talk to the fuckin' kid, be friendly, maybe offer him your pussy for dessert. What you say, kid?"

Frankie turned his head from the window. The devil was distracting him for his trial and he was succumbing. The policemen would come when he looked away at the demon and the temptresses.

Both women were dark, pretty, Mexicans maybe. He couldn't be sure. One was smoking and chewing gum at the same time. The man was dark too, but his hair was yellow, almost white, unnatural. All of them were looking at Frankie now.

They were the only customers in Wendy's. A fat young woman behind the counter was talking to a kid in a white shirt who was making something on the grill.

"Kid, you a deaf asshole?" the man called J.J. said. "I hate myself when I pull this shit," he said to one of the girls, who giggled. "But it's just in me. You know?"

"Whatever," said the gum chewer, flicking ash in the general direction of the aluminum ashtray.

"Let's just go, J.J.," said the other girl.

"We got no work for hours," J.J. said, shrugging her off. "This'll take a minute. We can all go get some beauty sleep."

The girl shrugged, resigned, and sat back looking at her fingers.

"Kid, you are pissing me off here," said J.J. "I'm jus' tryin' to have a little friendly conversation between strangers. This is a big, cold city. You make friends where you can find 'em."

"The Lord is all the friend I need," said Frankie.

"What?" said J.J., almost choking on his coffee. "You hear what he said? The Lord is all you need? What about at night when you start thinking of a nice piece of pie like Lauren or Jess here?"

"Stop now in the name of the Lord Jesus," Frankie said, clasping his hands together.

"I can't believe this," said J.J., getting up. "I didn't know they really grew fruitcakes like this anymore."

Frankie fixed his eyes on the window, beyond

the window to the front of the Clark Street police station. Two uniformed policemen, both black, came out and hurried around to the rear of the building.

"I'm gonna have to insist that you look at me when I talk to you, little Jesus," said J.J., taking a step toward Frankie.

The fat girl behind the counter picked up on what was happening and stopped talking to the kid in the white shirt.

"What's going on?" she asked.

"Nothing," said J.J. "Friend and I are just having a little fun here. We're just two couples cooling down after a night on the town."

The girl looked at J.J.'s false grin and then at Frankie, who did not meet her gaze. She started talking to the kid in the white shirt again but kept glancing back at J.J., who advanced on Frankie and leaned over on his table, palms flat, breath stale from rot and brimstone.

"Hey, kid, Jesus is fine but will he be there to go down on you when you need him?" J.J. whispered in Frankie's ear.

Before J.J. could really start his laugh, he felt himself flying backward as if the wall had exploded. Someone screamed and J.J. couldn't breathe, couldn't see anything but black, and then he felt the knee in his stomach, and again, and something in his ear.

"Get off, get off, you crazy bastard," the girl called Lauren screamed.

"Stop that," yelled the fat girl behind the counter.

Then the weight was off him and J.J. could see. Standing over him was a crazed, open-mouthed bloody thing. The thing was kicking him. The thing turned and punched Jess in the throat. She staggered back, holding her neck, trying to breathe. Lauren screamed, "Oh, my God," and went running for the door as the crazy thing J.J. had let loose grabbed a chair and threw it at her.

J.J. tried to sit up, but something was broken and he couldn't move.

Screaming, more voices.

The kid who was no longer a kid had picked up another chair and turned toward J.J., who tried to slide backward, gasping, "Hey, I was kidding, for God's sake. What the fuck are you doin'?"

And then the horror hit J.J. The horror that came with the realization that the kid had something raw and bloody between his teeth, the realization that it was J.J.'s ear.

"Oh," moaned J.J. "Help. Somebody, help."

The creature standing over J.J. spat out his ear and brought the chair down on him, crying, "Are you washed in the blood of the lamb?"

That was all J.J. Prescott remembered, that and the sight of Jess trying to cry and catch her breath. All he would remember until he woke up in the intensive-care ward of Weiss Hospital four days later.

Frankie was going to hit the demon again, but the Lord whispered in his ear that the bloody exorcism was complete. Frankie turned to the gasping woman, the one who had chewed gum and smoked at the same time. She staggered backward when he looked at her, fell back over a table, and hit her head against the window while trying to scream.

Frankie dropped the chair and ran for the door, the same door Lauren had run through seconds ago. He ran out into the street knowing that he was a bloody vision.

He raced through the cold, frightened an old woman on her way to the bus stop, and made his way to the refuge of his pickup truck.

He pulled the collar of his jacket up to cover part of his bloody face, forced himself to be calm, and turned on the ignition. In the rearview mirror he saw Lauren coming out of the police station with two uniformed policemen who weren't even wearing coats. They didn't look in Frankie's direction. The Lord was still on his side. Praise the Lord.

He pulled into the slow-moving traffic heading south into the city.

He had passed the latest test, had defeated the demon, and now he would have to return to his task. The Lord might well place many other obstacles in his path, but now he knew that it was within his power to smite demons and recognize tempters.

Frankie Kraylaw, with the help of God, would prevail. He would destroy the two policemen. He would wrench his wife and son from this city of evil. Then a new thought struck him, the voice coming as he was sure it had come to Abraham. When the task was completed, when God's will was done and Frankie had been rewarded on earth for his faith, God might well want him to sacrifice his firstborn son.

Yes, if God so bid him, he would sacrifice Charlie on the altar of the Lord though he truly loved his son as Abraham had loved Isaac.

Frankie wanted to say "Praise Jesus" aloud. He tried, but his throat was dry with blood and he choked upon the words.

There were four people at Maish and Yetta's 1950s split-level brick house in Lincolnwood when Abe arrived with his bag of bagels, bialys, and cream cheese. He avoided Bess's eyes and went to Yetta, who stood, her eyes red, a heavy woman who had given up any pretense of holding herself or her feelings together. She looked and felt in his arms like a sack of cotton left out in the rain.

Spindly-legged dark furniture and faded flower patterns, gray carpet throughout, two bedrooms, one of which had been shared by David and Edward until they each left for college, marriage, and their own families.

"Avrum," she said, clinging to him, almost knocking him over.

"Yetta," Abe answered, patting her head and trying to keep his balance.

Her pain came into him, a sudden wet shock,

and she cried. "I can't remember what he was like as a baby," she said, holding him at arm's length to make this statement that astonished her. "Can you remember Lisa?"

"Some things," Abe said, looking at Lisa, who stood across the room.

Bess, dressed in black, was now moving toward him and Yetta. She did not look angry. Bess was erect, slender, as tall as her husband and looking fifteen years younger than him, though only five years separated them. Bess was not a beauty, but she was a fine-looking woman, a lady. Her father had been a butcher on the South Side, but she carried herself as if he had been a banker. She had the soft, clear voice that telephone operators used to have.

Lieberman had done his best, which was not always very good, to keep his wife from being displeased with him, not because he feared her but because he felt the criticism of her common sense.

"Yetta," Bess said softly. "Come, let's have another cup of coffee and show the Reiffels the family pictures. Come."

Yetta nodded dutifully and started to turn, but paused to say to Abe, "Maish went to work."

"I know," said Lieberman. "I just came from there. He sent these."

Bess took the package and handed it to an overly made-up woman who could have been sixty or eighty.

"You remember Marge Reiffel," Bess said.

"Of course," Lieberman said with a smile, though he had no idea who this woman was. "How have you been, Marge?"

"Don't ask," Marge said, turning away with a wave of her hand and a tear in her voice as she headed for the kitchen with the bag.

Bess stood at Lieberman's side while Lisa led Yetta to the sofa, where an open book of family photos waited.

"Give him something to eat, Bess," Yetta called. "He must be starving."

"I will," said Bess, turning to her husband.

"I wanted you to sleep," Lieberman said. "I thought you could use a good night's rest for all this."

"I know," she said. "I figured."

"You look beautiful and you smell like perfect memories."

"You look terrible, Lieberman," Bess answered. "And you smell like mildew. You got time to go home, take a shower, change clothes?"

He shook his head no and watched his sister-in-law sitting with the photograph album on her lap, slowly pointing to a David of the past and telling the story of the lost moment.

"That's her history," Bess said. "That book, some memories of things that don't mean anything to anyone else. We teach kids about kings and wars but pay no attention to the history that will really count for them, their own lives."

"You're right," he said.

"You'd tell me I was right if I said your Cubs

deserve to lose a hundred games this year. I'm not mad anymore, Abe. We've got grief to deal with here. Are you all right?"

Lieberman couldn't answer.

"Are you feverish, Lieberman?" Bess said, putting her cool hand on his brow.

He closed his eyes. "Keep it there," he said.

She took her hand away and he opened his eyes.

"Can you stop by the house when Barry and Melisa come home, just before three? Todd's going to pick them up and keep them for a few days. Lisa got some time off and she's going to help me here, pick up Edward at the airport."

"Bess," he said. "I'm trying to catch the people who killed Davey."

"You want to make arrangements for the funerals, the burial, food, calls to relatives? Maish can't do it. Yetta can't do it. Carol is in the hospital trying to . . ."

"Enough," said Lieberman, holding up his hands. "I'll be home. I'll change clothes. I'll get the kids packed . . ."

"Lisa packed them."

"Then I'll sit there till Todd comes."

"At three-fifteen."

"I'll be there," said Lieberman. "I gotta go. I'm late."

"Stay a few minutes. Rabbi Wass is on the way."

All the more reason to get out of here,

Lieberman thought, but he said, "Can't. Bill's waiting for me."

He kissed Bess on the cheek and she stopped him to kiss him gently on the mouth. Her smell seeped into his being and made him feel like sex or sleep.

"Abe," she whispered. "Don't think that way."

Her face was in front of his, her brown eyes wide and unwilling to look away.

"What way?" he said with a patient sigh.

"The way you looked when that Puerto Rican girl was murdered. Like you're going to hurt someone, probably yourself."

"I'm late," he said.

"Three o'clock," she reminded him.

"Three o'clock," he confirmed, moving past her to kiss the seated Yetta, to accept a hug, and to nod to Lisa.

"You remember this one, Abe?" Yetta asked, pointing at a photograph of her two sons at the ages of about ten and thirteen and a younger Abe who looked in the picture exactly as he looked earlier that morning and as he had looked from his fifteenth birthday.

"Round Lake," Yetta said. "See, David's fishing in a bucket. You know why he didn't have a shirt on, didn't wear one all summer?"

Lieberman looked at the photograph for some clue, but saw none.

"He thought," Yetta explained, "that he was

going to be a superhero. He'd puff up his little tan chest and try to look strong."

"I remember," he said, looking at Lisa, who saw the same thing in her father's eyes that Bess had seen.

"Abe," she said as he stood.

"I know," Lieberman answered. "Your mother just told me about Todd picking up the kids."

"I don't mean about the kids."

"I know," he said. "I gotta go."

He was halfway through the crowd when Irving Hamel appeared before him. Irving was not a bad man, but he was an irritating one. He was also young, not yet forty, and a lawyer. He had all his hair and it was black. He wore contact lenses. He stood tall and worked out every morning at the Jewish Community Center on Touhy. His wife was beautiful. His two kids, a boy and girl, were beautiful. Irving Hamel might one day be the first Jewish mayor of Chicago or a Supreme Court justice, but to Abe Lieberman, he was generally a pain in the ass.

"My condolences about David," Irving said.

His suit was dark, perfectly pressed. His condolences sounded sincere, but Lieberman felt, as he usually felt about Irving Hamel, that there was another agenda that would come out in a prepositional phrase or an aside.

"Thank you, Irving," Abe said, patting the younger man on the shoulder and trying to move past him.

"How's Bess taking this?" Irving said softly,

sincerely. "No one ever thinks about how Bess is taking things. She's always a rock for others, but something like this . . ."

"She'll be fine," said Lieberman, now knowing where this encounter was leading. "My wife can take on death as well as she's taken on life."

"Oh," said Irving with an admiring shake of the head. "I know. Lord, I know. The woman is an inspiration to us all. But . . ."

"Irving," said Lieberman, invading the man's personal space by stepping toward him. "Bess isn't going to resign as temple president. She's not going to take a leave or have a breakdown. So you're not going to add a line to the community-service listing of your résumé."

"You think I . . ." Hamel said incredulously.

"I know you," Lieberman said evenly. "Do us all a favor, including you. Fight this another day and another way. Don't discuss this with Rabbi Wass unless you already have. And don't discuss it with anyone else but Bess. You want to take her on, be my guest."

With that, Lieberman sidestepped the man and strode toward the door.

Before he left the house, however, Lieberman slipped into the alcove near the front door and used the phone there to make a call. The call led to another call and then another until he reached a boy named Justo Carnito who gave him a time and a place. Lieberman wrote the time and place in his pocket notebook, said *"Gracias,"* and hung up the phone.

As he got into his car parked almost directly in front of his brother's house, Lieberman checked the side mirror and saw the familiar black Pontiac of Rabbi Wass, the young Rabbi Wass, who was forty-five years old.

Rabbi Wass was one of three pillars of Temple Mir Shavot on California Avenue just four blocks from where Lieberman and Bess lived on Jarvis. The second was eighty-five-year-old Ida Katzman, whose ten jewelry stores, left to her by the departed Mort Katzman, allowed her to make donations that had not only kept the congregation alive but also held the promise of a move in the near future to the former Fourth Federal Savings Building on Dempster in Skokie, in a neighborhood of younger families with growing children and new life for the temple. The third pillar of the congregation was Lieberman's wife. Bess was not only the president, but also head of the building-fund drive.

Lieberman's rear tires slipped as he backed up, and when he gunned the engine, he slipped further into an iced rut of his own making.

"Wait," called Rabbi Wass from the open window of his car; Lieberman was trapped.

Rabbi Wass parked in one of the many available morning spaces on the street of small homes and walked over to Lieberman's car, motioning him to roll down the window. He did.

"I'll give you a push," said Wass.

"Rabbi, I . . ."

"Gently in gear and I'll push. Strong back. My ancestors were farmers."

And Lieberman obeyed, worrying about the hour and knowing he would have to pay with a few minutes of conversation.

"Now," shouted the rabbi.

Lieberman stepped gently on the gas.

"Rock back and then we'll thrust on forward," shouted the rabbi.

Abe put the car back in neutral and then switched to drive and hit the gas. With Rabbi Wass pushing, the car belched out into the street.

"Thanks, Rabbi," Lieberman called through the window with a wave of the hand.

"A moment," called Rabbi Wass, moving to the passenger side of Lieberman's car, opening the door, and sliding in. "I need moments of activity like that. Thank you."

"I'm very late," said Lieberman, looking at his watch.

"Only a minute. I promise. I want to express my sense of loss to you and your family."

"Thank you."

He meant well, this earnest man with a round, bespectacled face, and Abe had come to look forward to the *Shavot* services on Friday night during which he could meditate, lose himself in the repetition of praise to God and the poetry of the service, and, if he was lucky, tune out the well-meaning rabbi.

Lieberman was not a religious man; he had considered himself a silent atheist as a young man, a closet Buddhist as an adult, a tolerant acceptor of the rituals of his people at the age of fifty.

The problem with the man at his side was that Rabbi Wass, like his father before him, was a bore whose sermons were definitely the low point of each service though the sermons always dealt with topical issues, including Israeli politics, Middle East peace, racial tension, and Jewish-American politicians. The subject of each sermon was relevant, but Rabbi Wass's observations were on a par with those of a cautious politician: people should learn to be tolerant, should give more to each other, should be open to new ideas.

"We'll have funeral services on Thursday," Rabbi Wass said. "I'm aware of what must be done by the police in such cases of violence."

"That's good," said Lieberman.

"I would like you to say a few words of comfort to the family," said Rabbi Wass, looking earnestly at Lieberman through clouded lenses.

"That's your job, *Rov*," he said.

"It would mean much to your brother, his family, Bess."

"I'll say a few words," Lieberman agreed. "Now, I've really got . . ."

"I understand," said the rabbi, touching Lieberman's arm. "I called the hospital before I left home. Dr. Friedman's on the staff. He's the son of Sophie and Nat. You know them?"

"Yes," said Lieberman.

"Carol and the child are almost certainly out of the woods," he said.

"Thanks, Rabbi."

Rabbi Wass smiled, sighed, opened the door, and said, "I'd better get inside. Remember Thursday. Just a few words of comfort."

He closed the door and Lieberman drove away wondering what words of comfort he could possibly give to his brother, to Yetta, to their son Edward. Maybe they shouldn't be comforted. Maybe they should face the pain for what it was and try to go on.

Maybe a lot of things.

Lieberman hit Lincoln Avenue forcing his way into traffic. He was definitely going to be late.

In the small, warm attic room on the third floor of his home and office on Sheridan Road, J.W. Rashish Ranpur, cardiologist, drank some tepid tea and looked around to see that everything was in place. The carpet was dark and clean, the music stand was in place, the heavy wooden folding chair with the cushion stood in the center of the room facing the window through which he could, if he chose, look out into the chill, solid white expanse leading all the way to the icy shore of Lake Michigan.

The tape and compact disc player stood next to the folding chair, and as he sat facing the two speakers, Dr. Ranpur glanced at the photograph on the wall, the autographed photograph of the Preservation Hall Jazz Band. He had gone to hear

and see them in concert last year and had difficulty holding back his tears of satisfaction as the
trombone player, an ancient stick of a man even
darker in hue than J.W.R. Ranpur and even older,
not only played but took solos, sang, and danced.
The memory made Dr. Ranpur's eyes fill with
tears.

He sat, picked up his trombone, which felt
sufficiently warm, made sure that the slide was
smooth and clear, and selected a compact disc.

The room filled with the sound of horns—
trombone, cornet, saxophone—and the rattle of
banjo, piano, bass fiddle, and drum.

Rashish Ranpur had one hour before his first
patient arrived, and in that hour, as he did every
day, he would play plaintive jazz songs along with
tapes and discs and even rise to sing "Silver
Dollar" or "St. Louis Blues." Dr. Ranpur played
the trombone passing well. He knew that. He was
also sure that if anyone heard him singing, with
his accent, they would have trouble holding back
a smile.

Wait, not anyone, he corrected himself as the
music began. He had the feeling that the sad-
eyed policeman named Lieberman who had come
to him during the night would not laugh, that he
would understand. He had seen the grief in those
eyes and knew that the man's physical ailments,
the high blood pressure, the chronic liver problems, the arthritis in his knees and fingers were
as nothing to the pain he endured with the horror

114

that had taken place just outside Dr. Ranpur's front door.

It was possible, when some time had passed, that Dr. Ranpur would call the policeman, ask him about his ailments, and invite him to hear the Preservation Hall Jazz Band, or an old King Oliver, Isham Jones, or Jack Teagarden record.

The sad, slow, dirgelike beginning of "Hindustan" made the walls of the small room tingle. This would be a session of sadness for the young people who had been shot in his yard only hours ago, a session of sadness and understanding and the celebration of a new life.

Dr. Ranpur began to tap his toe and lifted the trombone to his lips. He waited dutifully for his turn, and when the trombone solo came he joined in, merging with the soloist, and for an hour was lost in the near-perfect meditation of the music of now-old men.

Seven Minutes After Ten A.M.

The man and the woman sitting in the small comfortable waiting room both checked their watches.

The man's name was Lester Allen Wiggs. He called himself Anthony Simington. He was of medium height, slim, with impeccably groomed,

115

stylishly long brown hair combed straight back. His nose had been broken several times, which helped give him the look of a man who had learned the lessons of hard work and had graduated to the three-piece London suit he now wore. The woman was Jean Tortereli, who called herself Jennifer Simington and presented herself as Anthony Simington's wife or sister, depending on to whom the couple were speaking. She was efficiently elegant: black shoes, black knit dress, simple pearl necklace, an off-white sweater that matched the pearls. She pulled up the sleeves of her sweater at times in the conversation when it looked like hard work was called for. She had the beauty of an older model with, perhaps, just a bit too much angular definition to her cheeks, nose, and jaw, which could make her look a bit cold or quite efficient depending on which attitude best suited the situation.

"Bad feel here," said Anthony.

"The weather," Jennifer said, taking out her cigarette case, opening it, and then deciding against smoking. She closed the case, put it back in her purse, and put her hands together.

Anthony looked at her, admiring the confidence and efficiency that she emitted. They had been working together for more than two years. The partnership had been nearly perfect. Neither was physically attracted to the other. Anthony liked young, dark women with gutter diction, and they seemed to like him. Jennifer seemed to have no sexual interest in men or women.

"I say we give them . . ." Anthony began, but the door opened, interrupting him.

"Is this the right room?" asked the old man in the robe, looking a bit confused.

"Mr. Sachs?" asked Anthony, standing up. "You're in the right place. I'm Anthony Simington. This is my wife, Jennifer."

The old man stepped forward to shake the hands offered to him by the couple. Anthony closed the door. Jennifer guided the unsteady old man to a mauve leather-covered armchair. The old man and the couple sat facing one another. Though he seemed a bit frail, it was difficult to see this man as being in the final stages of terminal renal failure.

"Perry is supposed to be here," the old man said, looking at the door nervously.

"Your lawyer must have been a bit delayed. The weather is terrible," Jennifer said, leaning over to pat his hand.

"Is it cold in here?" the old man said, pulling his robe tightly around him. "To me it feels cold."

"Perhaps a bit," Jennifer said with a reassuring smile. "I'll ask them to turn up the heat the moment we leave."

"Thank you," said the old man. "Maybe you'll forgive me, but I don't always remember. . . . Why are we meeting?"

"It was your lawyer's idea, Perry's idea," Anthony lied. "To see to it that when the good Lord took you to him, whatever remained of your

117

worldly possessions would go to a worthwhile cause. We understand that you have no relatives who might survive you and to whom you might wish to give aid after you've gone. The Lord . . ."

"The good Lord has not been particularly good to me," said the old man. "I'm dying and I don't think I welcome spending eternity telling him how wonderful he is. It's much more restful to think that there might be no God."

Anthony Simington chuckled respectfully and Jennifer smiled in understanding. Jennifer found her briefcase on the floor, opened it in her lap, and began fishing out brochures and lists of numbers, which she handed to the old man. He took them in slightly trembling fingers.

"Don't have my glasses," he said. "Besides, I've got no more patience for reading, even the funny papers. I read the *Tribune* sometimes if I can lay it flat on a table. Last book I read was . . . something about a man whose wife falls through the window or something."

"All right," said Anthony Simington. "Let me explain. We represent a small group of organizations, organizations that help people, organizations that will benefit from your contribution and honor your name."

"What good will that do me when I'm dead?" asked the old man.

"None," said Jennifer somberly, holding out a brochure. "But that is not as important as knowing your assets will go to one of these organizations striving for success through hard work and a sense of human decency. Do you want the money you've worked so hard for all your life to simply go to the government?"

"I've worked hard," the old man agreed, looking at his hands. "And I've paid my taxes. Always paid my taxes. No shortcuts, you know what I mean?"

"We have the Taylor-Ives Children's Support Fund," Jennifer said, "the Cook County Friends of AIDS Victims, the Volunteers for the Disabled, the Commitment Society Against Drug and Alcohol Abuse."

"Each one of them," Anthony said, leaning forward toward the confused old man, "needs dollars to continue to do their work."

"I don't know," the old man said, looking at the brochures on his lap. In photos the sad, emaciated faces of black children looked up at him.

"Without Perry, I can't . . ." the old man began, but he stopped when he saw the office door fly open and a large, pink-faced man enter the room carrying a battered briefcase.

"Sorry I'm late," said Perry. "Court appearance. Emergency."

"That's quite all right," said Anthony Simington. "We've been having a fine talk with Mr. Sachs."

"They've been telling me I should leave my money to drug addicts, sick children, homosexuals with AIDS, and who knows who else," said the old man, shaking his head and looking at a spectacularly uninteresting painting on the wall, of a white bird in flight in a gray overcast sky.

Lawyer Perry fixed the Simingtons with a challenge in his eyes that came out in his voice.

"I see," he said.

Perry was dressed in a rumpled suit and had the look of a man who held his drink badly. In short, to the bogus Simingtons, Perry looked like a man who was not prospering.

"We would need legal advice on transferring money to the proper fund," said Anthony.

"Of course," echoed Jennifer.

"Paid legal advice?" Perry asked.

"A fee directly from dollars transferred," said Jennifer.

"A flat percentage," said Anthony.

"What are you talking about?" the old man demanded.

"Helping people," said Perry.

"People who need help," Jennifer said, catching Perry's eye.

"Well, should I do it?" asked the old man.

"These funds are all charities?" asked Perry.

"Yes," Jennifer said emphatically.

"Nonprofit?" Perry went on.

"Nonprofit," answered Anthony.

"We live off a small fee and other corporate work we do," explained Jennifer.

"I see," said Perry.

"See what?" asked the bewildered Mr. Sachs.

"You'd need a signed copy of the revised will," said Perry.

"And a small contribution in advance to show good faith before we alert our aided charities of the benefaction," said Jennifer.

"Made out to . . . ?" Perry asked.

"The organization of your choice," said Anthony, reaching over to take his wife's offered hand.

"Sounds fine to me," said Perry with a grin. "Mr. Sachs?"

"Me too," said old man Sachs, looking down at a photograph of a very young, bravely smiling black girl in rags.

"We have enough?" Perry said, standing.

"We have papers with us," said Jennifer, also standing with her husband. "Ready for signature."

"May I?" asked Perry.

Anthony went back into his wife's briefcase and came up with a folder that he handed to Perry. Perry opened it, glanced at the papers, and looked down at his client.

"Looks like we have enough," said the old man.

"Fine," said Anthony Simington, beaming.

"Not so fine," said old man Sachs.

"Well," said Jennifer, "if there are any details you'd like . . ."

"One," said the old man.

"And that is . . . ?" Jennifer said.

"You are both under arrest," said the old man.

Anthony smiled at Perry, but Perry wasn't

121

smiling. Anthony turned to Jennifer, but she wasn't smiling.

"Fraud," said Perry.

"Sergeant Hanrahan will read you your rights," said the old man, moving toward them.

"Wait . . ." said Anthony, backing away, a lock of hair starting to come loose over his ear.

Jennifer sighed, sat down again, took out her cigarette case, and lit up.

"I think you've misunderstood what my wife and I have been saying here," Anthony tried, his hair definitely moving toward the unruly.

Lieberman removed the robe and revealed a compact recorder hooked to his jacket pocket.

"This is ridiculous," said Anthony. "We want to see our lawyer. You have no . . ."

"Each fund which you describe is in your names, your real names," Lieberman said, looking down at the woman, who crossed her legs and continued smoking without looking at any of the men. "There are no charities. I'm going to say something, but more for me than you. Did you ever think even for a second or two that you're taking food out of the mouths of kids who may be starving?"

"That's not true," shouted Simington.

"It's true," said Lieberman as Hanrahan droned out the Miranda in the background. "Now, there are a couple of uniformed officers outside the door who will escort you to the station. You can call your lawyer before they even book you."

". . . will be used against you," Hanrahan concluded.

Jennifer rose from the chair, closed her briefcase, and strode to the door without a word while Anthony continued to crumble.

"This is . . ." he said, but was cut off by Jennifer turning to him and slapping him hard.

"No more," she said calmly. "Not another word. You understand?"

Anthony Simington had no more words. He nodded and followed her into the hall where the two uniforms stood waiting.

"Cuffs?" asked one of the uniforms through the open door.

"By all means," said Lieberman.

The uniformed policeman nodded and led the couple away.

"We could have gotten more out of them, Rabbi," said Hanrahan, loosening his collar.

"My mind is elsewhere, Father Murphy. You were late. I had three minutes of playing the doddering da."

Lieberman folded the robe and looked at his partner.

"Iris," Hanrahan said.

Lieberman nodded and said, "I was late too. It's one of those days. I think we've got enough on Tony and Jenny."

"Maybe," said Hanrahan.

"Maybe," agreed Lieberman. "We've got an eleven-thirty meeting with El Perro. Check in with Nestor on the desk and brief Kearney on the phone. Should give us enough time."

"El Perro," Hanrahan said, shaking his head.

"You got better?" asked Lieberman.

This time Hanrahan shrugged. "Eleven-thirty," he said. "God, Rabbi, you know the paperwork we're gonna have with those two?" Hanrahan nodded toward the door.

Lieberman knew. The paper trail on a con game was worse than on a homicide and an arrest report had to be filed within twelve hours. But Lieberman had volunteered for this one. First, because he was asked and looked old enough. Second, because Lieberman's mother had spent the last three years of her life in this very residence. His mother had nothing when she died, but if she'd had anything, the pair they had just arrested could easily have talked her out of it.

Lieberman moved to the door. Behind him Hanrahan said, "Abe, I've got to ask you. I know it's not the time, but it's getting to me. Tell me straight out what you think. Is Maureen ever coming back to me?"

Oh, God, thought Lieberman. It never gets easier. There had been a night five years ago. Just one night when William O. Hanrahan had been on a binge for almost a week, one night when Lieberman had almost found himself in bed with his partner's wife. It hadn't happened, but it could have.

"I don't think so, William," Lieberman said.

"I don't think so either, Abraham. Maybe I'd best be getting on with my life."

"Spoken like an Irish cop."

"Spoken like my old man," said Hanrahan. "Let's go."

It had taken the Lord little more than an hour to give Frankie Kraylaw his reward.

Frankie had driven to a park he knew off Rogers Avenue, a big park, half a block in from Clark Street. The park was empty. The wind was blowing sheets of grainy snow flecked with dirt over the hard, footprinted surface of the thick layer underneath.

Frankie had looked both ways after parking the car and then stepped into the snow to scoop up a cold ball just beneath the surface of thin chill. He washed in the snow, rubbed J.J.'s blood off and rinsed his mouth with snow, and then ran a thick handful of freezing ice on the bloody front of his coat. It was better. He was sure. Not perfect, but better. Maybe better enough not to draw attention to him.

He got back in the truck, checked the fuel gauge and his image in the mirror. The fuel gauge was fine. There were a few spots on his face and neck, however, that Frankie had missed. He spit on his fingers and worked at them, watching to be sure that no police car appeared in either direction.

He drove slowly, planning, wondering, and coming up with an idea. He made his way to

Christ Evangelical Church and Mission just half a mile away, north of Howard Street and into Evanston. The parking lot was almost empty, which meant nothing much was going on, but many of those who found solace here and a semisquare meal were people without a car, usually without even carfare.

An elevated train rattled by at the top of the embankment across the street. Frankie got out of the pickup and looked at the solid brick and dirty spire of the church. This was a church that had seen its day, a church that was now paying for its prideful early raptures. Churches should be simple. God was simple and wondrous. He didn't need shrines of gold or silver that mocked his everlasting truth.

Frankie went through the rear door of the church, listened for preaching, singing, or talking, and hearing none made his way to the rest room. The Christ Evangelical Church and Mission had recently gone through eleven years as a real estate office after forty years of failing as a church. The real estate office, like the church before it, had failed, in part, at least, because people felt uncomfortable talking about life and health insurance with a cemetery right outside the window. But the church was back now, catering to a new congregation of the homeless who shuffled up Chicago Avenue at odd hours day and night like an army of the living dead.

Frankie looked in the mirror, pronounced himself clean, and headed for the reading room, a good place to get warm and look at one of the dozens of books and simplified pamphlets with pictures that sat in the stands around the room. The room was about the size of a school class-room. Two long tables, both wood, not matching, stood in the center. Unmatched chairs lined up around them.

Eight people were sitting at the tables when Frankie stepped in. The cold had brought a rush of religion. One woman who Frankie didn't recognize coughed, a rasping cough. All eight had coffee mugs in front of them. All eight had a religious tract or the Holy Book open in front of them. One man with a gray stubble–covered face leaned against his right fist and snored gently.

No one paid attention to the snoring man nor did anyone look up to see who had entered, but Thomas C. Albright, long estranged from his native state of Tennessee, soon wished that he had and that he had made some kind of escape, even through the back door near the toilet and into the cold wind of the cemetery.

Thomas Albright's first sense of company was a shadow over his book. Though his eyes had deteriorated steadily for the last twenty of his forty-two years, Thomas did not wear glasses. He was a polished squinter.

"Frankie?" he said.

Frankie looked at the pudgy man in the ratty coat and nodded.

"I heard from Reverend Alonso that you went back home."

"I did go home," admitted Frankie. "But I got called back. I came for my family. I love my wife and child and they need me. A child needs his father. A wife needs her husband. Anything else is unnatural and not to be tolerated regardless of the consequences. The Lord does not take kindly to a coward."

"Sounds reasonable to me," said Albright, who had once witnessed Frankie's violence and had no intention of provoking it. Anything Frankie said or wanted would be fine with him. If he was lucky enough to get rid of Frankie, Thomas knew he would consider seeking refuge among the Unitarians for a month or two, even if it did mean walking another six blocks.

Frankie wasn't looking at Tom Albright. He was looking around the room, playing with his car keys and the plastic crucifix on his key chain.

"Can't find her," Frankie said. "Can't find my wife, my son."

"Cruel world," said Albright sympathetically, lifting the mug of coffee to his lips and marveling that he wasn't shaking, at least no more than usual.

"Got any idea where they might be?" asked Frankie.

Frankie was not a large man. He was a knot of barbed wire with a baby face. He was smiling now at Albright, smiling the smile of a buddy, and it chilled Albright like the world outside. It chilled Albright because he would have sworn that several of Frankie Kraylaw's teeth were stained

128

with a dark redness that looked very much like blood.

Albright had once been a stockbroker. There were remnants of memories of the art of lying and survival not far below the surface of his derelict exterior. Once he had known when to lie and when to tell the truth; but now all he could think of was survival.

"Angie the Polack," he said. "You know her? Great singing voice. Used to be one of the Sunshine Sisters back in the forties. Belts out the hymns like . . ."

"I know her," Frankie said, suddenly turning his eyes on Thomas, who almost dropped his coffee mug.

"I think Angie said she thought she saw your wife working a place somewhere near Wilson, you know, by the Indian Center. Angie gets a bed there now and again. Claims she's a Sioux. Hell, she's not even a Polack."

Frankie put his hand on Albright's shoulder and Albright came near to screaming. He looked around the table, trying to hide his panic, but all seven of the men and women were very busy minding their own business, drinking their coffee and keeping their eyes on the pages of salvation before them.

"It's wrong to call people names."

"Names?"

"She's a Polish person, not what you called her."

"She's a Greek," said Albright.

"It is wrong to use words of derision," Frankie said intently. "All Christians, regardless of nationality or color, can find salvation and sit with you in Heaven."

"You're right," said Thomas, shaking his head as if he had just heard something so profound it might take him at least a month to digest.

"On Wilson?" Frankie said, his face inches from Albright's. "Angie saw my Jeanine on Wilson?"

"Near Wilson, maybe," he said. "Near. Or maybe it wasn't near. And she only said she thought. She didn't talk to her or anything, but she thought."

"Strong thought, weak thought?"

"Frankie, how would I know? You wanna talk to Angie the P . . . Angie, ask the Indians. I wish you luck. I really do. A man should be with his family."

"A man should be with his family," agreed Frankie. "I'll be back."

Frankie got up quickly and strode toward the door, his boots clomping and echoing across the room, the sound ignored with the expertise of the homeless, who urged him out but wouldn't have been surprised to see Crazy Frankie Kraylaw turn, pull a gun from under his jacket, and shoot everybody in the room.

Thomas Albright closed his eyes and gripped the still-warm mug in both hands as the door closed behind Frankie. Thomas thought he might have peed in his pants but he wasn't sure. What he was sure of was that he would do anything short of violence to get a drink. He was dead flat broke and had been on the wagon for almost three months. But now he needed a drink and a warm place to stay where Frankie Kraylaw wouldn't find him if Frankie failed to find his wife.

Albright got up and allowed himself a cough. "God help her," he said aloud.

He shuffled across the room planning to stop at the clothes alcove near the front door where he could change his soiled pants for a pair of clean ones and maybe a sweater or two.

It wasn't fair that this was happening to Thomas Albright, who hadn't even thought of doing harm to anyone but himself for at least a dozen years, but fair, Thomas knew, had nothing to do with it.

Carol Lieberman woke up in panic, too weak to move, mouth dry, lips cracked, unable to call out.

"God no, God no, God no," she said to herself, moving her eyes, trying to blink, fearing someone would come in and find her paralyzed and think she was dead.

She couldn't move her arms, her head. Something was ping-pinging. The room was green.

And then a sound like the scratching of an emery board on a cracked fingernail came more from her chest than her mouth. She was breathing heavily, afraid.

The door opened and she turned her wide-open eyes toward the soft sound.

A thin, white figure swished toward her. The Angel of Death. Quickly, the angel would lean over, kiss her, take away her breath, and leave her dead. Was that an old tale from her grandmother Sadie? Was she making it up from a half-remembered nightmare?

The Angel of Death lifted Carol's hand and clutched her wrist firmly. Carol forced herself to look up at thick glasses, a pale green face. The witch in *The Wizard of Oz*.

Carol was awake now. She knew it was a nurse and not the Angel of Death and her breath came more easily.

The nurse let go of Carol's wrist and touched her chest with the cool metal of a stethoscope.

"Know where you are?" the nurse said, removing the cool metal from her chest and taking the stethoscope from her neck.

"Hospital," Carol croaked. "Water, please."

"We can wet your lips," the nurse said.

"Velma Anderson," Carol said after licking her dry lips with her cracked tongue. "Name tag."

Velma reached for the pitcher of water on the table next to the bed and wet a washcloth that came from nowhere.

"Feels good," said Carol after her lips had been dabbed.

"Amazing how something like a few drops of water on a washcloth can be so satisfying," said Velma, touching Carol's arm and smiling down.

"Amazing," Carol agreed. "Velma?"

"Yep."

"Everything's gone wrong."

"What can I tell you, kiddo? You're alive. Your baby looks as if he'll be fine. As bad as it is, it could be worse."

"David's dead. Someone said David's dead."

"Your husband's dead," Velma said, taking Carol's hand.

Carol tried to shake her head, but it hurt, a searing pain over her right eye.

"Why did he shoot me?" she said. "That was wrong. He could have killed the baby. He couldn't want to kill the baby."

"He probably didn't know you were pregnant," Velma said softly. "And honey, I don't know if it really makes any difference to these animals whether you're pregnant or not. It's getting as bad as Washington or Los Angeles out there sometimes."

"No," Carol said, tasting blood, dry blood from her cracked lips. "It doesn't make any sense."

"You expect people like that to make sense?" said Velma. "Maybe we'd better change the subject and calm you down or we'll have Doctor Anglin running in here."

Something thumped inside her and Carol winced.

"What is it?" Velma asked.

"My . . . I think the baby kicked," Carol said.

"Good sign," said Velma reassuringly.

"It felt angry," Carol said. "You think he feels it, what's happened?"

"No," said Velma. "I think you're a little light-headed from the medication."

Carol tried to take a deep breath. It came up short and she panted three times before her breathing felt normal.

"How can I tell the baby about his father?" Carol said, feeling the tears.

"When he gets old enough to understand, you'll find a way," said Velma. "Small kids are remarkably uncurious about the past till they're old enough to start making sense of it. I've got five of them. I've got to get back to my desk."

Carol's hand reached out, grabbed the nurse's wrist.

"He can't be born in this city," Carol said, her panic returning. "I've got to get out of here soon. Go somewhere where . . ."

Velma gently removed the hand and said, "You need sleep. With what you have in you, I don't understand why you're awake. Believe me. I've been doing this for almost thirty years. You need rest, sleep for you and the baby."

"You don't understand," Carol said. "My husband. David. Baby's father. Doesn't . . ."

"Close your eyes. Lie back and I'll stay with you a few more minutes. Deal?"

Carol nodded in agreement and closed her eyes. They'll find him, she thought, remembering the faces of the men who had killed David. They'll find him. Abe will find him. Then, then . . .

Before she could complete the thought, Carol Lieberman was asleep and dreaming.

"Two thousand, seven hundred and fourteen dollars," said Raymond, sitting back and looking at the mound of money on the table.

"Plenty," said George.

Raymond nodded. "Plenty," he said, but he thought, Not nearly enough.

"I'm hungry," George said.

"Man, you just ate thirty, forty greasy Egg McMuffins."

"I'm thirsty."

"Drink water."

"I don't care for water in the winter."

Raymond had a headache. Yesterday, he had a job and hadn't committed a felony in his life. Today, he had murdered a man. He had to straighten this out. Find Lilly. But first he had to deal with George. Raymond had picked up George for last night, had been sure he could control him, had been sure he needed help. And now he was saddled with this fool across from him, and had Russian drug dealers and the police looking for him.

Someone hit a car horn on the street outside. Raymond looked around the room. It was a nothing. The sofa where George had slept; his own small bed in the corner; table, couple of chairs, little black and white television, and two thousand dollars on the table. And the small bookcase filled with paperbacks he had devoured with a dictionary at his side, wanting to use these books to carry him from his color, his past, his accent, and the cripplingly low expectations he had almost let himself accept. Lilly had helped him with the words, had declared him not only beautiful but also smart. And then, when he had his chance, this fool of a worse-than-fool had brought down the life of Raymond Carrou.

George sensed that his dollars-and-breakfast-sandwich euphoria was not being picked up by the frowning Raymond. George flattened his Russian hat on the table and rubbed it over and over again.

"I got a mother back home, sister too," said George. "You know Back Sally Streets in Pointe-à-Pierre?"

Raymond nodded. He had heard about it.

"Won't be so bad. I'll go back there, get work. No one trying to put me in no electric chair in Trinidad. No winter. We shoulda stayed. I could be wearing a white shirt and a smile and playing "Who Knows Who Took Me Bones" on the guitar. Somethin'. You know?"

"Maybe," said Raymond, standing up and walking to the window.

Someday George would tell someone. His mother, his sister, a friend at a bar. Maybe George would get religion and tell a priest who'd get him to tell the police. Maybe lots of things. There was no other way. George would have to die. And die soon. There was too much to lose.

"Get your coat on," said Raymond suddenly.

George looked confused.

"Might as well go now as anytime. We'll drive to Florida. Car breaks down before we get there we'll take a bus. We've got the money. Then we'll get tickets in Florida and get a plane home. We'll be there in a week maybe, with a few dollars left in our pockets. Sound good?"

George stood up, picked up his hat, and said, "Sounds near perfect."

"Then get your things, put the money in your bag, and let's go," said Raymond, reaching for his coat on the chair.

"You trust me holding all the money?" George said, looking at the table.

"I trust you," said Raymond.

"Thanks," said George.

Raymond didn't answer. If things went the way he was planning, and if his nerves did not betray him, he would have the money and be rid of George in an hour or two.

Then he would find the hospital. Find the woman who had looked at him in disbelief when George had shot her. She would remember his face forever as it was then. Clearly. Raymond had to get to her, deal with her, or he might never sleep peacefully again.

Noon

"They play bingo here, *viejo*, you know? Old Mexican ladies there. Old Russians, Polacks. Bingo's all the same. Universal language. Know what I mean? For a dime a card you got here the United Nations."

Emiliano "El Perro" Del Sol was holding court in a storefront bingo parlor on Crawford Avenue a few blocks south of North Avenue. He sat on the raised platform playing with the revolving aluminum cage of white bingo balls with black numbers. The *chink-chink* of the balls turning in the cage rolled under El Perro's voice.

Lieberman and Hanrahan stood alongside one of the tables that filled the room. The tables were in three long lines, enough room for more than one hundred and fifty people to play each night and win cash, appliances, and anything else that Los Tentaculos had stolen and couldn't fence.

"How you like it, *viejo*? Take a look at the pictures on the walls."

Lieberman kept looking up at El Perro.

"Those pictures are real paintings, man," said El Perro, shaking his head. "Islands, the sun, religious stuff, shit like that, you know?"

"I'm impressed, Emiliano," said Lieberman.

"That's right. And you know who owns this legit business? You got a good idea? That's right," said El Perro with a satisfied grin, looking around at the three young men behind him who stood silent and nearly at attention.

Lieberman knew them all: Fernandez, narrow like the knife he carried and willing to do anything to please El Perro, who had taken him in when his parents had thrown him out; the hefty Carlos "the Crazy" Piedras, who bit off the tops of beer bottles; and Jorge "La Cabeza" Manulito, tall, good-looking, and usually careful enough to know how to stay on El Perro's survival side.

El Perro himself was a sight to see. He was dressed entirely in black today, shoes, socks, slacks, T-shirt. His face was a map of wild scars leading to dead ends. A scar from some ancient battle ran from his right eye down across his nose to just below the left side of his mouth. It was rough, red, and had probably taken an afternoon of stitches. His nose had been broken so many times that there was little bone, no cartilage. When lost in thought, which was seldom and frightening, El Perro played with the flesh of his nose, flattening it with his thumb, pushing it to one side absentmindedly. His teeth were white but uneven, except for his sharp eyeteeth, which made anyone who saw El Perro grin think of a vampire. El Perro's hair was always slick and brushed straight back.

"Your friend Mickey Mouse is staring at me again," El Perro said, pointing at Hanrahan. "Comes into my place wearing that excuse for a suit wanting a favor and looks at me like that.

139

You know something, Lieberman? I still think your partner he don't like me."

"Nonsense, Emiliano, he talks about you all the time, says he wants his yet-to-be-born grandchildren to grow up and be just like you."

El Perro laughed, a cackling laugh that the young men behind him picked up on and joined except for Manulito. When they laughed, Los Tentaculos were careful to watch their leader for a change in mood.

"You got balls, *viejo*," said El Perro, giving the bingo-ball cage a sharp final twirl as he rose.

"And they're withering fast from age and a tired prostate," Lieberman said.

El Perro clasped his hands together and stepped forward as if he was about to pray. "Sometimes I don't know what the fuck you talkin' about. *Habla, hombre.*"

"My nephew was murdered last night. His pregnant wife was shot."

"And you think Los Tentaculos . . . ?" El Perro shouted.

"No," said Lieberman. "The killers were black men. One was called George. They had accents, probably Islands accents. They took my nephew's hat, one of those Russian fur hats. Might be wearing it."

"*Siga,*" said El Perro, standing above the two policemen behind the bingo-caller's table like a priest of petty gamblers, considering whether to bless his supplicants with bingo and the gift of a portable radio with earphones.

"No place to go with it," said Lieberman.

"*Ah, yo veo, viejo. Quieres que nosotros vamos dentro las calles a buscar por sus Negros, verdad?*"

"*Verdad*, Emiliano. I want you to help us find these guys."

"They shoot pregnant women," El Perro said, shaking his head. "That's shit, you know?"

"It's shit," Fernandez echoed in confirmation.

Lieberman knew of at least one instance in which El Perro had beaten a pregnant woman, who had insulted him outside St. Bart's Church. The woman had been rushed to Cook County where she delivered a month prematurely. The baby lived, just barely.

The conversation seemed to trouble Carlos. Jorge leaned over to explain in Spanish what was going on.

"Your nephew. He was a good guy?" asked El Perro.

"A very good guy, Emiliano," said Lieberman. "His father is my brother."

"So this is a big favor?" said El Perro, stepping off the platform and moving toward the two policemen.

"Big favor," Lieberman acknowledged.

El Perro looked back at his men and scratched his neck.

"The streets are cold," he said, turning to Hanrahan and Lieberman. "And you ain't givin' me much to work with."

"All I've got," said Lieberman, holding open his hands.

"Vamos a ver lo que podemos de hacer."

"Gracias otra vez," said Lieberman.

Hanrahan stood stone silent, eyes fixed emotionlessly on the face of the swaggering young man across the table.

"No gusta, su amigo," said El Perro, returning Hanrahan's gaze.

"Pienso que el hombre creyó el mismo de usted," answered Lieberman.

"I can live with that," said El Perro. "I'll get back to you we find anything."

Lieberman touched Bill Hanrahan's shoulder and the two policemen walked slowly toward the door. Behind them they could hear the sound of the bingo-ball cage being nervously spun.

"Una cosa mas," came El Perro's voice as the policemen neared the door.

Lieberman had been expecting this, but he showed nothing on his hangdog face as he turned.

"Que quieres, Emiliano?"

"We find this guy for you, what you figure you owe me?"

Bill Hanrahan was about to answer, but Lieberman stopped him with a touch on his partner's sleeve.

"You or one of your *hombres* walks on the next misdemeanor."

El Perro shook his head and let a single finger trace the path of the long scar on his face.

"Two misdemeanors," Lieberman offered.

"Hey, man, we don't commit no misdemeanors," Jorge said.

El Perro turned on his man suddenly, fists clenched, shoulders tight with fury.

"*Despensame, jefe,*" Jorge said, taking a step back. "*Solamente una pequena chiste.*"

"*Callete tu boca, Pacito,*" said El Perro very softly. "*Mas tarde vamos a ver lo que pasa.*"

"*Perro jefe, yo . . .*" Paco started.

"What you say, *viejo*?" said El Perro, turning to Lieberman and Hanrahan. "I spin the cage, pull a number. If it's on the card I forget Jorge's insult. If it's not, *pues entonces . . .*"

"We don't have time for this bullshit," said Hanrahan.

Fernandez smiled.

"I'm spinnin', Jorge," said El Perro. "I'm spinnin' to see if I let you keep your fingers for embarrassing me in front of *el viejo* and Mickey Mouse."

"I had enough, Abe," said Hanrahan, turning and walking out the door.

El Perro took a bingo card from the table and sailed it over his shoulder as he faced Lieberman. The card fluttered past Jorge, who scrambled after it, his gold chains chinking.

"I'm spinnin'," said El Perro, reaching down for the cage full of balls and spinning it madly once, twice, three times.

Lieberman checked his watch.

"Two felonies," said El Perro. "We walk for the next two felonies."

It was Lieberman's turn to shake his head no.

"All right, all right," said El Perro, stopping

the metal cage, opening the latch, and pulling out a ball. "One felony."

"One felony with no assault," said Lieberman. "Which means no one, *nadie*, gets touched, not even a scratch, and nothing with weapons showing."

"Guns, *bueno*, no guns, but knife. Let's deal here, *viejo*."

El Perro threw the ball into the air with a yelp. The ball sailed toward Lieberman, who reached out his left hand and caught it.

"Muy bueno," said El Perro, clapping his hands and turning to be sure Fernandez and Carlos joined him, though Carlos did not seem to know what he was applauding. "You got a deal. Now what's the number on the ball? Don't keep my man in suspense up here."

Lieberman looked at the ball.

"B-4," he said, looking up at the stage as Jorge's dark, handsome face turned from sagging fear to an idiotic grin.

"I got it," Jorge said.

Lieberman threw the ball back to El Perro, who reached forward to catch it.

"One felony, no one getting hurt. No guns," said El Perro, returning the ball to the cage and latching it.

"Can't guarantee, but I'll do my best if you find George and his partner."

"Best is good enough for me," said El Perro. "You know something? I hate the fuckin' cold."

Hanrahan was in the driver's seat of the car

listening to Rush Limbaugh when Lieberman slid in and closed the door. Hanrahan turned off the radio.

"What are we doing, Rabbi? Notice I said 'we.'"

"Making deals with the devil," said Lieberman. "Picking my nightmares. Trading new pain for old. Father Murphy, the truth as I know it is I want the guys who killed David and shot Carol."

Hanrahan looked at his partner, who turned in his seat.

"What?" Lieberman said wearily. "What are you looking at?"

"You deal with the devil and you can count on a marked deck," said Hanrahan.

"Old Irish saying?"

"No, a Greek bartender named Gus at Bobbie Lavery's Tavern. You hungry?"

Lieberman nodded.

"Fajitas or gyros?" asked Hanrahan, pulling into Crawford Avenue traffic.

"Surprise me," said Lieberman, pulling his collar up.

The American Indian Center on Wilson looked like an old streetcar barn, two stories, dirty red brick. Bundled men and women with high cheekbones moved in and out walking slowly, hands deep in pockets. One skinny old man whose face was wrinkled beyond anything Frankie had ever seen, with the possible exception of Hickory John

Bassett, walked down the concrete steps, lit a cigarette, and looked both ways and up at the sky. Then he pulled up his collar, put his head against the wind, and moved to the west.

As Frankie got out of his pickup an El train rattled by down the street behind him and screeched like a tack on a slate into Wilson Avenue Station. There weren't many people out and those that did appear moved fast against the cold. That is, if they weren't Indians. The Indians didn't seem to have anywhere to go. The storefronts, almost all of them with Spanish names over their doors, were frosted. Frankie crossed the street and hurried up the stone steps, opened the door, and walked into semidarkness, his soles and heels clapping on the bare wood.

Two men and a fat woman, all of them Indians, stood in a circle near a stairway.

"Pardon me," said Frankie. "I'm looking for a woman named Angie. A Sioux woman."

"The Polack," muttered one of the men, who was red-eyed and maybe a little drunk. He was dressed entirely in unfashionably tattered denim, including a denim vest.

"Yes," said Frankie eagerly.

"What do you want with her?" the fat woman said. There was education in her voice and Frankie went wary and let the Spirit move him.

The fat woman was better dressed than the men, a dark, sacky sort of dress, clean, maybe even new or close to it.

"She's an old friend," he said. "I just want to say hello, tell her I'm back in town, talk to her."

"She's not here," the woman said.

"I . . ." Frankie began.

"She's not here," the woman repeated flatly.

"Can you tell me when . . . ?"

"I can, but I won't," the woman said.

"I beg your pardon, ma'am?"

"You're not her friend," the woman said.

The second Indian man, tall and lean with a dark ponytail, said something Frankie didn't understand. The Indian woman nodded but kept her eyes on Frankie.

Frankie smiled. The woman did not.

"You're burning with hate," the woman said. "It's not a friend you're looking for."

Frankie felt the surge of the wet, hot eel of anger, but he grinned. "Indian magic?" he asked. "You read minds?"

"No," said the woman. "I'm a social worker here. You've got the look of an angry drunk who tries to hide it with a false smile. Only you're worse. You're not drunk on whiskey."

Frankie took a step toward the woman, but the two Indian men stepped between them.

"I don't want any trouble," said Frankie, holding up his hands, his eyes darting between the men.

"Yes, you do," said the woman. "But we're not going to give it to you. Turn around, walk out that door, and don't come back here again, ever."

The two Indian men took a step toward Frankie, who backed up.

"You don't understand," he said, stopping, determined. "I'm doing God's work."

The woman puffed out her lower lip, said nothing, and shook her head.

Frankie was face to face with the larger of the two Indians.

"Big Bear was in jail," the woman said. "He lifted weights for four years. You want to find out if I'm telling the truth?"

"I fear only the wrath of the Lord," said Frankie.

"I wasn't trying to frighten you," the woman said. "I was telling you what you were up against so you'd consider your options more seriously."

"I've never insulted your people," said Frankie.

"That's good," said the woman. "I've insulted yours. Maybe you'll go to Heaven and I'll go to prison, but somehow I don't think so."

Big Bear's huge hands started to rise.

"Don't touch me," Frankie said through clenched teeth, trembling with rage.

"Don't touch him, Bear," the woman said. "He wants to walk, let him walk."

Frankie took a step back and then turned and went out the door and down the concrete steps. The heavy wooden door banged behind him.

Inside, Billy Blue Feather turned to Connie Sekajowa and said, "What the fuck was that all about?"

"I don't know," said Connie. "Go tell Angie that he was looking for her. Tell her what he looks like. Ask her if she knows him and then get her out the back and someplace safe."

"She can stay at my place two, three days," said Big Bear.

Connie Sekajowa, her eyes still on the door through which Frankie Kraylaw had fled, nodded again.

"World's full of goddamn crazies," Billy Blue Feather said with a sigh, starting up the stairs.

Outside Frankie hurried to his pickup, got in, and tried to control his breathing. He was panting, trying to catch his breath. She was in there. She was in there. No doubt. He could tell from the way the fat Indian woman had boned him. She had no right.

He watched the door and thought for a minute and then turned on the ignition and moved the pickup to where it couldn't be seen from the doorway of the Indian Center. He stopped in the driveway of a cleaning store on the corner, where he could watch the front door of the center and see down the street on the side of the building in case someone came out of the alley.

Frankie shivered from the cold and something else he did not give a name. The taste of blood from J.J.'s ear was still clinging like dry metal to his tongue. He had not slept in more than thirty hours and was not now tired. He would stay awake for days. He would pursue for the rest of the life that God gave him if he must, but Frankie

Kraylaw would endure and be rewarded. And if the Lord chose that he not be rewarded on earth then so be it. His will be done.

From the alley came the Indian named Big Bear, helping a tiny woman in a long cloth coat around the dirty mounds of ice and snow. It was Angie, no doubt.

"So," said George. "Let me see if I got this straight."

They were in the rattling car, not much heat and no energy, rambling down the Dan Ryan Expressway heading south in the general direction of Florida.

"Your cousin Celia, she married Massinet Hart," George went on, the Russian hat tipping back on his head.

"Yes," said Raymond, looking around for an empty field, something, somewhere he could get George out and shoot his fool head off.

"So," said George, holding up two fingers for no reason that Raymond could understand, "that makes you and me some kinda cousins, something like that?"

"No," said Raymond. "It doesn't make us cousins."

Raymond tried not to sound surly. But his life was on the line and he was driving away from the place he had to be, where he had the most important business of his life, driving away from Lilly. Raymond didn't like the way he had been picking up on the Islands accent that he had

150

worked so hard to lose. Associating with George had done that to him.

"Seems to me it does," said George, clutching the battered bag containing the few thousand dollars that he had stolen.

"Seems to you," said Raymond, nodding.

He hit the radio, hoping the sound of anything would stop George from talking. There weren't many stations the radio could receive. The antenna had long since been torn off by who knows who.

Someone, a man with a high voice or a woman with a strange one, was singing in Spanish. George shut up, listening or thinking.

"That corn out there?" George asked.

"Weeds," said Raymond.

George nodded, ingesting this important information.

"Raymond, you mind I ask you again?"

"What?"

"Why you shoot the white fella?"

"Why did you shoot the woman?"

"I asked you first off," said George. "An' you shot first."

"Thought he was going to give us a fight," said Raymond.

"Didn't look that way to me."

"It did to me," Raymond answered, raising his voice and hitting himself on the chest with his right hand. "Why did you shoot her?"

George tried to think about it again, to remember, to make sense.

"You shot. I shot."

"I had a reason," said Raymond.

"Not me," George said. "I just got bucked."

They were quiet for about five minutes while Mexican bands and singers wailed plaintively or sang so fast that the entire song seemed to be one word.

"What's that book you bring with you?" George asked.

"*What Makes Sammy Run?*"

"What it about?"

Raymond didn't answer.

"I think I'm hungry," said George.

"You got the McDonald's sandwiches."

"They don't taste so good anymore. I want something else. I don't know, shrimp maybe," said George.

There was a vast field of weeds on their right beyond which seemed to be some low buildings, probably houses. Set back on the left of the highway were factories that had signs near the road giving their names, but not what they did.

"We'll stop when we see something," said Raymond. "Maybe Indiana."

"I like Stuckey's. You been to Stuckey's, man?"

"If we see one, I'll stop."

"Even we don't see one I like 'em," said George with a smile.

"What are you so fuckin' happy about?" asked Raymond, unable to fully control his anger.

"We home free," George explained.

"Yeah," said Raymond, turning quickly to the right down a dirt road that seemed to lead nowhere.

"Where we goin'?" asked George. "We gonna pop a tire we do this way."

"I've got to piss," said Raymond. "Bad, and I don't see anyplace up ahead."

"Be cold, freeze your peck-dog," said George. "I heard of a guy his piss froze right when it come out of him. That's a fact."

The road got rougher, bouncier, and in the rearview mirror all Raymond could see of the Dan Ryan was the moving rooftops of cars going in both directions.

"Here," said Raymond, stopping the car.

"I don't see no place to turn around," said George.

"We'll back up if we have to," said Raymond, opening the door. "You coming? Might be a while before we come to a toilet."

"I guess," said George, opening the passenger door and stepping out, one arm firmly holding the closed bag like a football, the other rising quickly to keep the fur hat from being taken by the wind.

The snow wasn't deep. Maybe it had been blown by the prairie wind or cut by the millions of weed stalks.

Raymond walked ten yards ahead of the car, whose engine he had left running, shuddered, and unzipped his pants, feeling the sudden blue-cold icy touch of winter on his limp penis. One hand stayed with his penis. The other eased into his pocket and found the gun. Behind him, Raymond heard George step off the road, trampling crisp, frozen weeds.

"Oh, brother," George shouted. "This is one damnit-to-hell of a country, I can tell you that."

Raymond quickly zipped his fly and turned. George had his back to the road a few feet away. Raymond took two steps toward him and raised his pistol, holding it in two hands to keep himself from trembling.

"When I get back . . ." George began, his back still turned, a stream of urine steaming from him.

The shot from Raymond's gun finished the thought for George.

George jumped, not quite understanding what had cracked next to him, and then, still exposed, one hand still cradling the bag of money, he turned his head and saw Raymond, gun in hand, looking at him.

The second shot went through the bag, which George held up in front of his face, and took off the small finger on his left hand.

"What you doin'?" George demanded, backing away.

Raymond fired again. This time the bullet hit flesh and sank into George's right side. George looked down at his side, looked at Raymond, and adjusted the fur hat on his head.

"I'm killin' you, man," said Raymond, his accent returning in an angry rush, his voice vibrating with fear. "You just too fuckin' stupid to understand even when you're shot and looking at the goddamn gun."

He fired again, but George was already moving to his right, toward the field of weeds. He was moving but not running. Raymond went after him.

"Shit," said Raymond, as George stumbled ahead of him.

"You keep the money, man," cried George. "I'm droppin' it. You jus' turn around and leave me here bleedin' and all. I be all right. You stop shootin' me and I give you all the money."

Raymond didn't answer. George had the sense to crouch low so he might be hidden in the tall, thick weeds. And in spite of his size and the wounds he was suffering, George moved quietly. But what did him in was the blood that left a trail Raymond could follow slowly, patiently.

George suddenly stood up and ran, or rather, stumbled, trying to open the bag he carried as he did so. If he opened it, Raymond knew he would pull out his gun, change the game he had begun. Raymond fired at the fleeing figure, missing him twice but making him move so fast that he couldn't open the bag he carried.

Then, suddenly, as Raymond panted after George, his breath coming labored and hurting, George disappeared. He was just gone. One second there was his head and you could hear him breathing and gagging hard and heavy. The next, gone.

Raymond hurried now, following the trail of

red blood on white snow, knowing that George might be pulling out the gun right at that moment.

Raymond almost fell into the ditch. He started to slip, reached back with his foot, and grabbed a clump of weeds with his free hand. He sat down hard and cold with a grunt and looked around in panic, this way and that. A small stream of ice lay along the bottom of the ditch, a small stream of ice and George. George was not moving. He was on his back, eyes closed, blood spurting from his chest but still clinging to the bag, the fur hat still on his head.

This was not the way Raymond had wanted it. He had wanted to shoot George on a road or a path and leave him there to be discovered with the dead man's hat and almost all of the Russian drug dealers' money.

If it was warmer, Raymond would have sat there another few minutes thinking it out. If it was warmer and he felt more confident that no crazy farmer would be driving up the road and find his car sitting there, the motor running.

The ditch was about five feet deep. Raymond wasn't sure he could get out if he jumped down and took some of the money. If he jumped in he would have to walk in one direction or the other until he found some place to climb out and then, well, he might have trouble finding his way back to the road without the trail of George's blood.

He got up, his tailbone hurting, and looked

back for the car. He couldn't see it. He could hear the sputtering engine and the hooting wind.

No help for it, he decided. He took one more look at George to be satisfied that he was dead and turned to follow the red trail. He would have to call the police, somebody, 911, maybe the fire department, say he was driving down some road and heard shooting, maybe describe enough for them to find George's body.

He tramped through the weeds that he and George had bowled over and tried to think.

It would have to be.

He now thought of the woman in the hospital.

Life is crazy nuts, Raymond said to himself, moving closer to the chugging engine of the car. Crazy nuts.

He got into the car, closed the door, put his gun in his pocket, and began backing out down the narrow road. He fought panic and the desire to hit the accelerator, take his chances, and get the hell out of there. He fought and, with the exception of a few minor runs off the road, made it safely back to the Dan Ryan, catching some luck when he backed onto the road, there being no one in sight, and drove ahead looking for a turnoff he could make so as to get back to the city.

He would have to get rid of the car. It had left tire marks in the snow. They might be able to trace them. The car was no damn good anyway, but it was sure better than no car, but real is real.

Besides, Raymond had a plan that would get him a new car and something more valuable.

Twelve Forty-Nine in the Afternoon

George found himself looking up at the most incredible cloud he had ever seen. It was shaped like a feather, right down to the quill. He also had the dizzying impression that he was standing or floating and looking not up but straight ahead. The feeling made him want to throw up, but that would have to wait until he could figure out what had happened.

First, he still clung to the bag. That felt right. Second, he reached up and felt for his fur hat. It was gone. This sent him into a fury of reaching back, groping, feeling hard, cold dirt and stones and finally, finally, finding the fur with the tips of his electric-pained fingers.

George sighed and closed his eyes in relief.

Then he remembered. Raymond had shot at him, chased him, tried to kill him. Where was Raymond? Why wasn't George dead? Why hadn't Raymond taken the money? What other reason would he have for shooting George? Since George had been planning to shoot Raymond when the opportunity arose, he was not angry, only puzzled. He knew Raymond was smarter than

158

he was, but George had counted on being more crafty. Obviously, he had been wrong.

It was when he tried to sit up that George knew he had been shot. Since his hands were both almost frozen, it took him a second or two longer to discover that he had lost a finger. He looked at the stump, which was bleeding only slightly thanks to the winter cold, and then felt his side. It was bloody, but it was not bleeding heavily. Maybe the winter again. It would be strange, thought George, forcing himself to his knees, to be saved by the very weather that he hated. But he wasn't saved yet, and getting up from his knees almost turned his temporary survival into irony.

Moving was difficult. What was equally difficult, considering that he was probably in shock, was that he seemed to be in the bed of a small river with a bank at the height of his neck. Were he not shot George knew he could scramble up the embankment, but he was shot and having trouble keeping his eyes open.

He began stumbling to his right in the direction he thought might be south, toward Florida, toward the Gulf. Even in his pain and confusion he did not think he could walk very far, but he might as well head in the direction he wanted to go. No sense turning back to Chicago.

And so he staggered, clinging to the bag, hat pulled over his head, the hand with the missing finger plunged into his coat pocket, throbbing.

Someone was singing. It wasn't just the wind. Someone was singing and George recognized the voice. He almost called out and then realized that it might be Raymond. It might be some trick. Then he knew that the voice was his own and this frightened George very much. He had been singing without knowing it.

He clamped his mouth closed, biting his lower lip, and staggered on, trying to move faster.

Two Minutes Past
Three P.M.

"We're home."

Barry's voice came through the sound of Lieberman snoring. Lieberman opened his eyes as a rush of frigid air slapped him in the face and ran down his body.

"Close the door," he said.

Barry closed the door and he and Melisa stood looking across the room at their grandfather, who sat dazed in his living room chair.

"Fell asleep," said Lieberman.

Barry and Melisa dropped their books and began to take off their coats. Then Barry paused with one sleeve out of his coat and looked at the two suitcases standing next to the closet.

"Leave the boots on," Lieberman said, checking his watch and trying to come fully awake. "Your father's coming for you. You'll stay with him a few days."

160

"Grandma Bess doesn't like us to walk in the house with boots," said Melisa, looking at him.

"Then take them off," said Lieberman, making an effort to stand.

"They're hard to put on," she answered.

"Then leave them on and stand at the door. I'll bring you provisions to keep you from starving for the next four or five minutes."

"But you don't understand," Melisa whined.

"Listen," he said, taking a few steps toward the girl. "I went through this with your mother. I'm too old to go through another generation of damned-if-you-do. You understand?"

"I understand," said Barry.

"Good," said Lieberman, looking at the boy. "Explain it to your sister over a pastrami sandwich. I made some."

Lieberman padded toward the kitchen with both children following him, both wearing boots.

"I don't want a sandwich," said Barry.

"We'll stick it in a sack and you can take it with you. What about you, little bird?"

"Put mine in a bag too," said Melisa.

"Fine," said Lieberman, pushing open the kitchen door. "You can both watch me eat."

Lieberman went to the refrigerator and pulled out a bottle of some off-brand pineapple juice. The sandwiches were on the table, encased in Handi-Wrap.

"I'll have some juice," said Melisa, sitting.

"Me, too," said Barry.

"Got it," said Lieberman, plucking three paper Dixie cups from the holder over the sink.

Back at the table, Lieberman dropped three sandwiches into a brown paper bag.

"One for your father," he said, reaching for one of the two remaining sandwiches and starting to unwrap it.

"Grandpa," Barry said slowly.

"Yes."

"Are you supposed to be eating pastrami sandwiches?"

"No," said Lieberman, taking a bite, his teeth going through the fresh pumpernickel and sinking into tender meat. "Nor am I supposed to drink, not even a glass of wine on *Shavot*. In fact, if the dreary truth be known, I'm not supposed to eat anything with fat or cholesterol or calories or alcohol."

He took another bite of sandwich, savoring the sharp tang of mustard on his tongue.

"I see," said Barry, soberly.

Melisa drank her pineapple juice and remained silent.

"That leaves me a lifetime of carrot and cucumber salads," said Lieberman. "Which are not bad things. You know George and Ira Gershwin?"

Melisa shook her head no.

"I think so," said Barry. "They make records."

" 'Methuselah lived nine hundred years,' " said Lieberman. " 'Methuselah lived nine hundred

162

years, but who calls that livin' if no gal will give in to no man what's lived nine hundred years.'"

"That's dirty talk, Grandpa," Melisa said.

"No, it's not," said Lieberman, returning to his sandwich. "It's common sense. Sometimes you've got to eat a pastrami sandwich. Now, what is it you want to talk about?"

"How did you know we wanted to talk?" asked Barry, looking up at Abe with Todd Cresswell's eyes.

"I'm a policeman," Lieberman said.

"Can we talk about David?" asked Barry, looking down.

"We can talk," said Lieberman.

"We called him our cousin, but is our mother's cousin our cousin?" asked Melisa, pushing her empty paper cup away from her.

"Yes," said Lieberman. "That's it? That's the question?"

"No," said Barry. "Cousin Carol's still got the baby, right?"

"Right."

"Is Uncle Maish going to die?" asked Melisa. "And Aunt Yetta?"

"Of grief?" asked Lieberman, slowing down on the sandwich to savor the last few bites. "Or natural causes? Of natural causes, yes, but I couldn't tell you when. Of grief, no, but I can't tell you for sure what it will do to them."

"What are you going to do when you find the person who killed David?" asked Melisa. "Are you going to shoot him?"

"Should I?"

"You're answering a question with a question. You said we shouldn't do that," said Barry, who had not touched his juice but was playing with the cup, scraping off wax with his fingernails.

"I don't know what I'll do when I find him," Lieberman admitted.

"I say shoot him," said Barry.

"I think you should put him in jail in a cell all by himself," said Melisa. "Forever, with no one to talk to and no television. Only books that are good for you and food that's good for you but tastes bad so he'll live a long time and be sorry."

Lieberman, finished with his sandwich and drink, leaned back in his chair and looked at his granddaughter. It sounded like a good plan to him.

The doorbell rang but no one moved.

"We should go to the funeral," said Barry. "The services. I should go. I'm almost thirteen."

The doorbell rang again.

"You'll have plenty of them. This is one you can skip. You wanna let your father in?"

Melisa slid off her chair and left the kitchen while Lieberman got up, scooped up the crumpled plastic and a few crumbs, and dropped them in the plastic garbage container in the corner.

The doorbell rang once more and then Barry and Lieberman could hear the outer door open and the voice of Todd Cresswell.

Lieberman handed Barry the brown bag, touched his cheek, smiled wearily, and guided

164

the boy through the kitchen door into the dining room.

Todd, a slender man with a handsome, slightly lopsided face, straight cornstalk hair, and rimless glasses, stood at the front door, his arm around Melisa's shoulder. Todd was wearing a furlined denim jacket and a blue knit cap. He looked like an ad for All Spice.

"Abe," he said. "I'm sorry about David."

"Thank you," said Lieberman, guiding his grandson toward his father.

Todd smiled sadly and touched the boy's cheek in much the same way that Abe had done.

"How are Maish and Yetta taking it?"

"Not too bad," said Lieberman.

" 'Death of manhood cut down before its prime I forbid,' " said Todd, picking up one of the suitcases. "Sorry."

Lieberman had requested on more than one occasion that his son-in-law not quote Greek tragedy. This time he simply shrugged.

"Can we go to a movie or bring home some tapes?" asked Barry, putting on his coat.

"Maybe," said Todd.

"Come on in and have a sandwich and some coffee," Lieberman said.

Todd adjusted his glasses and looked toward the door.

"I can't, Abe, not now."

"Someone waiting in the car?" asked Lieberman, keeping his eyes on Todd as Barry and Melisa finished putting their coats on.

"Yes," said Todd.

"A lady?" asked Lieberman.

Todd didn't answer.

"Who's in the car, dad?" Melisa demanded.

"A lady I work with," said Todd. "She's going to have dinner with us. How about pizza at Barnaby's? My friend likes pizza."

"I don't really care what your friend likes," said Melisa. "I think I wanna stay here."

Melisa, Barry, and Todd were all looking at Abe, who felt a strong desire to take a hot bath.

"I'll help you carry the bags out," he said.

"You don't . . ." Todd began, but Abe had already moved to the closet by the front door and was plunging his stockinged feet into his boots.

"Let's go," said Lieberman, throwing on his coat and taking the suitcase from Melisa.

The sun was trying to turn the afternoon into less than a disaster but the sky was overcast and it didn't stand a chance.

"Careful on the steps," said Lieberman, almost slipping.

"Abe, I want to talk to you about . . ." Todd whispered, as the children moved cautiously toward the car whose engine purred at the curb in front of the fire hydrant. There was a woman in the front seat. She started to get out.

"Faye," Todd said too heartily and much too loud when the woman was out of the car and facing them, "this is Abe Lieberman. And this is Melisa and Barry."

"Nice to meet all of you," said Faye, shivering.

She was wearing a denim jacket just like Todd's and a knit hat, but hers was bright red.

Lieberman did not have to check the faces of his grandchildren to know that Todd Cresswell was in for a few rocky days.

"I had plans for tonight," Todd said, squinting first at Faye and then at Lieberman. Faye moved to the back of the car and opened the trunk with a key she pulled out of her pocket. "I couldn't . . ."

"You don't owe me an explanation," said Lieberman.

"I just didn't want you or the kids to think . . ."

"Can't stop people from thinking, Todd," Lieberman said, plunging his hands in his pockets. "Besides . . ."

The line didn't need finishing. It had been Lieberman's daughter, Lisa, who had left her husband. It had been Lisa who refused to get back together with him. There was no right or wrong to it as far as Lieberman was concerned. Todd didn't owe him an explanation.

Faye took the suitcases from the children, placed them in the trunk, and closed it as Todd said, "Faye's comedy. I'm tragedy. Lisa's tragedy too. I . . ."

Abe touched his son-in-law's arm and Todd stopped.

Faye moved to the side of the car, opened the door, and held her palm out with a smile to usher the children into the rear seat.

"We take turns sitting in the front," said Melisa.

"Melisa, I . . ." Todd began, but this time Faye cut him off.

"Fine with me," she said. "Barry, why don't you go in the front? Melisa and I can talk in the back."

Barry hurried into the front seat and Melisa reluctantly let herself be guided into the back.

"Good to meet you, Mr. Lieberman," Faye said, waving. "Please accept my condolences."

"Thank you," said Lieberman as the woman closed the back door of the car.

"I know what you're thinking, Abe," said Todd, not meeting Abe's eyes.

"What am I thinking?"

"Oedipus," said Todd.

"I was thinking gas from pastrami, Todd," Lieberman said. "But since you mention it, Faye is a little older than you are. Or, put another way, I'd say Faye is a little younger than I am."

"I've got to go," said Todd.

"I like her," said Lieberman. "At least what I see. You tell Bess or Lisa that and I'll call you a liar. Are you happy?"

" 'Count no mortal happy till he has passed the final limit of his life secure from pain.' The last line of *Oedipus Rex*. Let's say I'm doing better than I have been."

"This is getting awkward and I'm getting very cold," said Lieberman. "I'll talk to you tomorrow."

Todd nodded and ran around the car, relieved at escaping with so few bruises.

Through the window of the car, Abe could see Faye listening seriously to something Melisa was saying. Then Faye looked up at him. Her smile slipped away and there was something of a plea in her eyes as they met Lieberman's in the few seconds before the car pulled away from the curb.

When Todd had turned the corner heading north toward Evanston, Lieberman went back into the house, prepared for about fifteen minutes of cleaning up the slush-stained floor where the kids had trod. But before he could get his shoes off again, the phone began to ring.

Nestor Briggs had a lot on his mind and his hands. A woman speaking Russian or Polish or something stood in front of the intake desk at the Clark Street police station and jabbered away.

Behind the woman, who was dressed in what looked like an Indian blanket with sleeves, stood a tall, bald man in his forties wearing an overcoat. The overcoat, lined with something that looked to Nestor like black fur, was open and under it was the best-looking gray charcoal suit and matching tie that Sergeant Nestor Briggs had ever seen in his more than thirty-five years as a Chicago cop. The tall, bald man was red-eyed and kept checking his watch, looking for help from God through the ceiling, and biting his lower lip. Nestor wanted to hear the man's story. He wanted to answer the phone. He wanted to take a piss, but he had to listen to this woman yak at him in angry Serbian or Greek.

She wasn't a bad looker, a little too thin for Nestor, who hadn't had a woman in more than six years, but what the hell. She was dark with a long neck and high cheekbones.

"What language you talkin', lady?" Nestor asked with mock patience, trying to catch the eye of the weeping man who might sympathize with his dilemma, might even, miraculously, speak Albanian or Croatian.

The woman shouted louder, took off her jacket, and rolled up the sleeve of the blue and yellow plaid shirt she was wearing. Her arm was bruised and yellow. Nestor put on his glasses, stood up, and leaned over to look. There were no needle tracks.

"Over there," Nestor said slowly, pointing to the wooden bench against the wall. "Go sit over there."

The woman paused, looked at the bench, looked at Nestor, rolled down her sleeve, and answered Nestor in her language as he had spoken to her, slowly, clearly, as if speaking to a half-wit.

"I'm a patient man, lady," he said, "but I got business to . . . hold it."

He picked up the ringing phone, holding the woman off with hand gestures and a finger pointed at the bench.

"Clark Street," he said. "Right."

Nestor pulled his pad in front of him. There

were already eight messages on it. He folded the pink pad back with his free hand, which gave leave to the Czech or Latvian woman to advance again.

As the person on the other end of the line spoke, Nestor wrote the message for Lieberman.

"I'll let him know," Nestor said, now holding his right hand over his ear to drown out the screams of the exasperated woman who was pounding on the desk.

"Shut up, shut up, shut up," the bald, well-dressed man behind her suddenly shouted.

The woman paused in her diatribe and turned to face the man. Nestor couldn't see her face with her back turned but he was sure that there was something akin to Rumanian madness in her eyes.

"Shut up?" she said in almost flawless English.

The phone was ringing again. Blankenship, Foster, and Meridiani came through the front door dragging a young Hispanic man whose eyes were open wide and blank and whose hands were handcuffed behind him. The Hispanic wasn't fighting. He was a lump, a 250-pound lump of flesh wearing what looked like a World War II army uniform.

Nestor came around the desk as fast as he could, which was none too fast considering the reason he was behind the desk in the first place was a ten-year-old hip operation that had left him with a permanent limp.

"One of you guys give me a hand here," he

called as Foster, Blankenship, and Meridiani lugged their silent load across the floor.

"On your own," Blankenship grunted. "This asshole's come to life three times and tried to kick the shit out of us. We're locking him."

The Hungarian or Ukrainian woman was advancing on the weeping well-dressed man. She was silent, which, as Nestor well knew from experience, was a bad sign.

The sound of the Hispanic man's shoes scraping across the tile floor was cut off as the three cops got him through the door leading to the lockup. The door slammed behind them.

"Hold it there," Nestor called as the woman kept moving on the weeping man, who held his ground looking angry.

"Shut up?" the woman said softly.

"You think you have problems?" the man asked, hyperventilating. "You think you have problems? My wife just took every penny I've got, everything, right out of the bank, the drawers, every goddamn thing. And you know where she went? She ran away with my kid brother who hasn't had a job for more than two fucking days in his life."

Nestor was between the man and the woman now, holding his hands up to stay the woman who, it was now clear, stood almost a head taller than the desk sergeant, who wanted nothing more than to get through the day alive, feed his cat, grill a chicken burger, and watch the *Tonight* show.

"Ma'am," Nestor said. "Just back it up. Sit

down over there and I'll find someone who can speak . . ."

Then the tall, bald guy said something behind Nestor, but Nestor couldn't understand it because it was in the same damned language that the woman had jabbered in, or one close to it.

The woman exploded in fury, trying to claw her way past Nestor, shrieking.

Nestor took a scratch on his right cheek and a knee to the thigh. He threw his arms around the woman and shouted, "Help out here."

The weeping man was now pulling at Nestor's shirt, trying to get past Nestor to the woman.

A punch went by Nestor's face and hit the woman flush on her right ear.

"That's enough," Nestor shouted, losing his glasses and control of the situation.

The woman reached over Nestor, tore at his shirt, and tried to grab the thin man's hair, but there wasn't enough there for a meaningful attack.

Then, suddenly, the weight of the tall, thin man behind him was lifted away. Nestor stepped back and the woman swung at him. Bill Hanrahan stepped in to grab her arm. Since Hanrahan's right arm was engaged in a choke hold on the tall, bald man, he had to cope with the woman with his left. It took some doing, but she obliged by moving into him to get at the bald man.

"Cuff her, Nestor," Hanrahan said wearily.

With some effort and another scratch, Nestor cuffed the woman. He stepped back, touched his cheek, looked at his scratch, and prayed fast to Jesus that the woman wasn't HIV positive.

"Where is everybody?" Hanrahan asked.

Nestor, breathing hard now, tried to talk normally but couldn't.

"Don't know . . . Foster, the others, came . . . I called. The damn phones."

The phone was ringing.

"I thought we were gonna be goddamn automated," Nestor said, pulling the jabbering woman to the bench and forcing her to sit. "I thought everyone called nine-one-one these days. Nobody calls nine-one-one. They call me. They call me and they tear the shirt off my back."

He turned to Hanrahan and pointed to the bald man, whose face had turned crimson. Hanrahan loosened his grip and the man began to cough.

"All these people speaking who the hell knows what," said Nestor Briggs, brushing back his few remaining hairs. "And they can't remember a simple goddamn number. They look up Nestor Briggs. They call the other stations and ask, 'You know where I can find Nestor Briggs? I wanna make him earn his pension.'"

Hanrahan led the gasping man to the bench on the opposite side of the lobby and sat him down.

"I want back in lockup," Nestor said. "I got years in. I got a right to some respect, don't I?"

"You got a right, Nestor," Hanrahan said patiently.

"You're goddamn right I got a right. I'm telling Kearney. He don't like it I can go over his head.

174

I got friends. I . . . you think she's a hooker, this one?"

Hanrahan looked at the foreign woman who sat, her hands manacled behind her, glaring at the two policemen and the gagging man.

"No," said Hanrahan.

The woman shouted something and Hanrahan looked at Nestor, who had found some Kleenex on his desk and was dabbing away at his wounds.

"I don't know what she's talking about," Nestor said.

"She says she just killed her husband," the bald man said in a rasping voice. "He's better off. I'd be better off if my wife had just killed me."

"What's she talking?" Hanrahan asked.

"Bulgarian." The bald man wept.

"I knew it," said Nestor.

"I'll send someone out for them," said Hanrahan. "The phone's ringing."

As Bill Hanrahan went up the stairs to the squad room, Nestor picked up the phone. He had completely forgotten the call for Lieberman.

The squad room on the second floor of the Clark Street stationhouse was hot. No one knew how to regulate the temperature though many had tried and almost as many man-hours had gone into trying to get the maintenance crew and their bosses downtown to take care of the problem as had been spent in the investigation of armed robbery. The heat brought out the worst in the room, which still looked relatively new though it was more than a decade old. The smell

175

of bodies, tobacco, forgotten lunches. And the room was full. Cold weather was supposed to keep people at home and out of other people's pockets, but this day was an exception.

"Hoff," he called. "Nestor needs a hand."

Hoff, the new kid on the block, lean, black, and ready to take on anything, nodded, put down the report he was reading, and moved to the door through which Hanrahan had just come.

Hanrahan moved to his desk in the corner. Lieberman, who had the desk across from him, wasn't in. His desk was a mess of reports, files, and scribbled notes. Hanrahan's work was in a neat pile in front of him. He took off his coat, draped it over the chair next to his desk, and sat down.

In one corner of the room, Pascalini and Ryan were talking to a frightened-looking dark young woman who looked like a hooker. She was smoking and looking around as if she expected something really bad to happen. From the look on her face, Hanrahan figured it already had.

Porter and Berogoski were working on a report a few desks down. Berogoski, the fat one, was standing over the shoulder of Porter, the thin one, telling him that he was misspelling everything.

Hanrahan took the first folder off the pile, opened it, and looked down. He should have gone home, made the bed in the living room, done the dishes. He should have . . . and that's when Hanrahan, listening to one cop correct another's spelling and a hooker sobbing about some "loony," had a sudden revelation.

"Decisions," he said softly, aloud. "I can't make decisions."

He was on the verge of exploring this insight when the words of the excited hooker broke through.

"I told you. I told you."

"Tell us one more time, Jess," Ryan said, his pock-marked Irish face as concerned as Spencer Tracy in any one of his priest roles.

"He was kind of skinny, had on this, I don't know, jacket," she said. "Young, hair over his eyes, like pictures of that guy, you know, killed all those Jews back who knows."

"Hitler?" asked Ryan.

"With the little mustache, yeah," Jess said, crossing her legs and taking a deep drag. "Light blond hair, blue eyes, maybe gray, looked real crazy. Just sitting there looking out the window at Wendy's right out there."

She turned in the chair and pointed at the wall.

"Wendy's?" said Pascalini, who looked a little like a picture Hanrahan had once seen of Edgar Allan Poe.

"Yeah, right," said Jess. "Then, out of nothing, J.J. says, 'Hello kid, how are ya?' Kid goes nuts. I never saw anything like that. Jumps on J.J., bites his fuckin' ear off, and then starts beating on him with a chair. The way he looked at me . . . He's still out there. I ain't goin' out there. He might be waiting for me."

"He have an accent?" came the next question.

The two detectives and the woman looked up at Hanrahan.

"Accent?" asked Jess nervously.

"Like foreign or from the South," asked Hanrahan.

"Yeah," Jess answered, remembering, "but more like . . . I don't know, not like white nigger talk, you know?"

"His nose," said Hanrahan, "maybe pushed over to one side just a little?"

The young woman looked up at Ryan, who nodded that she should answer the big man's questions.

"Maybe," she said. "I don't know. Maybe."

"What did he talk about?" asked Hanrahan.

"Talk about?" Jess asked, looking at what was left of her cigarette. "He was a nut, a religious loony. Jesus stuff, you know. You run into them all the time. Some of 'em junkies who found religion. They're the worst, man."

"I've got a picture to show you," Hanrahan said, going back to his desk.

Ryan waited a beat and then went back to his questioning.

Porter pulled the report he was working on out of the typewriter and Berogoski took it from him gently with two fingers, saying, "Work of art."

Bill Hanrahan sat for a beat looking over at the young woman. Then he got up again and moved across and out of the room. He was back in less than five minutes holding a five-by-seven photograph in his hand. He walked over to Jess, who stopped in midsentence and looked up at Hanrahan as he turned the photograph toward her.

"Yeah," she said, her voice shaking. "That's him. That's him."

Hanrahan handed the photograph to Ryan, who turned it over to check the name. Hanrahan went back to his own desk and called Lieberman.

It was Hanrahan's call that Lieberman had come back to after watching the kids, Todd, and Faye drive off.

"How's it going, Rabbi?" asked Hanrahan.

"Surviving, Father Murphy, surviving."

"Frankie Kraylaw's back in town," said Hanrahan.

There was no answer on the other end of the line, so Hanrahan loosened his tie and went on, "He bit a guy's ear off in Wendy's next door to the station. Hooker who was there says he was watching the station. Way I see it there are maybe a couple of hundred reasons why he might be sitting in Wendy's watching the station, but only one of them makes much sense."

"Looking for us," said Lieberman.

"Us, Jeanine, the boy. One of us should find him, Abraham."

"Take it, Father Murphy," said Lieberman.

"You're lookin' at me like maybe I'm gonna do something you're not gonna like, right?" asked Emiliano Del Sol, expecting no answer but the

179

one in the eyes of the very black man with the little beard who sat before him. "I mean am I right or am I wrong? I know that look. Like this a little. You tryin' to look tough, *macho*, *pero dentro de su corazon, tiene miedo, verdad?*"

"What you want from me, man?" asked Christian Velde, holding a cup of coffee to his lips, ordering his hands not to quiver. "And don't talk to me in no Spanish. I don' understand no Spanish."

They were in the Dominica Pierre Jamaican Restaurant on Howard Street and the place was empty except for El Perro, two of his Tentaculos, Carlos and "La Cabeza" Manulito, and Velde. Carlos and La Cabeza stood next to the booth at which El Perro and Christian Velde faced each other. In front of Velde was a deep-dish sweet potato pie and a white telephone.

The restaurant was long and narrow with five booths along the right and six tables lined up on the left going to the back of the restaurant where the kitchen was.

Someone in the place was cooking. It smelled sweet.

"What's that shit you're eatin', man?" asked El Perro, pointing at the plate in front of Velde.

"Sweet potato pie," said Christian, wishing now that he had brought someone with him, at least Henri Gommier and his 9mm Ingram Mac 10, the sight of which would make most Spanish piss ants crap in their pants and run for the doors, cursing.

Velde, however, was a smart man who had survived forty-three years as an extortionist and drug dealer by knowing how to gauge those who opposed him. If Henri were here, Christian was sure he would have to kill these three and get the hell out of the States fast. But Henri was not here and Christian had come for his payment and a bite to eat in his favorite restaurant in what he considered a safe neighborhood, his neighborhood. These Mexicans were crazy to come here, but it was clear to Christian that they were, indeed, crazy, at least the one across from him about whom he had heard but never until this dark moment met.

El Perro reached over and dipped his finger in the custardy dark brown dish in front of Christian. Then El Perro stuck his finger deep into his mouth, extracted it, swallowed, and pronounced, "Not bad shit, man. Jorge, we take seven or eight of these things with us."

"With my compliments," said Christian.

"That's O.K.," said El Perro, reaching over for another fingerful of pie. "You gonna do us a bigger favor."

"A bigger favor?" Christian said, sliding his sweet potato pie across the table and handing El Perro a fork.

Christian had heard about the mad leader of Los Tentaculos, his temper, his changing moods, the people he had maimed or murdered for good reasons and for no reason at all. He had also heard that El Perro had a patron in the police.

Christian looked up at the two young men standing next to the booth, blocking any thoughts he might have of exiting or being seen by anyone hurrying by on the street.

"It's cold out there, man," El Perro said, shaking his head and talking with a cheek full of pie. "I'm tellin' you. You know? And I got guys out on the streets, on the phones for I don' know how many fuckin' hours. How many hours, Jorge?"

"Little over four," said La Cabeza.

"I gotta tell you somethin'," El Perro whispered, leaning over the table. "You look fuckin' great."

Christian nodded and touched his small dark beard. As always, he was well dressed, conservatively dressed, a businessman on his rounds patronizing a favored restaurant. His suit was a three-piece charcoal from Polo, his tie a perfect swirled silk paisley with matching socks. His shoes were custom made.

"I gotta tell you somethin' else," said El Perro, wolfing down the last of his pie and looking at Christian's coffee.

"Baptiste," Christian shouted, "bring my guests some drinks. Coffee, Mambi?"

"Coffee," El Perro said, looking at the kitchen and nodding to Carlos, who turned to face the kitchen door, his hand under his coat.

"Baptiste is the owner," said Christian.

"*Espero que si,*" said El Perro with a grin.

A heavy black man in a white apron and cap pushed open the door almost instantly. He carried a tray with three steaming cups. Baptiste's eyes did not meet those of Christian or the three men. He set the cups down, dried his hands on his apron, and hurried back to the kitchen.

"Pick one," said El Perro, pointing up at Carlos without looking at him.

Carlos pointed to one of the three cups.

"Drink it," El Perro said to Christian Velde.

Christian smiled. "You think I keep cups of poisoned coffee in the kitchen here?" he asked.

"I don' think nothin'. I think you gonna drink that coffee."

Christian nodded, reached for the coffee, and took a sip. It burned the roof of his mouth and his throat, but he downed the entire cup in four gulps.

"We wait now to see if I die?" asked Christian.

El Perro reached for another cup and downed it, ending with a deep, satisfied sigh.

"Jorge," El Perro said, his eyes never leaving those of the Jamaican. *"Bebe."*

La Cabeza took the cup and drank.

"I'll get another cup for . . ." Christian began turning his head toward the kitchen.

"No," said El Perro. "Carlos needs his hands free. He can't think about more than one thing at a time, you know?"

Christian nodded. "How can I help you?"

"We been drivin' for four hours, seein' people, businesses, restaurants, bars. We been talkin' serious to people from the Islands, from places like . . . tell the man, La Cabeza."

Jorge stopped drinking and rattled off, "Barbados, Grenada, Guadeloupe, Antigua, Haiti, Dominica, Martinique, Trinidad . . ."

"Basta," said El Perro, holding up his hand.

Christian thought the madman across from him was truly remarkable. He had not blinked once nor turned his eyes away from Christian from the moment he had eased into the booth.

"Jorge's got a memory on him," said El Perro proudly.

"Impressive," said Christian.

"We're lookin' for a big fool black guy from the Islands," said El Perro. "Guy's name is George. Couple people say maybe they seen him. Lotsa guys named George. But this morning, my George, he got himself a fur hat like those Russians. One, two people think maybe they seen this George with another black guy. Good-lookin' guy. I wanna find George and this guy. These people I been talkin' to say you can maybe help me find them."

Christian nodded wisely. "What did these two do?"

"Killed a guy and shot *una mujer con nino.*"

"You mean a pregnant woman?"

"That's what I jus' said."

"That's bad luck," said Christian.

"Fuckin' A when we find him," said El Perro, crossing himself. "We gonna save him one of those prostrate operations like my old man he

184

had to have. We gonna make him eat his own *cojones*."

Christian Velde was quite sure that the lunatic meant exactly what he was saying.

"I'll make some calls," Christian said. "Sure you don't want anything to eat?"

"Nada," said El Perro, looking around at the paintings on the walls. All of them were by the same artist, dark women in colorful Islands dress, some of them with baskets on their head or in their arms. All of them happy, happy.

It took five short calls by Christian. When he hung up on the fifth call, he looked up at the three men and said, "Don't know George's name. The other man is Raymond Carrou. From Trinidad. Good looking. Goes to night school. Likes chicks. Black, white, slants. You name it. Has a straight job."

"He changed careers this morning," said El Perro with a broad smile.

"I got the name of a few places he hangs out, place that he works downtown. I maybe can get his address if I look around."

"Look around," El Perro said.

Christian nodded, carefully removed a leather-bound notebook from his jacket pocket, opened it, and with a gold-plated fountain pen began writing in clear, precise block letters. Los Tentaculos stood silently. Someone opened the restaurant door. El Perro did not look up, but Carlos and Jorge turned. The couple, both white and dressed for business, looked at the dark men

185

facing them and exchanged a few words before they turned and left, trying to make it look as if they had forgotten something or wandered through the wrong door.

"Here," said Christian, tearing out the sheet and handing it to El Perro.

"*Gracias*," said El Perro, starting to rise as Christian carefully screwed the top of his pen back on and placed pen and notebook in his jacket pocket.

"Two things more," said Christian as El Perro handed the sheet of paper to Jorge. "One, you owe me."

"*Verdad*," said El Perro.

"Two, you don't front me again. Never. You front me again and we're at war. *Comprende?*"

"*Comprendo*," said El Perro.

"I'm gonna tell some people that if someone does me, they find you and put you down even if they have to bomb every Mexican restaurant and apartment building in the city."

El Perro was grinning now. He nudged Jorge, who joined him in the grin.

"Hey," El Perro said over his shoulder, walking away from the booth as Carlos backed away with him keeping his eyes on both the kitchen and Christian Velde. "I think I come back here sometime for those pies. Maybe we run into each other. Maybe the stuff you give me is bullshit and we talk some more."

"It's straight," said Christian, adjusting his tie.

"*Pienso que si*," said El Perro, moving out of

the door Jorge opened to the swishing noise of Howard Street.

"I like that guy," said El Perro when they were back in the new blue GEO Prism they had come in. El Perro changed cars every month or so, always different from one another so no one could get a fix on what he rode in.

He sat in the front seat next to Jorge who drove while Carlos sat in the back so he could have plenty of room if he needed to use his weapon fast or drop it out of either window.

"*Yo tambien,*" said La Cabeza in the backseat.

"I think maybe we give him a favor sometime and give him his war, too," said El Perro. "*El viejo* Lieberman, I think maybe now he owes Los Tentaculos a big one."

"Where are the arresting officers?" Fiona Connery asked Nestor Briggs as he made his way through lockup on the way to his locker.

"Who?" asked Nestor, looking at the frail redheaded girl from the public defender's office. She wore a no-nonsense skirt and jacket but she still looked too young to be a lawyer. Too young to go to high school.

She was playing weary, put-upon, overworked, all of which she certainly was, but Nestor had other things on his mind.

"Lieberman and Hanrahan," she said.

They were in the small alcove where two rooms were reserved for lawyers and clients in the lockup. The alcove smelled of paint and steel.

The room in which Jean Tortereli sat smoking and waiting for Fiona Connery smelled no better and was no more inviting, with just a small table and four chairs. No windows.

"Out," Briggs said. "A Murder One. Miss, I'm not working lockup anymore and I've had a hell of a day. So if you'd just . . ."

Nestor tried to walk around her but she cut him off with her briefcase.

"Tell Lieutenant Kearney that if I don't see a statement or talk to the arresting officers, I'm filing for false arrest."

"Sounds reasonable to me," said Briggs, and he went through the door marked MEN'S LOCKER through which she could not follow him.

Fiona checked her watch. She did not date often. In fact, she hadn't had a date in more than three months. Or was it four? The job, the caseload for which there weren't enough hours in the day, the fatigue, not to mention that she hadn't been asked until yesterday, all contributed to her limited social life. Amend that, she thought. My nonexistent social life.

The minutes were flying and she had to get home, change, put in her contact lenses, and be ready in little more than an hour. She lived only fifteen minutes away in a cheap but clean apartment in Albany Park a few blocks from North Park College. Paul Nathan was not Mel Gibson, but he wasn't Charles Durning either, and he was smart, polite, and a successful doctor who had testified on behalf of one of her clients a few weeks ago. She could live with a little baldness. She couldn't go on living without a date.

Fiona tucked her notebook under her arm, adjusted her glasses, and went into the conference room, where Jean Tortereli looked up at her.

"Well?" asked Tortereli, her businesslike exterior definitely wilting with each hour of uncertainty.

"I'm going to try to reach the lieutenant in charge, get him to dismiss charges," Fiona said, sitting and folding her hands, forcing herself to speak slowly. "However, I doubt if he will dismiss the charges. Nor do I think a judge will dismiss until the case goes to prelim tomorrow."

"So, I sit in here and rot?" Tortereli said.

"And, I must tell you, the chances of your walking away from this one without doing some time are remote," said Fiona. "You've got two priors. Lester Wiggs, who I am not representing, has a long list of priors. The two detectives who handled the arrest are veterans with clean records and they were principle parties to the felony."

"I can't believe this," Tortereli said with indignation.

"Believe it," said Fiona. "I'll do what I can, but I can't promise much. We can plea, maybe get you off with probation, but you'd have to agree to testify against Lester Wiggs. No guarantees."

Fiona held her breath and succeeded, she was sure, in not looking anxious or looking down at her watch.

Jean Tortereli looked down at Fiona angrily, her red, recently repainted lower lip quivering. She reminded Fiona of Snow White's step-mother.

"I've got to think about it."

"My guess is that the same offer is being made to Mr. Wiggs. His lawyer is Peter Michaelson. He was a classmate at DePaul. Same criminal-law classes. Since Wiggs's sheet is longer than yours, the state attorney's office will probably accept your offer of testimony. If he does, they put it to Mr. Wiggs and Mr. Michaelson and Mr. Wiggs is advised to plea to a lesser offense. You don't tie up a court date, the time of the public defender's office, and the cost of holding you."

"I'll do it," Tortereli said, reaching for the package of cigarettes she had left on the table.

"All right," Fiona said, standing slowly and tucking her notebook into the briefcase her mother had given her when she graduated two years ago. "I make a call. You'll stay in here tonight if you sign some papers, or you can get taken to the women's lockup at County."

"Here," said Tortereli. "I've heard about County."

"I'm fairly confident, if Mr. Wiggs pleas, that we can have you on the street with no charges by tomorrow afternoon. Questions?"

"What if he tries to pull me down with him?" Tortereli asked, shaking her head and trying to light her cigarette at the same time.

"His lawyer will advise him not to," Fiona said.

"It wouldn't do him any good since you'd both start increasing the ante and telling more than the police already know."

"So, you're saying I should hold something back if I've got it, something that will keep Lester from trying to take me with him?"

"I'm saying what I've said," Fiona answered. "You can interpret it as you wish."

"O.K.," said Jean with a big sigh.

"Good," said Fiona. "I'll see you early tomorrow."

Fiona didn't wait for any more conversation from her client. She opened the door and called for the lockup turnkey, who ambled over from wherever he had been taking a rest.

If she hurried, Fiona had just enough time to fill in the waiver of transfer of Jean Tortereli, leave a message for Kearney, and get home in time to be ten, fifteen minutes late for Peter Nathan, tops.

George was standing on the hill at the Eastern Market in Port of Spain. His mother was on an outcrop of brown rock from which a thin waterfall tumbled musically down to the stream. She was leaning over, elbows on her knees in her white dress, to get a better look at the old woman by the stream. The old woman was cutting leaves from a dachine plant. His mother would get some leaves and mix them with crabs, okra, and herbs to make callaloo soup.

George smiled in delight, his tongue going over

his lips in anticipation of the meal. About thirty people, all of them black, most of them women, looked down at the old woman in black cutting the dachine leaves with the help of her sons.

Around George on the hill were his aunt, his sister, and people he didn't know, all of them watching the cutting of the dachine leaves.

There, a woman stood wearing a black dress with white circles, with a matching bandanna. There, a woman in a purple dress with a white lace collar that left her smooth brown shoulders and back showing. Below, a man in a straw hat stood with his arms behind his back next to the stream. There was a large colorful basket at the man's side, a basket, George knew, that waited for the leaves.

A woman in a purple dress and a purple bandanna stepped in front of George. He tried to move to one side, but she moved too. He moved to the other side. She followed without looking back, continuing to block his view.

There were too few moments like this to have a thoughtless woman ruin them. George grew angry, instantly angry. He looked to his mother but she was still leaning over trying to watch the old woman cut the leaves. Everyone but George could see. An "Ahh" escaped from the crowd, but George did not see what caused it.

His heart was pounding with fear and anger as he approached the woman in front of him. A small push and she would slide down the wet rock, get out of his way. His hands went out. He could see them. They were not the hands of a man. They were the thin brown hands and arms of a small boy. The fingers were almost touching the woman now. The smell of callaloo was sickening now. George's knees were shaking and he was afraid he would fall and everyone would turn to him and laugh.

Just before his fingers touched the woman, she turned. The turn was sudden. George backed away, almost falling, and let out a yelp. The woman was white. Her belly was big. She was smiling at him. It was the woman he had shot. There was the hole. Right there in her stomach.

Panic. His mother must not know, must not see this.

He turned from the smiling white woman and found himself facing the two men from whom he had taken the money. They were sitting at a table, the same table they had been sitting at when he took their money.

George looked for his mother and saw Raymond among the dark faces. Raymond was holding a gun. The gun was pointed at George. Raymond said something and George howled and opened his eyes to see a different white woman, a white woman in a white dress looking down at him.

"You are one lucky man," the woman said.

She was heavy, more old than young, with hair too yellow to be natural.

"Callaloo," George tried to say, but it came out a dry rusty blur of pain. The pain was surrounded by a dream. The pain was in his chest, in his nose, in his arms.

"You speak English?" the woman asked.

George nodded.

"Your throat's a little sore. Tube. It's out now," the woman said, checking the glucose bottle that dripped into a tube leading to George's right arm. "Can you understand English?"

George nodded.

"Good. Can you talk? Softly. Not a whisper."

"Yes," George rasped. "I am in a hospital."

"Very observant," said the woman, moving to the foot of his bed and picking up a chart.

George turned his head as far as he could to the right. It wasn't very far. There was another bed in the room. The other bed was empty.

"Man wants to talk to you," the nurse said, returning to his side and lifting his wrist to take his pulse.

"Man?"

"*The* Man," the woman said. "Police. You had a couple of bullets in you. They have a certain curiosity about such things."

"I'm very tired," said George, closing his eyes.

"Man says he'll only be a minute. Doctor says if you're up and can talk we can go for it. I'll cut in after a minute or two."

"Wait," rasped George as the woman turned and left the room.

George tried to pull his thoughts and lies together. It was a difficult task when he was well, whole, and undrugged.

The door opened again and a man came in. The man was Chinese or something, in a leather jacket. He was hefty, compact, and about forty.

"George," the Chinese guy said, moving toward the bed. "You look terrible."

"I been shot."

"I know. Who shot you?"

George shrugged.

"You don't know who shot you?"

"Man," said George. "White man. Robber."

"A white robber took you on in the middle of a prairie," said the Chinese man. "Did he say what he wanted?"

"Money," said George.

"Then why didn't he take it?" asked the man.

George's eyes blinked and looked around for an answer. "He didn't take any money?"

"That I can't say," said the man. "But you were found on the side of the Dan Ryan Expressway with a bag of cash in your arms. Another question after you tell us who shot you: Where did you get the money?"

"I am very tired," said George, closing his eyes.

"I'll bet you are," said the cop. "Talk with your eyes closed."

"I am very tired," George repeated.

"Doctor says you should be dead," the Chinese cop said. "Another question: Where did you get that hat?"

George's hands went up to his head. The movement tugged at the needle in his arm and pulled at the stitches in his back. The hat was gone.

"Robber," George groaned wearily.

"White guy who didn't take your money," the cop said flatly. "He gave you the hat?"

"Yes. Well, no, man. He drop it or somethin'. Where am I?"

"La Grange."

"Is that near Florida?"

"Close," said the cop.

George smiled, ignored the cop, and let himself be carried back to drugged sleep.

The policeman, whose name was Martin Fu, stood for a minute to be sure that George was really asleep, then he left the room and went to the nursing station.

"Phone," he said.

"Local?" asked the older nurse with the tinted hair, looking at him over her glasses.

"Chicago."

"All right," the nurse said with a sigh, going back to the chart she was working on.

Martin Fu took his notebook from his pocket, fingered through it for the number he needed, and placed the call. What he heard on the other end when the ringing stopped was a harried voice saying, "Sergeant Briggs, Clark Street station."

Beyond Briggs, Martin Fu could hear some woman screaming in Russian or something, then a man with a quivering voice in English.

"Lieberman," Fu said.

"Not here," said Briggs.

"Give him this message. My name's Fu, La Grange police. Got a guy in the hospital here fits the description that went on the line this morning."

"Right," said Briggs, as the woman and man in the background raised the ante, again.

Fu left his phone number and started to say that it might be urgent, but Sergeant Briggs had already hung up.

"Thanks," said Fu. "One more call. Local."

The nurse nodded and Fu called the station and informed his duty officer that he would be at the hospital waiting for a call from a Detective Lieberman in Chicago.

"How's the day, Francie?" asked Fu.

"Long," said the woman on the other end of the call. "Long."

Fu hung up, nodded at the top of the nurse's head, and moved back to the door of George's room. He had no real concern about George getting up and leaving, nor any real concern about whoever shot him tracking him down to finish the task. But if this was a suspect in the murder that had hit the noon news, it would not be a good idea to leave him unguarded.

Fu found a chair inside George's room and moved it outside the door. From the pocket of his leather jacket, he fished a compact electronic Tetris game his daughter had given him for Christmas. He pushed the button, heard the small ding, and sat down for what he hoped would be an hour or so of quiet meditation.

The heater had stopped working in the pickup truck, so Frankie had to give up his view of the entrance to the apartment building where Big Bear had taken Angie. The apartment was in a three-story, yellow-brick-courtyard walk-up. Frankie had watched the windows when the Indian and the old woman had gone in and in the near darkness of the Chicago winter afternoon he had seen the light go on in the apartment on the second floor.

The only thing left to do was wait and pray, but Big Bear didn't come out and the heater didn't work and Frankie knew he had to get out of the truck or freeze.

He didn't think it could possibly be colder outside the truck, but it was, so he decided that he would have to go up to the apartment even if Big Bear was there. He would simply carry the shotgun under his coat, and while it would stick out a little . . . He was opening the door to get the gun when he saw the lobby door open and the big Indian hurry out, hands in his pockets, collar up. He trotted out of the courtyard and onto the sidewalk as Frankie ducked behind the truck and watched until Big Bear was at the corner of the block at least forty yards away.

Then Frankie walked quickly to the entrance, entered the lobby, and tried the inner door. It was locked. He would have punched a hole in one of the door's glass panes but someone had beaten him to it. He reached in through the

198

broken pane and unlocked the door from the inside. As he stepped in he smelled mildew and chill.

The steps were covered with ragged carpeting and the light bulb on the first landing between the two apartments was bare, yellow, and dim. The second floor was the same. Very slowly, patiently, he tried the door of the apartment where the light had gone on. It was locked. He knocked.

"Big Bear," he called.

No answer. He knocked again.

"It's me. Frankie."

Still no answer.

"Come on," Frankie coaxed. "I've got the money for you."

Beyond the door he heard movement, the creak of wooden floorboards.

"Who's there?" came Angie's frightened voice.

"Frankie. Tell Big Bear I've got the fifty dollars. I just want to give it to him and head back to Wyoming tonight."

"Fifty dollars?"

"Fifty," he confirmed.

He had used the devil's own tool, turned greed and corruption on the woman, tested her, and now, he was sure, she had been found wanting. A chain slipped, a lock turned, and the door opened just wide enough for Angie's face to show. The face was a puffy white, the eyes brown with a near yellow where the white had once been. Her hair was straight, gray-white, and less tangled than

Frankie had vaguely remembered. She squinted at him.

"I know you from someplace?" she asked.

"Not that I know of, ma'am."

"Give me the money. I'll give it to the Indian."

Her hand came out of the crack of the partly open door.

"Where is Big Bear?" Frankie asked with a smile, looking around the hall to be sure no one was listening.

"Out," she said. "I'm a friend. I'm stayin' with him. I'll give it to him."

"I can't," said Frankie with a sigh. "No offense, ma'am, but I don't know you or what's in your heart. I'd say it's a good heart, but the devil does have powers."

"I do know you from someplace," she said.

"Well, now that I see you clear you look familiar to me, too, ma'am," he said with a smile. "But I can't be sure. Listen. Big Bear and I have a secret place we put money. You turn your back and I'll put it there and when Big Bear comes back you just tell him Frankie was here and left the money in the hiding place. Fair?"

"I don't know," Angie said.

Frankie's hand was on the door now, applying gentle pressure.

"I'm sorry. I wish I could wait but I just don't have the time and I know Big Bear needs the money, but if you say no, then . . ."

The door opened and Angie, clutching the top of her purple sack of a dress, backed away to let him in. Frankie came in, closing the door behind him.

"Thank you," he said. "Now, you just turn your back."

Angie turned her back to the wall and Frankie looked around the apartment. It was neat, uncluttered. The furniture was old but clean. A faded Indian blanket covered the sofa and on the wall of the small living room was the photograph of an Indian family in full tribal dress. Frankie crossed to the sofa, bent down pretending to stuff something behind the pillows, and then stood up.

"You can turn now," he said, facing Angie, who shuffled about to face him.

"Wait," he said, looking at her. "Sure, I know you. You're Angie, met you once or twice at the church in Evanston. You know, St. Catherine's."

"Yeah," she said, rocking on her feet and pointing at him. "I thought you looked familiar. You work there or something, right?"

"I do God's work," Frankie said. "I must go now. I've been traveling, trying to get work. Came back to Chicago to find my wife and boy and bring them to Wyoming, but . . ."

He shrugged.

"Can't find 'em?" she asked.

He nodded his head yes, his eyes misting, a sincere mist of beginning tears.

"Her name's Jeanine. I heard she was working at a McDonald's, but . . ."

"Jeanine," Angie said with excitement. "I know her. I know her. I seen her."

201

"No," said Frankie.

"Yes," said Angie. "Honest to God. On Western, up near what's that street, Granville, something. Working the McDonald's. Right there behind the counter. She's the one who's husb . . ."

Angie's mouth snapped shut.

"Bless you," said Frankie. "The Lord must have guided me to you. Repay an old debt and be rewarded."

Angie's putty face was wrinkled now with thought and the recognition of some memory about Jeanine's husband.

"I'm thinkin' something here. Rememberin', you know. Ain't it that she run away from you, somethin', you know?"

"No," said Frankie. "I just had to do some traveling. Spreading the Lord's truth."

"No," Angie said, pointing at him with one doughy hand, holding her collar closed with the other. "You're the one the Indian said was lookin' for me. Oh shit, God. Christ."

Angie began to shake, to cry as Frankie came around a small table in the middle of the room and moved toward her. Suddenly, with a yelp like Ab Grunner's dog when the semi ran over it, the old woman ran to the corner of the room and through the door. Frankie lunged after her but was a step too late as Angie threw the bolt on the bathroom door.

"If I had time," he said, standing in front of the bathroom door. "But I do not."

Beyond the door Angie was sobbing, an echoing sob. Frankie was sure she was sitting in the bathtub.

He turned, found the kitchen, opened it, and pulled out a half-full jar of raspberry jam. He went back into the living room and, to the sound of frightened sobbing and wails, put his finger into the jam and moved to the wall, where he painted a jagged raspberry cross. He filled it in in the proper places, stepped back to admire it, and strode across the floor and out of the apartment.

Six P.M.

One glass of rum. That was all Raymond drank and he drank it slowly, sitting at one of the tables at the Biabou Restaurant on Division Street, being sure to eat all of his bean soup and sandwich.

Others around him, all black, many with the accent of the Islands, ate chicken or fish, drank, and laughed amid photographs of the white Monastery of the Ancient Order of St. Benedict, a steel-drum band on the docks greeting tourists, and the Coroni Swamp, where he had seen oysters growing on trees, crabs crawling on branches, and pink-white egrets plucking shrimp from the shallow, murky waters. The one photograph that he did not like and that he was always careful to have behind his back and out of sight when he ate at the Biabou was of a street in the old section of Port of Spain, with its red-rusted roofs and wooden fence. It was like the street on which he had spent the first twenty-one years of his life. It was an image that he had been painfully erasing during the ten years he had spent in the United States, the last eight years of which were as an illegal alien.

Raymond knew that he would have to return to work soon, that he would need to act as if nothing had happened, that he would need to blend in and wait.

He looked at the book propped open before him to ward off conversation. The problems of Sammy Glick seemed less than meaningful.

Raymond felt very tired. Was it yesterday, only yesterday when he had not yet committed a violent crime, had not yet killed one man, possibly two?

He needed another rum, but the Biabou served no liquor, only food. You had to bring your own bottle and Raymond had done just that, but it was a bottle he had taken from the apartment, a bottle with but two small servings left in it, and it was now empty and he was still feeling pain.

"You not eatin' enough," Henriette said, standing over Raymond, who looked at a couple at the next table trying to get their children to eat.

"I'm not hungry," said Raymond.

Henriette, large, young, very black, and dressed in colorful Islands pink and red, shrugged. Like many other girls from the Islands she had a fancy for Raymond, but even if he were not worrying for his life, Henriette wouldn't interest him, never had. Too young, too round, happy outside, ready, he was certain, to weep at the slightest cause. Raymond could not abide crying women—or crying men for that matter.

"You want me to take de bowl?"

"Take the bowl," said Raymond.

"What happened to your friend?" Henriette asked, cleaning away the dishes.

"Friend?"

"Big fella. You know. George, from Trinidad. You come in with him few days back."

"Just someone I ran into," Raymond said uncomfortably, trying to coax a few more drops from his bottle of rum. "No friend of mine."

"No matter to me," Henriette said, shrugging again. "Mama and Doc-Doc said they seen him with you this morning in you car and he be wearin' a furry hat and a look on his face like a scared owl."

Raymond didn't bother to answer.

Henriette shook her head and carried the dishes away toward the kitchen.

All I need, Raymond thought. All I need.

He got up, paid with some of the money he had taken from the body of the dead man, and headed for the door, almost bumping into two Latinos, one big, dumb, looking for a fight, the other nervous, thin, hair brushed back. Raymond avoided them as they headed for the kitchen. When their backs were to him, Raymond saw that the big dumb-looking one had an octopus painted on the back of his leather jacket. The thin Latino turned suddenly, looking toward him, but Raymond managed to avoid his eyes and step into the cold.

The sweet smell disappeared behind him in the crackle of icy air. Raymond's ears went cold and he reached into his pocket to fish out the red earmuffs.

The car was around the corner past a grocery that sold both Islands and Chinese food. He had once bought a bottle of Chinese medicine in the store when he had a headache. It had cured his headache and every other headache he got until he ran out of the pills. When he had gone back to the store, the Chinese woman had said they could get no more of the pills from China, that they had a substitute. The substitute had not worked. Raymond had never gone back into the store.

He slid into the car and turned on the heat. The gas gauge showed almost empty. The fan barely turned, sending in air almost as cold as the outside.

He had no choice now. It would be dangerous, but he had to go to the hospital, find her. He had things he deserved in life. Raymond had been cheated too many times by his own bad choices and the promises of others.

George was gone. Raymond deserved to be safe.

He would go to the hospital and when he did

what he must do he would walk out into the nightmare of winter with some hope for the future.

Raymond drove. He would drive until it was time. He would not go back to the apartment until it was safe, until he had dealt with the woman. Yes, he would wait until late, work out the details of his plan.

Warm air was coming through the vents now. The air had an angry burnt smell to it and Raymond was beginning to feel drowsy. The two glasses of rum did not help. Well, in one way they did. In another, they made it difficult for him to drive through the narrow, unplowed, ice-layered streets.

Though he had wanted to distance himself from Trinidad, calypso music, and steel-drum bands since he stepped on the boat to New York a decade ago, at times of weakness he found himself remembering snatches of songs he had despised as a teen. One particularly haunted him. It had been created by Lord St. John-Pelly and on more than one occasion he had heard Lord St. John-Pelly sing it on the street.

"A man he trusts a woman trusts his faith to the wind. A man he trusts a woman is lost before he can sin."

Frankie almost missed his wife.

The six o'clock shift was just coming on at the McDonald's on Western near Granville where Jeanine worked. He saw her through the window, wearing a stupid uniform that made her breasts stick out. There she was smiling at men, taking orders, serving burgers and fries and drinks. On display. People could just look at her, even touch her hand.

He had found a spot in the parking lot where he could watch the counter and where Jeanine was not likely to see him. She had no reason to be looking for him, no reason to know that he had a pickup truck, that he was back. And if she did spot him, he would have to take her right there, make her tell him where Charlie was. If anyone tried to get in the way, so be it. Frankie touched the chill barrel of the shotgun. The Lord would take his hand and people would die, and if they were good Christian people the Lord would take them unto his bosom.

But Jeanine did not see him. She moved behind the grill and disappeared. He considered getting out of the truck, making his way through the dinnertime crowd to be sure he knew where she was, but that might be dangerous and it probably wasn't necessary.

He was sure it wasn't necessary when Jeanine, wearing a heavy, furry-looking coat he had never seen, suddenly appeared about a dozen yards to his right talking to a guy dressed in a bulky jacket.

Jeanine was laughing.

Frankie slunk back into the corner of his seat, into the shadows behind the steering wheel.

"And when Burns told me to take the mop,"

the young man said, "I said, 'Sure, who you want me to take it to?'"

Jeanine laughed. It hadn't been funny, what the man-kid said, but she had laughed to please him.

From the shadow Frankie watched the young man open the door of a Ford Festiva parked two cars away. Jeanine got in and the young man came around quickly to let himself in. He had trouble getting his Festiva started. Even with a car between them and a grinding engine, Frankie could hear Jeanine laugh.

Frankie prayed for the car to start, and eventually it did.

Following them was easy. Watching them as he followed was hard. Did she move toward the man? Touch his arm? It was hard to see through the slowly defrosting window of the Festiva, but was she laughing, talking? Jeanine's mouth was opening and closing fast. He had never known her to talk a lot or to laugh, but she was doing both now. He was sure of it. What else was she doing? What else had she been doing?

They drove straight south on Western. Frankie had to run a red light on Lawrence to keep up with them because he was keeping two cars back now. Then, at Wilson, the Festiva signaled for a turn. Two cars went around the turning car and Frankie was on his tail again, but keeping his distance.

They drove past a hospital, turned right, and went two blocks before the Festiva stopped.

Frankie pulled into a spot five cars behind them in front of a fire hydrant and quickly turned off the lights and the engine.

Was it a minute? Two? The passenger door opened and Jeanine stepped out, laughing. She reached back in with the door open. Touching the man's face? Shaking his hand?

And then she withdrew, the door closed, and the Festiva sat, motor running, while Jeanine crossed the street, moved through a low iron gate, went up on the porch of a small, well-lighted house, and fumbled in her pocket for a key. When she found it, she smiled and held it up to show the man in the Festiva.

Only when she was in the house and the door closed did the Festiva pull away.

Frankie waited, counting to two hundred, praying, wanting to plan but unable to think of anything beyond getting his wife and son, having them next to him even if he had to tie them down, and heading west.

Frankie got out of the car and looked both ways. There was no traffic on the residential street. Cars filled the spaces on both sides. Frankie crossed the street about forty yards from the front of the house Jeanine had entered. He walked slowly, watching the door of the house, listening for the sound of approaching cars or footsteps. Nothing but the distant swoosh of tires on Wilson Avenue two blocks away.

In the dark snowy patch between the house Jeanine was in and the dark one next to it, Frankie stood on his toes trying to look into a window. He couldn't see much, but what he saw was sufficient. Charlie's head moved by. Not talking but walking. Jeanine came next, saying something Frankie couldn't hear.

Whose house was this? What was his family doing here? Slowly, carefully, warning himself, Frankie moved toward the front of the house and, ankle-deep in snow, stepped over the low iron fence and tiptoed up the steps. Through the window on his left he could see an open sofa bed, the blankets a mess. Jeanine, still in her uniform, was talking and starting to make the bed.

Was it Charlie's? Had his wife slept in it? Alone?

No longer worried about noise, Frankie ran down the stairs and looked at the mailbox. There was no name on it. He opened the box and pulled out a handful of mail. The streetlights had come on a few minutes earlier but there wasn't enough light for Frankie to read the name. He stepped back, holding the top letter close, and made out the name William Hanrahan on a bill from Commonwealth Edison. The name. Frankie was sure he knew the name. He found another letter, this one also to William Hanrahan, from Publishers' Clearing House, the name in big, clear, bold letters.

Frankie dropped the mail in the yard and strode across the street to the cab of his pickup. He removed the shotgun, cradled it in his arms, and recrossed the street, ready to drop the weapon to his side if someone should appear.

He carried his own lightning now. And he would wield it as the Lord moved his hands.

Frankie moved onto the porch and knocked at the door, his feet tingling inside his boots, his mouth tin dry. She was coming. Yes. The door opened and there she stood. It took her a beat to recognize him. By the time she had gathered herself enough to close the door, Frankie had pushed it toward her.

Jeanine's laugh was gone. It was replaced now by the familiar look of fear as she backed away.

Frankie stepped in, shotgun in his arms, and kicked the door closed.

"What sins have you committed during my exile by the heathens? What sins with that policeman who expels me from the city so he can fornicate with my wife?"

"I haven't . . ." Jeanine said in panic, looking around for help that wasn't there as Frankie took another step into the room.

Charlie appeared in the doorway behind Jeanine. The room behind the boy was a dining room set with three places. Charlie's look did not change. He stepped into the room, blinking and expressionless, and now stood with no sign of emotion as his mother clung to him, sobbing.

"Get your things, fast," said Frankie. "Get a bag, a box, and throw things in. I'll give you five minutes."

Jeanine was shaking her head no, not defiantly but as if her world had come apart.

"No back talk," said Frankie, pointing the shotgun toward the doorway to the dining room. "Move. I hear a window open, a door open, and I come letting the Lord dictate what my finger does with this tool of vengeance."

Neither Charlie nor Jeanine moved.

"You forsook me, Jeanine Peasley Kraylaw," said Frankie.

Frankie took another step toward them before he was aware of another presence in the room, a person standing in the doorway behind Frankie's family.

"It would be best if you and Charlie stepped back," said Hanrahan.

The policeman's face was red. His jacket was open and in his hand, pointing toward the ground, was a gun, a black-gray gun.

Frankie raised the shotgun in the direction of the policeman who had stolen his family.

"Best move now," said Hanrahan gently. "Better if the boy's not in the room."

Jeanine looked at Frankie and then at Hanrahan. Then she guided Charlie behind Hanrahan.

"The Lord has delivered you into my hands," said Frankie. "He means me to punish you for breaking commandments with my wife."

"And you mean to punish her and the boy, too?" asked Hanrahan.

"I mean to," Frankie said. "It's my right, my obligation."

"The Lord didn't send me, Frankie. I followed you from McDonald's. You left an easy trail, starting with the man you almost killed at Wendy's. When I knew you were in town and looking for me and Abe, it didn't take much to figure what you might be up to. I don't know how you found her, but . . ."

"The Lord Jesus Christ led me," said Frankie.

"If he did," said Hanrahan sadly, "then I think God's got a sense of humor I can't figure out."

"I'll pray for your soul," said Frankie, raising the shotgun.

"I'll need it," said Hanrahan, gun still at his side as Frankie Kraylaw pulled the trigger of his father's shotgun.

Lieberman and Bess walked into Temple Mir Shavot on California Avenue just four blocks from their house. As always, Bess adjusted the *yarmulke* that bobbed on top of Abe's curly hair before they went into the low-ceilinged, fluorescent-lit reception hall. There were tables of food under the windows and people milling around, all familiar faces, talking softly. Word had gotten around quickly.

It had been Bess's idea to have an open house before relatives and a *minyon* gathered at Yetta and Maish's apartment to sit *Shiva*. As president of the synagogue, Bess had certain unstated rights. Rabbi Wass had not hesitated to approve and support the idea and to get both the Women's Auxiliary and the Men's Club to get on the phone and put out word of the tragedy and the get-together.

Abe agreed that it was a good idea. It got Maish busy catering for the event and pulled him out of the T&L. It nudged Yetta into dressing herself, making some plans.

"Elliott Ness is here," Herschel Rosen said, stepping up to the Liebermans with his wife, Sarah, at his side.

"This is a time for jokes?" Sarah Rosen said, pushing her husband.

"It's all right, Sarah," Bess said, taking the woman's arm and walking her away.

"I'm trying to lighten up a little," explained Herschel. "It's my way. Besides, who knows what to say at times like this? You know what I mean? I've seen wives, brothers, kids, everyone die. You never know what to say. You know how I feel for you and Maish, Abe?"

"Thanks, Hershy," Lieberman said, touching the little man's shoulder. Herschel Rosen shrugged and lost himself in the small crowd.

Hymie Fried, the cantor, who looked like a former middleweight contender but sang almost like Jan Pierce, was wolfing down a bagel oozing with cream cheese as he talked to Rabbi Wass, who looked vaguely like a pudgy Claude Rains tonight.

Alter Cockers, even Howie Chen, dressed in jackets and ties, stood near the far wall drinking coffee. They nodded at Abe as he wended his way forward looking for his brother. Manny Resnick with the bad hip, who still owned the hardware store on North Avenue next to Slovotny's Meat Shop, found a hole in the crowd and grabbed Abe's hand in both of his, pumping.

"A shame," he said. "Whatever I can do, Abe. Whatever. I told Maish. Same goes for you. Whatever."

"Thanks, Manny."

Resnick reluctantly released Lieberman's hand and edged back as Abe moved forward.

"Abe," came Lisa's voice at his side.

There was something in his daughter's voice beyond grief, something Lieberman would prefer not to face.

A woman, thin, well dressed, and smelling of dark perfume, put her arms around him and kissed his cheek. The woman was weeping as she said, "So young. So young."

Someone pulled her back.

"I think that was Levan's first wife," he said, turning to face Lisa.

"Abe, you saw her," Lisa said as if she were establishing the initial, essential premise of a syllogism.

"Her?" asked Lieberman.

"Abe," Lisa said with exasperation.

Lisa was dressed in appropriate black, her hair tied back, looking very sober, serious, and professional.

"You talked to the kids," he said.

"I talked to Melisa. Barry wouldn't tell me anything."

The crowd buzzed, kept their distance for the father-daughter talk. Through a cluster of heads Abe saw his brother, hound-faced and nodding to someone hidden by a wave of mourners and sympathizers.

"Her name is Faye," said Lieberman.

"I knew that. I told you that," said Lisa. "What does she look like? What's she like?"

"Look," said Lieberman with a sigh, "I saw her for a minute, maybe . . ."

"Abe."

"Nice-looking lady, around forty-five, maybe even older. Weight around one-fifteen or -twenty. Hair short, gray-brunette. Good smile. Teeth her own, unstained. Doesn't smoke. Stands erect. I'd say she exercises regularly. Skin color is good. Steady hands. Eyes, hazel, meet yours when she talks. Definitely not Jewish. Her . . ."

"You want me to scream, Abe? Right here? Right now?"

"It's not in you, Lisa," he said with a sad smile. "I think I'd like to see you just let go and scream."

"You want me to say 'please'?" Lisa said, looking around to be sure no one could hear their conversation.

"Hell, no," said Lieberman. "You say 'please' and I pay for it the rest of my life. O.K. I liked her. She handled the situation well, the kids well, doesn't seem to push Todd. There was a look in her eye, asking for an even break. I think the lady's been through a lot in her life."

"Pretty?" asked Lisa, biting her lower lip.

"Pretty yes, beautiful no," answered Lieberman.

Lisa shook her head and folded her arms.

"My cousin is dead and I'm worrying about who Todd might be sleeping with."

"He's your husband."

"I walked out on him, Abe. I took the kids and walked out on him."

"I know," said Lieberman. "You're all living at my house, remember? Now you think maybe you made a mistake."

"No," said Lisa. "I think I did the right thing, but it doesn't make it hurt less when someone like Faye comes along and you think she may be a better wife for your husband."

"Nothing's easy, Lisa," Abe said as Maish saw him and waved. "Maish wants me."

Abe looked at his daughter, who met his eyes and smiled the smile of the perplexed.

"I always preferred biochemistry to tragedy," she said softly. "'How hard, abandonment of my desire. But I can fight necessity no more.' *Antigone*. After fifteen years, it rubs off. Go take care of Uncle Maish. I'm being selfish."

Lieberman made his way through a half dozen more condolences and found his brother, Yetta, and Bess standing in front of Ida Katzman, who sat on a bridge chair, her cane standing in front of her held erect by her thin befreckled hands.

Abe gave Yetta a hug and touched her cheek. There was nothing to say. Yetta held back tears.

"Death," said Ida Katzman.

Ida Katzman, eighty-six, looked into the hound-dog eyes of Abraham Lieberman, and repeated, "Death."

As the temple's principal benefactor, Ida was seldom contradicted. Since she seldom spoke, and when she did it was to observe and not to dictate, contradiction was seldom even contemplated by those who dealt with her.

"Yes," said Lieberman, taking Bess's hand.

Ida shook her head. "Mort and I had no children," she said. "You know that."

"I'm sorry," said Lieberman.

Ida shook her head. "Not that we didn't like children," she went on. "Children are the heart of our belief, of our religion."

Ida's frail hand moved to her chest to tap the heart about which she spoke.

Lieberman nodded.

Ida shook her head again, the hand that had been at her heart returning to help balance her cane.

"Times like this," she said. "The pain of losing a child. I remember when Woodrow Wilson was the president, when that actor with the bad breath . . ."

"Clark Gable," Lieberman supplied, in spite of a warning squeeze of his hand from Bess.

"Clark Gable had bad breath?" asked Ida.

"So I've heard," said Abe, "but you had someone else in mind."

"I don't remember," said Ida, looking at her cane for help down the path of memories. "Oh, times like this when I can't imagine the hurt of such a loss."

Everyone was looking at Lieberman now. Yetta, Maish, Bess, Ida Katzman. Somehow, as a policeman, as a man who had seen more death than anyone in the room with the exception of Isaac Pankovsky, who had survived Auschwitz, Abe Lieberman was expected to make a meaningful observation.

"I can't feel," said Maish before Abe could speak. "There's no pain. I want it to come, but . . . I'm what you call numb. You think we have enough coleslaw?"

Yetta wept and clung to her husband's arm.

Bess let go of Abe's hand to comfort Yetta, and someone touched Abe's arm.

Abe turned to face Whitlock, the old black man who served as janitor and all-purpose handyman for the temple.

"Telephone," Whitlock whispered. "Rabbi's office."

"Excuse me," Abe said.

Neither Ida Katzman, Yetta, or Maish seemed to notice as he turned to leave. Bess's eyes met his and let him know that she had the situation under control.

Lieberman followed Whitlock through the

crowd, touching an extended hand here, feeling a sympathetic pat on his shoulder there.

Whitlock ushered Lieberman out of the room.

"I want you to have my condolences," said Whitlock as they turned to the right and headed down the short corridor past the sanctuary.

"Thank you," said Lieberman.

"I've got a sense of what your brother must be going through," said Whitlock. "Lost one boy in Vietnam. The second is fine, but I worry."

"I know," said Lieberman, entering the tiny carpeted and book-lined office.

Whitlock left, closing the door behind him, and Lieberman took the three steps across the room and lifted the phone.

"Lieberman," he said.

"Briggs," said Nestor wearily.

"What are you still doing on the desk?"

"Corsenelli's got her period, something. I don't know," Briggs said wearily. "Lieutenant Kearney says I can make it up on Saturday. Bill called in. Said to tell you he's getting somewhere. If you need him, call him at home or leave a message with me. He'll call in. That skinny public defender kid with the red hair . . ."

"Connery."

"Right," said Nestor. "Looking for you and Bill and Kearney. She left a message. She'll be in in the morning to talk about her client turning evidence. You ask me, the state attorney and the public defender will let her walk and put him on probation. You ask me. Steal old people's pensions, Social Security, savings, and what do you get?"

"What else you got, Nestor?"

"Someone named Emiliano, no last name, called. Crazy spic. Could hardly understand him. Said he had something. He'd find you later. Let's see. What else? Oh, yeah, an Officer Fu in La Grange called, said he read the APB, thinks he's got the guy with the hat. I don't know what the hell he meant but I said . . ."

"Where is he?" Lieberman asked.

"Fu?"

"Fu."

"La Grange Hospital. Waiting for you."

"You read the APBs today, Nestor?" asked Lieberman.

"Who's got time?" asked Nestor.

"Goodbye, Nestor. I'll call in later."

Lieberman hung up and looked at his hand. It was shaking. The door to the rabbi's office opened and Bess stepped in. She looked at her husband's face and hand, closed the door behind her, and moved to the desk. She took the trembling hand in both of hers.

"Abe?"

"I'm fine," he said. "I've got to go."

"Maish wants you to meet him at Weinstock's Funeral Home at eight to make arrangements," she said.

"Skokie?"

"The one on Broadway near Lawrence."

Lieberman nodded and stood up.

"If I can get there, I'll be there."

He patted his wife's hand and stood her in front of him.

"I'm fine," he repeated.

She looked in his eyes.

"You won't do anything foolish?"

Lieberman smiled and kissed his wife.

"Providing I can tell the difference between smart and foolish, I won't do anything foolish. The problem is recognizing that it's foolish without having you to check it with."

"Pick up the phone," she said.

"Maybe I will."

Frankie pulled the trigger on both barrels of the shotgun and there was nothing but the neat metallic click of a clean weapon.

"Take the boy upstairs now," Hanrahan said to Jeanine without taking his eyes from Frankie, who broke open the shotgun and saw both chambers empty.

Hanrahan could hear the young woman and her son hurrying away behind him.

"Told you I followed you," said Hanrahan. "Saw your truck. Saw you go to the house. While you weren't looking, I was unloading."

"You're working for him," Frankie cried, pointing toward the floor, his face turning red.

"You're not gonna give up, are you, Frankie?"

"Never," said Frankie.

"We put you away and someday you'll get out

and I'll be older and your wife and boy will be that much more scared with waiting."

Hanrahan's clenched left hand came up. He held it open to reveal the two red shotgun shells he had removed from Frankie's weapon.

"God's will," said Frankie.

Hanrahan threw a shell across the room. It bounced off Frankie's chest to the floor. Hanrahan threw the second one. Frankie bobbled it a bit and then pulled it in. Hanrahan said nothing, but he shifted his gun and crossed himself.

Frankie, breathing hard, knelt for the shell on the floor, stood, loaded both barrels, and, as he raised the weapon, Detective William Hanrahan obeyed the voice inside him, the voice of his father.

"Remember," James Hanrahan had said. "When you get to the point when you know you're going to have to shoot someone, it'll come fast. Your breathing, your heartbeat will be racing with excitement and fear. That's natural. But it can make you flinch. Take my word, William, when you see a perp with a weapon in his mitt, your urge'll be to grab the trigger. Fight the urge. Level your weapon. You're right-handed, so cock the gun with your left thumb to keep from disturbing your firing grip. Use both hands. Fight the flinch, William. It'll be there some. Don't ignore it. Fight it. Look down the barrel. Then squeeze. Pull the trigger straight back. Don't grab. You do it right and you'll hear the bang loud and the thump of lead hitting home. Stay with the sighting through the recoil. Level and fire again. Always fire at least twice and remember to squeeze every time you fire. I'm telling you all this slow, but you go over it, imagine it, do it on the firing range until you don't even think the words, and if the time comes, and God willing it won't, you'll do it right."

The first shot staggered Frankie and his mouth dropped open. Hanrahan fired again. Frankie's fingers tightened on the twin triggers and Hanrahan stepped back into the dining room. Pellets went wild, spraying the living room, shattering photographs, windows, the television screen, lamps.

As he stepped back into the room, Hanrahan fired his third shot. It entered Frankie Kraylaw's face just above the mouth. Frankie fell back against the front door and slid to the floor, the shotgun clattering against and badly scratching an end table Maureen's parents had given them on their wedding day.

Hanrahan knew the young man before him was dead, but he had too much from his father and had seen too much in his life as a police officer to take any chances. He fired once more. The bullet entered just above the stomach. Frankie's body jerked once and then was perfectly still.

"He's coming," Carol cried.

This time Velma was in the room almost instantly, just as Carol was sitting up on her elbows, eyes wide, looking toward the dark corner of the room and the partly open door of the bathroom.

"Nobody's coming," Velma said softly, comforting, easing Carol back down, touching her perspiring head.

"David," Carol whispered, resisting the strong, thin hands that urged her back.

Seven-Thirty in the Evening

Lieberman just missed rush hour, which allowed him, in spite of the winter treachery of the Tri-State Tollway, to get to La Grange in about an hour. He hadn't made the trip in at least a year. No reason to go before now. This time he had barely noticed as he drove past the old Polish church, downtown with the odd illuminated windows of the Sears Tower, miles of factories south of the Loop, the old and new Comiskey Park.

He listened to the news until they reported nothing he didn't already know about the death of his nephew and the condition of his nephew's wife. When a fast-talking reporter came on with basketball news, Abe switched stations. He had no quarrel with the Bulls or the Bears, but the

Cubs were his love, had always been. Somewhere deep in a drawer lay a baseball signed by both Hank Sauer and Frankie Baumholtz. He had autographs of Roy Smalley, Ernie Banks, Andre Dawson, Ron Cey, and Bill Nicholson on programs tucked into one of the cardboard boxes in the basement. But Lieberman was not wedded to the past. He loved the present Cubs as much as he had loved those of the past. He didn't even mind that, regardless of a constant parade of talent, they inevitably faded and failed in the closing stretches of each season. Whoever donned the uniform fell under the Cubs curse, to be talented and loved and fail to win. It reminded Abe of one of Todd's Greek tragedies, but he couldn't remember which one. Maybe all of them.

David had gone to some of the Cubs' games with Lieberman when David was a kid. Maish could take or leave baseball. Lisa fought against joining Abe after the first time he had coaxed her into going. He had even bought his daughter a blue satin jacket with CUBS emblazoned on the back. But his nephew David, a short, pudgy kid with a serious round face, had loved to go. He watched each game with a scorecard in hand, keeping careful track of each pitch and accepting hot dogs, cotton candy, peanuts, and Pepsi handed to him by his uncle.

Abe had taken his nephew only half a dozen times, had bought him both a jacket and a cap. Now he wished he had taken him more often. He also wished he could remember the face of his nephew as a grown man, but he couldn't. All he could imagine was the round face of the little boy turning to him in slow motion with a smile when Wayne Terwilliger or Ron Santo drove in a run.

For the last ten miles or so before he hit the Ogden Avenue exit and went east toward the hospital, Lieberman listened to WJJD and sang along with the oldies, the real oldies. Bess had told him repeatedly that he had a good voice, but Abe had no illusions and so he sang along respectfully with Peggy Lee, Rosemary Clooney, Bing Crosby, Teresa Brewer, Tex Beneke. He sang, remembering most of the words, "Again," "Moonlight and Roses," "Till the End of Time," "This Old House," and "Rose, Rose I Love You."

When he pulled into the hospital parking lot, Lieberman was reasonably calm. He hadn't eaten at the temple reception, but he wasn't hungry. He hadn't allowed himself to dwell on what had happened, at least not until this ride to confront the man who may have killed his nephew. He had done his best to think of this as a standard investigation, not one involving the murder of the pudgy child of his only brother. He had done his best, but it hadn't been enough.

The hospital was small, and Lieberman had no trouble finding the right floor. And he had no trouble finding Fu—the hospital was not teeming with Oriental men. Fu was seated in front of the door to George DuPelee's room, which the duty nurse had pointed out after Lieberman had properly identified himself.

Fu, who looked tired, turned off his Tetris game, put it in his pocket, got out of the chair, and stood with his hands at his sides as Lieberman approached.

Lieberman introduced himself, holding out his hand.

Fu took it and said, "I think it's your guy. Fur hat mentioned in the bulletin has the initials D.E.L. sewn in."

"David Eugene Lieberman."

"Weapon we . . . He a relative?" asked Fu, pausing.

"Nephew."

"Sorry."

"The weapon," Lieberman prompted.

"A thirty-eight Smith and Wesson Terrier. It was in his pocket. State troopers have it," Fu went on. "Should match the gun that killed the victim and shot the wife."

"Different weapons," said Lieberman. "Wife was shot with a thirty-eight. David was shot with a forty-five."

The smell of the hospital corridor taunted his empty stomach.

"That a fact?" said Fu. "I'll have our people check the bullets we took out of DuPelee. Maybe we'll get a forty-five match there."

"Wouldn't surprise me," said Lieberman.

"Guy in there should be dead," said Fu, shaking his head. "Shot twice in the back, missed the spine, vital organs, unless you think the gall bladder is a vital organ. I don't even know what the hell it does."

Lieberman knew, knew what every organ was responsible for and capable of. In the last decade, each one of Lieberman's organs had demanded attention.

"Well," Fu went on when Lieberman didn't speak. "Short on blood. Son-of-a-bitch walked maybe two miles bleeding inside and out. He's lucky it was so cold. Blood froze."

"He can talk?" asked Lieberman.

"Doctor says if he's up to it, he can talk."

"Let's try."

Fu pushed open the door. The room was dark except for a night-light over the bed where George DuPelee lay on his side with his eyes closed. The two detectives moved closer to the bed.

Fu whispered, "George, open up. You've got a visitor."

The patient tried to turn away from the voice. Pain surged through him and he groaned, opening his eyes.

"Hurts like a goddamn. You know what I mean?" George said thickly. "Like a goddamn. Who you?"

"Sergeant Fu and Detective Lieberman," said Fu.

"Water," George said, licking his lips.

"I'll ask the nurse when we go," said Fu.

"Detective Lieberman has a few questions for you."

And so, standing at the bedside of George DuPelee, Lieberman spoke as Fu took out a Sony pocket recorder and turned it on.

LIEBERMAN: Your name.
GEORGE: George Anthony DuPelee.
LIEBERMAN: Where were you born?
GEORGE: La Brea, Trinidad.
LIEBERMAN: How old are you?
GEORGE: Twenty-seven.
LIEBERMAN: Do you know why we're talking to you?
GEORGE: Man, he shot me. You want to find him.
LIEBERMAN: Yes.
GEORGE: I never seen him. He give me a lift, shot me. All I know, man. Could use some water now.
LIEBERMAN: What did he look like?
GEORGE: Young, white, skinny, jumpy.
LIEBERMAN: He didn't take your money.
GEORGE: I think it was one of those, you know, race things, hate crime, you know? This guy he call me names, everything.
LIEBERMAN: Where did you get the money?
GEORGE: Worked, all cash. Jobs here,

there. Shining shoes, busboy, like that, you know?

LIEBERMAN: The hat.

GEORGE: Hat?

LIEBERMAN: The one you were wearing. Where did you get it?

GEORGE: Hat? Let me think. I'm hurtin' now, you know, my memory? Hat. I remember. Someone give it to me this mornin'. Yes, big fella like me. Said he jus' got it but it didn't fit. Nice guy.

LIEBERMAN: A woman named Carol Lieberman was shot this morning. So was her husband. The husband died. She didn't. I'm going to take your picture and show it to her. What do you think she'll say?

GEORGE: Don't know. I think I better get me some sleep now.

LIEBERMAN: I think the gun you had in your pocket is going to match the bullet they took out of the pregnant woman.

GEORGE: Got to sleep. Weak.

George closed his eyes and Fu turned off the tape recorder.

"Let me talk to him for a minute," Lieberman said wearily. "Won't take more than a minute."

Fu looked at George and then at Lieberman

before he shrugged and said, "Two minutes."
Then he left the room. Lieberman turned to
George again.

"Few more questions, George," Lieberman
said gently.

"Later, man."

"Now, George," said Lieberman. "Open your
eyes and talk or I'll shoot you."

"Man," groaned George, opening his eyes. "I
don't have to . . ."

He saw the weapon in Lieberman's hand. It
was pointed at George's face.

"You crazy, man? Why you gonna shoot me?"

"David Lieberman was my nephew,"
Lieberman said calmly. "Now, I'm going to tell
you something and then ask you questions. You
lie or I think you're lying and as miserable looking
a piece of breathing flesh as we both think you
are you will look even more miserable."

"I wanna see the Jap cop."

Lieberman slowly shook his head no and put
the barrel of the weapon against George's forehead.

"You would not shoot me," said George.

"Yes, I will," said Lieberman evenly. "David
went to ball games with me. His father is my only
brother. I'm tired and getting old fast and full of
lies I can tell after I blow your head off. So, who
did you shoot, David or Carol?"

"What I get from I tell you this?"

"To live," said Lieberman. "And maybe a
good word about your cooperation."

George closed his eyes again.

"Raymond shot the man," said George. "Got no call to protect him. He shot me, too."

"Why?"

"Why what? Why he shoot me? I don't know. We was goin' back to the Islands and he . . ."

"He's from Trinidad."

"Yeah, that's right. He shot your kin, not me."

"No," said Lieberman, "you shot a pregnant woman."

"I was confused. Shooting. Screaming. Confused."

"Where can we find Raymond?"

"He got a place over in the city, over a store. I don't know streets so good. 'Sides, we packed up and left that place."

Lieberman put his gun back in his holster.

"I think," said George. "I bes' see me a lawyer."

"That would be best," Lieberman agreed, moving to the door. "Get a good one. I'd say you don't have much of a case, shooting a pregnant woman during a robbery."

"Can't think now," said George.

"Get some rest. Get a lawyer."

"Yeah. Say, I didn't mean to kill nobody. Never hurt anyone in my life. Then this. I didn't want to go way up there and rob someone. Didn't want to rob nobody, but Raymond got me going. I thought he was my friend till he shot me in the back."

"Things like that do get in the way of a friendship," said Lieberman.

"Maybe you see him you jus' shootin' him down like the wild dog he is," said George, licking his lips and closing his eyes again.

"Maybe I will," said Lieberman, moving across the room.

"Don' forget about my water," George said in the glare of the lamp. "I think I be talkin' too much. Delirious. Don' know what I be sayin' here."

"Tell your lawyer," said Lieberman, opening the door.

In the hall, Lieberman briefed Fu on what George had said. Fu didn't ask how he had persuaded George.

"I think maybe I'll get George some water and talk to him again," said Fu, shaking Lieberman's extended hand.

"I'll stay in touch."

On the way back to Chicago, Lieberman didn't listen to the news or golden oldies from the big-band era. He didn't listen to talk-show hosts hanging up on callers. He listened instead to a voice within him speaking in a deep Islands accent telling him something he didn't want to hear.

Lieutenant Kearney sat in the kitchen of William Hanrahan's house drinking a cup of coffee. Kearney was forty-two years old, roughhouse good-looking with a broken nose and a reputation for common sense that had earned him the promotion and move to Clark Street. He had been in line for even better things, a comer, well connected, well liked, engaged to Carla Duvier, whose father owned a good part of the North Side of Chicago and its suburbs. And then, a few months ago, it had all blown up when Kearney's former partner, Bernie Sheppard, had gone mad, killed some people, ruined Kearney's reputation, ended Kearney's relationship with Carla Duvier, and put his promotion to captain on permanent hold.

Kearney was considered by those who worked with him to be a good cop, a patient cop, a cop with nothing to gain and little to lose, a cop who backed his men as he had not been backed by those above him when the going got rough.

Kearney sat across from Bill Hanrahan and waited. He had time and the coffee was newly perked and hot.

Hanrahan's fingers played on the cover of a record album he had retrieved from the ruins of his living room. It was *The Music Man*, Maureen's favorite. The record was shattered now, shattered by a shotgun pellet.

"Good coffee," Kearney said.

Hanrahan nodded. Maureen had loved freshly ground coffee. Ground, unground, instant—it had made no difference to Hanrahan, but Maureen seemed to know the difference and each morning of the last six years of their life together he had ground the beans, half regular, half decaf, before he left for his shift. It was one of the marriage habits he had continued partly, he knew, to keep things from changing or to make them change as slowly as possible. Now . . . He ran his finger over the rough hole in the album, his eyes watching dreamily.

Hanrahan could hear the team from downtown going through the debris of his living room, could hear their feet crunching glass, their voices trespassing on memories. Upstairs, Iris was comforting Jeanine and Charlie while a policewoman took their statements. Cold air raced through the broken windows of the living room and chilled the working cops, including Kearney, who wore his coat fully buttoned.

"He broke into the house," said Hanrahan, fighting back the unreasonable urge to excuse himself and clean up the living room, do his best to make it look the way it had an hour ago.

"And?" Kearney prodded.

"He had the shotgun. I sent the girl and her son upstairs. Kraylaw said he was going to shoot me. He shot and missed. I shot him."

"Missed with both barrels of a shotgun?" Kearney almost whispered.

"I must have shot first. Maybe he was going down when he shot. I think I ducked into the kitchen when I fired."

"You shot him more than once."

"He still had the shotgun."

"He had emptied both barrels."

Hanrahan shrugged wearily.

Kearney got up, stretched, and looked down on Hanrahan, who had pulled out the shattered record and was putting the broken pieces back together in front of him like a jigsaw puzzle.

"O.K.," Kearney resumed. "What else?"

"Nothing else," said Hanrahan.

"Look, if . . ." Kearney began, but stopped when he saw Donna Wheeler, the uniformed policewoman who had been taking Jeanine's and Charlie's statements, come down the stairs off of the kitchen. Wheeler was young, hair short, stocky, daughter of a cop, a pit bull eager to please.

"What you got, Wheeler?" Kearney asked.

Wheeler, not quite at attention, opened her black notebook, scanned what she had written, and said, "Both the mother and the boy say Kraylaw broke in, told them he was taking them. Detective Hanrahan came in. Kraylaw said he was going to shoot. Hanrahan sent them out of the room. Then they heard the shots."

"He said he was going to shoot?" Kearney asked.

Hanrahan looked up and nodded his head yes.

"That's what Mrs. Kraylaw and the boy say," said Wheeler.

"For the record, Bill," Kearney said. "One more time."

"Yes," said Hanrahan, covering the jagged pieces of the record with the bright album cover. "He said he was going to shoot."

"O.K.," said Kearney, rising again. "Thanks, Officer."

Wheeler turned and made her way back up the stairs.

"Hanrahan, on the record, you look like you need some help. Off the record, you look like shit."

"Yeah," said Hanrahan.

"Got someone to talk to?"

"I think so, maybe," said Hanrahan, touching his chin. He needed a shave now. When had he shaved last? This morning? In the tub?

"Do it," said Kearney, heading toward the living room. "Full report in the morning. Details."

"Details," Hanrahan repeated.

And Kearney was gone.

Bill Hanrahan didn't move. He listened to the movement in the living room, went through in his mind what he would have to do to clean up. Cardboard box for the broken glass, Hefty bag, maybe more than one, for whatever was broken. And the door. Last summer some young woman with an accent from lower New York State had come to his door and sold him a gallon of something that was guaranteed to get rid of any stain. Eighteen dollars it had cost him, but she had demonstrated on a coffee stain on the sofa and he had bought it. Four or five clean rags, a few sponges, the stuff in the gallon container, and he would get rid of the blood.

He went slowly up the stairs to the bedroom

on his right, the room that had been his older son's. The door was partly open and Jeanine, seated in the orange University of Illinois chair, was talking to Officer Wheeler, who knelt before her. On the bed, Iris sat next to Charlie, her arm around the boy, talking to him softly. Charlie had not shed a tear. Nor did he look frightened. His expression was blank. Shock. And then the boy sensed Hanrahan and looked up. Their eyes met. Hanrahan forced a small smile. The corners of Charlie's mouth twitched slightly in response.

And then Jeanine was aware of him. She looked over Wheeler's shoulder at Hanrahan. Her eyes were moist and red, her hair a mess. She was still wearing her McDonald's uniform. Their eyes met and Jeanine gave him a pained smile.

"I've got to go out," Hanrahan said.

Wheeler turned and nodded, but he had not spoken to her.

"You want me to go with you?" asked Iris.

"No," said Hanrahan. "I . . ."

He wanted to kiss her, put his head in the curve of her shoulder and neck, be comforted, but he knew he wouldn't do it, not in front of others, maybe not even if they were alone.

"I'll take them to my apartment," Iris said. "I called my father. He said it would be all right."

Hanrahan nodded, turned, and left, deciding when he got to the bottom of the stairs to go out the back door rather than to go through the living room and witness what he had done.

Nine-Sixteen P.M.

The room in which they sat reminded Lieberman of the inside of a musty jewelry box his mother had kept in the top drawer of her dresser until she died. The box that he and Maish had always wondered about and were never allowed to look inside of turned out to hold no surprises. It was lined with purple felt, contained a not-very-good gold ring, a locket with a cameo, and four silver dollars.

Abe remembered touching the cameo, running his fingers over it the day after his mother's death when he had roamed her small apartment alone. He had always liked smooth sculpture, smooth stones or rocks, finely polished wood, and flawless glassware, thin and fine. He had, with Maish's agreement, kept the cameo which now rested on the bottom of his dresser drawer. He had no idea if Maish still had the box. But this room had the feel, the smell of that box.

". . . the casket. You agree?"

Abe realized that the question was aimed at him, but he had no idea what it was. He turned to Mr. Myslish, the funeral director, who was dark suited, businesslike, efficient, too rotund for his own health, and at least double the age of David Lieberman, whose funeral arrangements they were discussing.

241

Abe looked at Maish seated at his side. Maish was lost in his own memories. Abe tried Rabbi Wass, who looked at Lieberman as if the answer to the question was vital to the continuation of civilization as we know it. Abe was not at all sure at the moment that he wanted civilization to continue as he knew it.

"I agree," said Abe.

"Good," said Myslish, breathing a heavy sigh of relief. "Then you will say a few words and Rabbi Wass will close and invite everyone to go with us to the cemetery for interment. Because of the weather, we'll need a tent."

"I will keep the graveside service brief," said Rabbi Wass. "Unless the temperature goes up significantly."

Maish looked around the room. The ceiling seemed particularly interesting to his more than usually moist eyes.

"The only question is who rides in the limousine," said Myslish, "and what the order is for the family cars."

"David doesn't care," said Maish.

"But," said Rabbi Wass, "it will mean something to the way you remember, your wife, his wife remembers."

Maish shrugged.

Everyone sat quietly for several seconds in Mr. Myslish's study, which looked uncannily like the inside of Becky Lieberman's jewelry box.

"So," Myslish said, jumping in to fill the dead silence. "We also have the question of who sits where during the service, which will be held in the large chapel. With all of your friends and relatives and David's and Carol's coworkers, I think we'll need the large chapel."

Voices came through the softness of the purple walls, muffled but harsh, rapid.

"The family, father, mother, uncle, aunt, cousin," said Rabbi Wass, "will sit in the front row. Whether we designate . . ."

The door to the study opened and a man who looked very much like Myslish and was, in fact, his son backed into the room. He was immediately followed by Emiliano "El Perro" Del Sol and the Tentaculos Carlos and La Cabeza. El Perro was wearing jeans, a blue button-down shirt, and a green sports jacket. Carlos and La Cabeza both wore jeans, T-shirts, and heavy black zippered jackets. All three were wearing black *yarmulkes* on their heads, as were the men already in the room.

"*Viejo,*" said El Perro, grinning, his scar shining as the grin stretched his young dark face.

Myslish had pushed himself to his feet and was hurrying around his desk to aid his son, who stood trembling in the middle of the room.

"Gentlemen," said Lieberman, still sitting, "this is Emiliano Del Sol and two of his associates, Carlos Piedras and Jorge Manulito. Emiliano, we are all very impressed by your entrance. Now, please make a less colorful exit and wait for me outside."

Emiliano paid no attention. He stepped farther into the room, with Piedras behind him.

"I never been in a place where they got funerals for Jews," said El Perro, looking around. "But I thought we should dress up a little. Out of respect for you, you know. That's why we put on these little hats from the box out there. We get to keep them or we supposed to put them back?"

"You put them back," Lieberman said calmly. "And this isn't the chapel," said Lieberman. "This is the funeral director's office."

"It's O.K. That's a rabbi over here, right?" asked El Perro, pointing to Rabbi Wass, who stood and faced him.

Abe had to admire Wass, maybe for the first time. There wasn't a trace of fear in the rabbi's eyes.

"This is a private meeting to make funeral arrangements," said Wass.

"Who's that?" asked El Perro, pointing to Maish, who hadn't even turned around to look at the intruders.

"My brother," said Abe, still seated. "It was his son David who was killed."

"I'm sorry," said El Perro. "We're all sorry. Ain't you gonna ask how I found you here, *viejo*?"

"Emiliano is also known as *El Perro*, the dog," Abe explained to Rabbi Wass and the Myslishes, who had taken refuge together behind their massive dark desk. "There are various reasons given why he has such a nickname, but most of them deal in some way with the idea that he has

244

been known to engage in carnal and uncontrolled violent acts."

"He talks good," said El Perro, standing in the center of the room with his arms folded over his chest, legs apart, a torn grin on his face.

"Emiliano likes to pose," said Lieberman. "He has an image to maintain and it derives mostly from old movies and mentors who were themselves influenced by old movies about Mexican bandits."

"I think you are being a little rude now, *viejo*," El Perro said with a sign of dwindling goodwill. "That's not like you."

"It's been a long day, Emiliano," said Lieberman. "Now please wait outside that door."

"O.K., but you should be more careful who you talk to like that," said El Perro.

Carlos continued to stand behind El Perro, hands at his sides, not at all sure of what was going on and decidedly uncomfortable about being in this unfamiliar world.

"I know," said Lieberman. *"Pero, por favor, Emiliano. Yo vengo muy pronto."*

El Perro considered the request for a moment and then turned suddenly and left the room with Piedras and Manulito at his side. Piedras reached back and closed the door behind them.

"The big one's name means 'stone,'" Lieberman explained.

"Entiendo," said the younger Myslish. "What . . . Maybe we should call the police?"

"My brother's a police officer," Maish said

with a sigh. "He knows killers and crazy people. It's his job."

Abe nodded.

"He's a police officer," Rabbi Wass confirmed.

"Go on without me," said Abe, standing. "I'll get rid of Emiliano."

The Myslishes looked relieved. Rabbi Wass nodded and Maish did nothing.

Stepping into the corridor outside the study, Lieberman closed the door. There were four doors in the darkly carpeted corridor. All were closed. El Perro was seated on a bench covered in what looked like red satin. Carlos stood at his side looking decidedly uncomfortable. Jorge adjusted his *yarmulke* and stood, legs apart, hands folded in front of him like a Secret Service agent protecting the president.

"Nice friends you got," said El Perro.

Lieberman stood silently until El Perro continued, with a grin, "I got your guy."

"George DuPelee shot my niece," said Lieberman. "My nephew was killed by a man named Raymond."

El Perro was still grinning.

"What have you got, Emiliano?" Lieberman said.

"Raymond Carrou," said El Perro. "I got his address, but he moved out fast."

"And?"

"I know where he works," said El Perro.

"And that's important?"

"You think I come bustin' in here, messin' with

your grief, if I didn't have somethin' big? I trust you, *viejo*. I give you information. You owe me bigger than we been talkin'."

"What have you got, Emiliano?" Lieberman said with unfeigned weariness.

"I heard the news on the television," El Perro said, fingering his scarred face. "All about what these guys done. And then when we find about this Raymond, it hits me like this."

El Perro suddenly clapped his hands together. The clap went dead in the draped corridor.

"Oigo," said Lieberman.

"Your friend Raymond works in the newspaper and candy stand downstairs at the Stowell Building. Been working there almost four years," said El Perro. "I seen the news on TV about the shooting, your family, and I put things together, you know?"

Lieberman folded his hands in front of him to keep them from shaking.

"Is that worth something or is that worth something?" asked El Perro.

"Yes," said Lieberman. "It's worth something."

"I figured it out jus' like that," said El Perro with pride, snapping his fingers with no more effect than he had achieved with the clapping of his hands.

"I owe you," said Lieberman.

"And you think I'm a *loco* fuck," said El Perro, rising. "Somebody here is even more nuts than me or even more stupid than Carlos."

Carlos stood stone-faced, waiting.

"We're goin'," El Perro went on. "I forgive you for insultin' me. You got a lot on your mind."

"One more thing," said Lieberman. "A favor."

El Perro turned with curiosity and listened to the request.

"If the baby is a boy," Yetta Lieberman said slowly, carefully, as if stating something she had been thinking about for a long time, "we should name him David. If Carol agrees, of course."

Her eyes were long beyond red and puffy. Her entire face was pink and looked to Lisa as if it had been stuffed with cotton balls. Her aunt was calm now as they sat in the kitchen of Abe and Bess's house, the house in which Lisa had grown up and into which she had recently brought her children.

Bess was sitting next to her sister-in-law. Yetta wore a baggy, thrown-on off-white dress with faded purple and red flowers in repeating dull patterns. Bess wore a dark skirt, a white blouse, and a string of pearls. Perfect. Hair perfect. Attitude of concern toward the grieving mother, perfect. And, Lisa conceded, sincere.

Lisa Cresswell had neither her mother's delicacy, grace, nor looks. She didn't have her mother's sense of humor nor her comfortable assurance and leadership. What Lisa had was her children, her intelligence, determination, and a husband she had probably already lost.

Lisa poured more coffee for her aunt and

mother and tried to pay attention to Yetta's rambling.

"You think Carol will say yes?"

"When she's up to it, we'll ask her," Bess said softly. "Maybe she and David had another name picked, one that David particularly liked."

Once again, her mother had said the right thing. If Bess hadn't been there, if the question had been asked of her, Lisa would have said that the decision to name the baby was Carol's and Carol's alone, that it wouldn't be right to try to tell the mother what to name her child. No one had told Lisa. It was she who had chosen the names of her own children. Todd, who had mounted mild campaigns for more Grecian names for his children—Cassandra, Electra, Orestes—had given in to Lisa's determination.

It was also Lisa's determination that had led her to take her children and leave Todd. Dissatisfied with what she had and not knowing where she wanted to go, she had acted abruptly, uncharacteristically, and with apparent certainty.

Before she was forty she had to leave Todd Cresswell. Todd the depressing and often depressed. Todd the apologetic. Todd who escaped to ancient Athens when things got too rough in contemporary Chicago.

She had left determined and now she stood, coffeepot in hand, not knowing how she looked or what she was wearing, wondering if her husband was in bed with a woman named Faye while Lisa's children slept in the next room. She had to admit that she was still almost certain that she did not want Todd back. She also had to admit that she was less disturbed by the vague image of Barry lying in bed with his eyes open listening to his father and Faye in the next room than she was by the more vivid image of Todd in bed with this woman. What made it worse was that Abe had liked the woman.

". . . is what I think," said Yetta. "What do you think, Lisa?"

"That we should wait till tomorrow after we've had some sleep to think about it," said Lisa, not knowing what she was supposed to think about.

Three women drinking coffee in the warm, familiar kitchen. Tragedy, Todd's kind of tragedy, had brought them together. Tragedy or not, Lisa felt comfortable, the warm coffee cup in her hand, the erect assurance of her mother across the table, the slouching dismay of her bewildered aunt.

The house was too warm. It was always too warm.

Lisa reached out and touched her aunt's shoulder. The corners of Yetta's mouth twitched into a pained smile and she reached up to touch her niece's hand.

"I don't know if I can face all those people tomorrow," Yetta said.

"I know," said Lisa.

"You'll do fine," said Bess. "We'll be right at your side."

"David's dead," Yetta said, looking at Lisa.

"Yes," said Lisa.

"I keep asking myself," said Yetta, looking at a photo of Aspen on Barney Weitzel's insurance-company calendar next to the refrigerator, "Why would anyone shoot David? Who would do such a thing?"

"I don't know," said Lisa. "People are . . . I don't know."

"Abe will find out, Yetta," said Bess.

Lisa nodded, but it was not her father roaming the frigid streets nor the rush of icy air that would take his breath as he turned corners that she imagined. It was Todd smiling, content, in the arms of some woman whose face Lisa couldn't conjure.

Raymond really had no place to go for another hour at least. He couldn't go to his apartment for fear that something might lead the police to him. He had taken what little there was of value in the three small, bleak rooms. The trunk of the car was full. The little black and white television sat on the backseat looking up at him with a cold, cataracted eye of disapproval whenever he turned around.

Raymond had spent more of the dead man's money on gas but he was not sure where he should go to wait out the hour. He was afraid to go too near the hospital. A policeman might see him with his motor running and wonder what a black man was doing in this neighborhood at night and Raymond, whose mind was racing madly, might not be able to come up with a suitable lie. Keeping the engine running was essential if he was to have enough heat in the car to stay alive.

The radio said the temperature had dropped to fifteen degrees and would go down to nearly zero.

He could not go back to his job. He would call in and say that he had to go back to Trinidad to be with his family, that he could take no more of the cold. Old Wycheck wouldn't mind. He'd find another black or maybe a Mexican for less than Raymond was getting.

He told himself that in a week, two weeks, a month, the police would search less hard if he could stay hidden, and the newspapers and television would have long forgotten.

It was not hard to hide if you were black, smart, and stayed out of white neighborhoods. Raymond had learned that. It was the money that bothered him. The money, and her eyes, looking up at him when George had shot her.

He went down a dark street past a Jack-in-the-Box and found himself next to a high school. He parked half a block down, close enough to the Jack-in-the-Box so that if he was approached by a policeman he could say that he was about to get out of the car to buy some cheeseburgers. He would even get out and buy the cheeseburgers and would explain that the parking lot had been full when he pulled up.

Raymond needed sleep, but he dared not sleep. It wasn't that he feared nightmares, the sight of the dead man with the fur hat, the sight of George lying on his stomach in the frigid ditch of dirt and snow. He feared dreaming of warm breezes and a white sandy beach, of his sister calling him from the street where he was playing cricket with his friends Bryan and Jason, using a dead tennis ball and planks from banana crates, of the cocoa-colored body of the girl named Zeal whose beaded sweat smelled of sweet sugar the afternoon they made love in her father's house. He feared dreaming these dreams and waking to the nightmare that was now his life. And he longed for Lilly.

Raymond turned on the radio. It crackled, and a woman's voice came on.

". . . seems to me that if you can't be safe on the street in a good neighborhood of this city when the temperature is minus zero then you might as well pack it in and . . . when I was a kid in Buffalo we never . . ."

Raymond changed stations until he found music, an old song, a voice that sounded as if it came from the past, a band of mellow brass and memories.

"Just one more chance," the man on the radio crooned, "to prove it's you alone I care for. Each night I say a little prayer for . . . just one more chance."

The walls of the office of Father Samuel Parker of St. Bart's on Granville were filled with photographs, mostly of football players. All the photographs were signed. One, which Hanrahan had seen before, was of himself in uniform, or someone about twenty who used to be him, someone big, erect, confident, with the open face of a boy to whom nothing could happen and for whom the future was open and sunlit.

Hanrahan had parked in the small lot of the church, which had been neatly and efficiently shoveled, probably by Whiz Parker himself. There were two other cars in the lot.

The front door to St. Bart's had been open, and when he entered the warmth of the church interior had drawn him in. Hanrahan had looked at the crucifix inside the door, crossed himself automatically, and looked for the stained-glass window above the door. During the day the window let in blue-red light and cast a dancing image on the wooden floor in the open lobby. Now the glass image of Jesus being taken from the cross had the pale gray cast of winter. The dark lead that formed the crown of thorns on the head seemed faded and the four women in the glass looked weary and defeated, particularly the woman who reminded him of Maureen.

He had been in St. Bart's several months ago, and had had his first confession in more than twenty years. A woman had died, and though Hanrahan had come to the church in search of a witness, he had stayed long enough to confess to Father Parker his own sense of guilt over the murder. Bill Hanrahan had been assigned to watch the victim's apartment. He had gotten drunk at the Chinese restaurant across the street. He had gotten drunk and met Iris and the woman he was supposed to be watching had died. The next day, after confessing to Father Parker, Bill Hanrahan had gone on the wagon, cold, flat, frightened but determined, and he had remained on the wagon. No AA, no talks with the Overton district shrink.

Tonight Hanrahan had walked through the door in the church lobby and down the aisle past a lone skinny woman praying on his left toward the back and an old couple up in front on their knees looking up at the Virgin Mother.

Hanrahan knew where he was going and turned to the right several rows behind the praying couple, turned to the left, eased down the aisle of wooden pews, and moved past the confessional booths to the dark alcove behind which was Father Parker's office.

He had knocked, afraid that Parker wouldn't be there, afraid that he would fall apart and run for the nearest bar on Devon. But Parker had been in, lean, black, welcoming, and dressed in denim jeans, blue cotton shirt, and sneakers.

"Bill," he said, holding out his hand.

"Father," said Hanrahan, stepping into the office.

Parker looked at him for a few seconds, still holding the big policeman's hand.

"I'd like to say it's good to see you," said Parker. "But from what I can see, I'd have trouble getting it out."

"You got time to talk?" Hanrahan said.

"It's my job," said Parker.

"You were on your way out."

"Park district. Basketball league," explained Parker. "My guess is they can play a half without me. Given the weather and the fact that the team we're playing is from South Shore, I have a feeling there may be no game. Have a seat. I'll go make a call and be right back."

It was when the priest was gone that Hanrahan had roamed the room looking at old football photographs, some of which included a Whiz Parker who looked not much younger than he did now. The difference was that the Whiz Parker in the photos was still running on his own right knee, not one made of plastic, pins, and metal joints.

"Sorry," said Parker, coming back into the room and closing the door. "Coffee? Tea? Water?"

"Nothing, Father," said Hanrahan, sitting.

Father Parker didn't move behind his desk. Instead he pulled up a chair and sat a few feet away facing the troubled policeman.

"The ball's yours, Bill," said Parker softly.

"I killed a man tonight, Father," Hanrahan said, looking toward the dark window beyond the desk.

"You want to confess?" Parker said softly.

"That's the problem, Father," Hanrahan said, looking back at the priest. "I don't want to confess. I murdered a man and I don't feel guilty. I murdered a man because I was sure that if I didn't he was probably going to wind up killing his wife and his son."

"And . . . ?"

"And," Hanrahan repeated, shaking his head, "the wife and son lied for me. I killed the woman's husband, the boy's father, and they lied to save me."

Hanrahan remembered Jeanine and Charlie beside him when Frankie Kraylaw pulled the trigger on the empty shotgun chambers, felt them, saw them.

"What do you want from me, Bill?" Father Parker asked.

"Should I let them live with that lie?"

"Are they Catholic?"

"What difference does it make?" Hanrahan said irritatedly.

"Let's put it another way, Bill. Do you want me to talk to them?"

"I don't know. Should I let them live with that lie?"

"Can you?"

"I ask you a question and you ask me a question and nobody answers questions. Nobody ever answers the damn questions and I can never make the damn decisions. Can you for Chrissake just tell me what to do?"

"No, for Christ's sake, I can't," said Father Parker.

"Then tell me what you think."

"I think if you hadn't killed this man, God's will would have been done."

"Sam, he would have killed them," Hanrahan said, getting to his feet and turning his back on the seated priest.

"Maybe," said Parker. "Maybe you could have done something else."

"Maybe," echoed Hanrahan. "Then again, maybe not."

"It's a question of belief, Bill."

"That it is," Hanrahan agreed, looking at the framed photograph of Willie Galimore with his arm around a small black boy who was certainly the priest sitting behind Hanrahan.

"Father, you can't believe if you don't believe. God built that in. Frankie Kraylaw said God talked to him, Jesus talked to him. He believed."

"He was wrong," said Sam Parker with a confidence that turned Hanrahan to face him again.

"How do you know you're not wrong?"

"I have to answer that?" asked Parker, getting out of his chair.

"Another question answers a question. No," said Hanrahan, rubbing his face. He needed a shave. He needed to make up his mind. "Faith. You've got to have faith."

"You've got it or you don't," said Parker. "I can't just hand it to you. You can go through the motions, hedge your bets and make the right moves, but if you don't believe . . ."

"How about I just do the right thing to start with?" said Hanrahan. "And hope the rest comes."

"Pray the rest comes," the priest amended. "How many times have you been through this conversation since you were a kid, Bill? Straight answer."

"With a priest?"

"With anyone."

"Five, six. Couple of times with my father before he died. It's come up once or twice with my partner. There's a case. Abe's a Jew, a good man. Maybe he's got faith in his God. You can't both be right, Father."

"How old are you, Bill?"

"Half a century."

"Make a decision, Bill."

The two men sat in silence and Hanrahan felt it coming a long way off, the memory of Maureen, the choking he felt when he listened to Sarah Vaughan tapes. The first sobs were small. He tried to hold them back, but they wouldn't stop. He looked up at Parker, whose face showed patience, patience and maybe sympathy.

"God damn it," Hanrahan sobbed.

"Let's hope not," said Father Parker.

The tears were coming now, not heavy yet, but coming beyond Hanrahan's control. He put his head in his hand and cried, "Jesus Christ."

"Well, for him you've come to the right place," said Parker softly.

Hanrahan let the tears come now.

"Father, I'd like to confess."

"We can do it here," said the priest.

"No," said Hanrahan, wiping his eyes with the

back of his hand. "Let's do it right. Like last time. Cassock and collar."

Ten Thirty-Seven P.M.

Getting into the hospital had been much easier than Raymond Carrou had expected, much easier than he had hoped for. In the car he had forced himself to come up with excuses to use if he was stopped. It would have depended on who stopped him. A nurse, a doctor he would have told that he was a new man on the cleaning staff. He was even prepared, if stopped by a security guard, to claim that he was a visiting physician in search of the radiology department. He had purchased a clipboard and some paper at a twenty-four-hour Walgreen's on Montrose and he consulted it frequently as he made his way through the hospital avoiding conversation.

Raymond's stomach had gurgled and twisted with fear. The gun had sagged conspicuously in his pocket. But no one had challenged him. People were too busy and he had moved briskly with the air of someone who knows where he is going and is running a bit late. He made sure, when passing anyone, to check his watch and clipboard and shake his head. What they saw was a tall, confident, good-looking black man whose face they would not remember.

The most difficult part was finding the woman.

He had been in hospitals, when his uncle Monroe had the cancer, when his mother had the women's problem. He knew there was an intensive-care unit and that Carol Lieberman had been taken there. This he had discovered with a phone call to the hospital and the explanation that he was one of her coworkers who had heard about the tragedy on the radio. The directions to the ICU were clearly marked on walls and in the elevator.

When he got to the third floor, he made a right turn off the elevator and found an empty corridor. The ICU was at the end through double doors. Luck stayed with Raymond. He pushed through the doors and faced the nursing station expecting to see someone formidable behind the desk. But there was no one there. He could hear the authoritative voice of a woman coming from the open door of one of the rooms.

His plan had been to ask which room Carol Lieberman was in, because a flower delivery was coming. He would hold up his clipboard, look impatient, check something off, look at his watch. If that did not work, he would wait for a shift change and someone else at the desk. But the desk was empty and on a slate board behind the desk, written in ink on rough pieces of white adhesive tape, were the names and room numbers of each patient in the unit. Carol Lieberman was in Room 316. He turned, found 316 on his left, and quickly made his way back through the double doors to the corridor when he heard the authoritative voice of the woman through the open door say, "I'll check with Dr. Saper. If he says you can have juice or water, I'll be right back. Just lie still. Relax."

Back in the third-floor corridor, Raymond found a custodian's closet. The door was open. He stepped in, turned on the light, and found that luck was still with him. Hanging on a peg was a pale gray custodian's jump suit. It was probably too big for Raymond, but that was far better than being too small. He changed quickly, quietly, heart beating faster and faster, and decided that he would watch the door to the ICU for the right moment, perhaps the ward nurse going to the toilet. At worst, he would slouch over and walk in carrying a mop and tell the nurse that there was an old woman in the waiting room holding her chest and looking for a nurse.

Few people passed while he waited. A bald man with glasses, wearing white, looked like a doctor. He had a bad cold. A limping little man in a robe hobbled by dragging a rolling stand with an IV connected to his arm. With his other hand, the old man did his best to keep the hospital robe from flapping open to show his skinny ass. Another old man in a rumpled shirt and jacket came off the elevator. He looked a little like a sad dog as he walked slowly to the double doors of the ICU and went in.

Raymond waited a few minutes more and checked his watch. It was 10:37. The doors opened as he looked up and a thin, gray-haired nurse with a pair of glasses dangling from her neck by a chain came out and made a turn to her left, moving quickly out of Raymond's sight.

He took a deep breath, checked the gun in the pocket of his custodian's uniform, stepped out, and moved quickly to the double doors.

Inside, in the dark hum of the reception area, he turned to Room 316 and was reaching for the door when a voice whispered behind him, "No, Carrou."

Raymond turned quickly, starting to pull the gun from his pocket, but hard metal drove into his stomach.

"That's the barrel of a gun that can make a very big hole in your stomach," Lieberman said. "A lot bigger than the ones you put into David Lieberman."

"You don't understand, old man," Raymond said, his hand still on the weapon in his pocket.

"Keep your voice down, Raymond," Lieberman said. "And turn around, walk through the doors, and turn to your right. Don't say anything else, just walk, now."

Raymond turned and felt the barrel of the old man's gun in his back now, low, cold. He walked through the double doors and, as he was told, turned right.

"You got to let me talk," Raymond said.

"Walk, don't talk," said Lieberman.

Raymond moved down the empty corridor, deciding that when they got to the exit door he would have to try, have to make his move, turn quickly, knock the old man's gun away. If he could do it quietly, he would drag the old man into the stairwell and kill him somehow. Then he would have to move quickly, get to Carol Lieberman, even if it meant killing the nurse. There were no more choices. It was all madness and survival now.

"Stairwell," Lieberman said, and Raymond turned, pushing the hand of the old man to one side.

Raymond Carrou stood at least four inches taller than the man, outweighed him by twenty pounds, and was more than thirty years younger. Once the gun hand was pushed away, it should have been easy. The only problem should have been keeping the old man quiet.

But when he caught a glimpse of the sad hound face before him, Raymond hesitated. There was no fear, no panic, and the gun, which should have gone flying into the wall, was still in the old man's hand.

The old man's right hand came forward in a tight fist ramming deeply into Raymond's gut. Raymond staggered back, putting his hands behind him to keep from crashing into the ceiling-high windows at the end of the corridor. The old man stepped forward quickly and put the barrel of the pistol into Raymond's right ear.

"The man you shot this morning," Lieberman said softly. "He was my nephew."

"I got to tell you . . ." Raymond gasped.

Lieberman put his hand over Raymond's mouth and said, "Shh."

The stairwell door opened and Raymond looked up in the hope of seeing someone who would protect him from the crazy old man with the gun. Two young men came through the door. One was big, a dull blank look on his face. The other was wiry with a wild grin and a scarred face. Both were Hispanic.

"He's gonna kill me," Raymond gasped.

"Viejo," said El Perro. "You gonna kill this brother?"

Lieberman backed away, removing the gun from Raymond's ear. Raymond stood up, his stomach in agony.

"I'm a custodian here, man," Raymond said, finding the roots of his down-home dialect. "This ol' mon he got seeds in his gourd, think I'm someone named Rayman. My name's Walter, see here, right on my uniform. This here is one crazy ol' mon, I tell you."

"Well," said El Perro. "You come to the right place, man. My partner Piedras here and me, we're like special deputy police. You come with us. *Viejo* here won't hurt you."

Raymond staggered toward the two Hispanics and looked back at the old man, who had pocketed his gun and now watched without expression.

"He's a crazy ol' mon," Raymond said as Piedras led him through the door to the stairwell.

When the door was closed, El Perro looked at Lieberman and said, "You owe us big already, *viejo.* This one is free, for the pregnant lady."

Lieberman said nothing, did not move. When El Perro had disappeared through the stairwell door, Lieberman turned and moved slowly down the corridor to the ICU.

The thin nurse with gray hair and the glasses on a chain sat behind the desk again looking at a chart. She glanced up when Lieberman came in and said, "No more than ten minutes, officer."

"No more than ten minutes," Lieberman agreed, and he opened the door to Room 316.

The room was dark except for the soft blue light over the head of the bed. A machine with a gray screen and a moving green blip sat on a cart next to Carol's bed. It pinged softly, somewhat like the sonar Lieberman remembered from his two years in the navy.

Carol lay, eyes closed, facing him. Lieberman closed the door and stepped to her side.

"Carol," he said softly.

She twitched in fear, uttered a gasp, and opened her eyes, looking feverishly around the room until she saw Lieberman. Her hair had been brushed back, but even in this light he could see that she was pale, very pale. Beneath the blanket he could see the bulge of the baby.

"Abe?" she said weakly, looking up at the shadowy figure a few feet from the bed. "I had a nightmare."

"Raymond," he said.

"Raymond?" she repeated, letting her head fall back on the pillow. "Who is . . . ?"

"Raymond Carrou. The nightmare."

Carol blinked and squinted at him.

"He works in the Stowell Building, where you've got your office," Lieberman explained. "He's worked in the lobby shop for almost four years. Only shop in the building. You must have seen him hundreds of times. Good-looking black man."

"Yes," Carol said. "I know him, but . . ."

"He's the one who shot David," Lieberman said.

"He's the one who . . ."

"And you didn't recognize him, couldn't identify him," Lieberman said flatly.

"It was dark, Abe. I was . . . He had just shot David . . ."

"You gave a description of the man. It doesn't match Raymond Carrou."

". . . I'm tired, Abe. I don't feel . . ."

"It was dark, a bad situation," Lieberman said softly. "Lots of confusion. Maybe it was just a coincidence that Carrou picked you and David this morning. Maybe he panicked when he recognized you and he and his partner decided to kill you both."

"Oh, God, Abe. Do you think . . . ?"

"Or," Lieberman went on, "maybe he followed you. Maybe he planned to rape you, he and his partner. Maybe he'd been watching you and followed you. But David put up a fight and Raymond panicked."

Carol's eyes were closed now and her head was shaking.

"How many months pregnant are you, Carol?"

She opened her eyes again and looked at him in confusion.

"Six months," she said.

"More like eight months," Lieberman said. "I looked at the surgeon's report."

"I can't believe . . ." Carol tried, but Lieberman interrupted her again.

"Eight months ago, that would have been in the middle of the summer. David was still in Spain for the Olympics all summer. Network assignment. His big break."

Carol said nothing.

"I'll tell you how it could have been, Carol," Lieberman said. "David was gone. Raymond Carrou was there. Something happened. You. Him. Both of you. Someone got carried away. Someone wasn't careful and you got pregnant."

Lieberman paused. Carol's eyes were closed again. Her lips were dry. She ran her tongue over them but it didn't help.

"You could have had an abortion, but you didn't," Lieberman said. "That's the part I . . ."

"Raymond said he loved me but if I killed the baby, he'd tell David and I'd have to run away with him," Carol said, so softly that Lieberman had to step forward, straining. "If I didn't have the baby, if I tried to abort it, he'd tell David. But the second the baby was born, David would know it wasn't his. I couldn't . . . I couldn't leave everything, run away with Raymond. He . . ."

"So," Lieberman said, "you decided to kill David."

"I didn't think of it that way," Carol sobbed. "I didn't know what to do. I . . ."

"David would be dead. You'd be a grief-stricken pregnant widow. You'd want to go away from the city where he was murdered, away from the memories, go somewhere alone to have your baby. Then we'd get a call or a telegram saying you were coming home, saying the baby hadn't lived."

"No," said Carol. "You make it sound so . . . so simple. I was going to tell all of you that I was going to stay with my sister in Arizona to have the baby."

"Then you and Raymond were going to live happily ever after in Arizona or Trinidad on David's insurance money," Lieberman said.

Carol was shaking her head no.

"I never wanted more than . . . I'd been married for eight years, Abe. Eight years. David traveled. David was busy. David was with other women when he traveled. David was kind, but David wasn't a lover. And David didn't need me. I couldn't think of anything to do."

"Except murder your husband."

"David wasn't a saint," Carol sobbed. "I could tell you things . . ."

"Don't," said Lieberman.

Carol was crying softly now.

"What are you going to do?" she asked.

"Raymond Carrou has disappeared," said

Lieberman, his voice wavering. "I have a feeling he might never be found. When you get out of the hospital, you go to your sister's farm and have the baby. Don't come back. Put the baby up for adoption. Keep it. Up to you. But don't come back. You understand?" he said again.

Carol looked up at the dark figure at her bedside, straining to see his face in the shadows, sure she heard anguish in the voice.

"You'd do this for me? After what I . . ."

"If Maish or Yetta find out about this, it would kill them," Lieberman said.

"I was crazy, Abe," Carol said, reaching her hand toward the dark figure.

He took a step back as the door behind him opened.

"Ten minutes are up," the gray-haired nurse said softly.

"Did David ever tell you he loved baseball?" Lieberman asked.

Carol pulled her hand back, a puzzled look on her face.

"Baseball?"

"Yes," said Lieberman.

"No," said Carol, tears filling her eyes.

Lieberman took one last look at the woman in the bed, turned, and walked past the nurse. He took the stairs slowly to keep his knees from rebelling. He also took them slowly because he wanted to think.

As he went up the last short flight of stairs, he could hear Emiliano Del Sol shouting into the wind, "Then go ahead, man. Fuck you. Only reason I don' have Piedras throw you off is *viejo* would bite off my *cojones* and spit them in my face."

Opening the door with the wind pressing against it was damned hard, but Lieberman managed to get enough room to ease through. The door slammed behind him, almost catching his hand.

He turned into a fierce blast of freezing air that took his breath and threatened to knock him over. The roof was deep in snow. Only the footprints of El Perro, Piedras, Jorge, and Raymond broke the smooth night whiteness, telling the story of their movements.

Raymond stood about twenty feet away at the edge of the roof. His footprints showed a direct long-stride line. El Perro had been pacing, as he now was. Both Piedras and Jorge stood silently shivering, waiting for orders.

"Goddamn, *viejo*. Where you been? We got a little problem here."

"I see," Lieberman said with a shiver, feeling the high snow seeping down his pantlegs.

"Way I see it," said El Perro, jacket open, ignoring the weather, "we let the son-of-a-bitch bastard jump. Hell, he doesn't jump we throw him off. That way it's all done. Jus' like that."

"What did you tell him, Emiliano?" Lieberman said, looking over at Raymond, whose shivering looked more like shock than cold.

"Scared him a little. Warm him up a little for you. That's all," said El Perro.

"Thanks," said Lieberman. "It was very helpful."

"Our pleasure. Besides, we got a deal."

"We've got a deal," Lieberman said. "Wait here. *Por favor*, Emiliano."

Lieberman fought the wind and took a dozen steps toward Raymond, whose oversized hospital custodian's uniform billowed and flapped in the wind.

"Don't come closer or I swear I'm gonna jump," Raymond shouted.

Lieberman stopped, scratched his neck, pulled his knit hat from his pocket, put it on his head, and pulled it over his ears. He plunged his ice-pained hands into his pockets and said nothing.

"I'll jump. I swear to you on my mother's life," Raymond repeated.

"You can walk out of this alive, Raymond," Lieberman said. "If I wanted you dead, you'd be dead."

"But not tortured," shouted Raymond, looking at El Perro. "You know what he said he was going to do to me?"

"I can imagine," said Lieberman. "Hey, it's cold and you're standing too near the edge of the roof. No one's going to hurt you."

"I'm stayin' here," Raymond repeated.

"Suit yourself," said Lieberman. "You come down with me and I'll say you turned yourself in, that you felt guilty about what you did. I'll agree to testify that you cooperated and showed genuine remorse. I'll talk to the state attorney's office about not asking for the death penalty."

"Why would you do that for me?" Raymond asked.

"One condition. You keep Carol out of it. Her working at the Stowell Building is just a coincidence. You don't know her."

"Hey, *viejo*," El Perro shouted behind him. "It's cold up here."

Lieberman ignored him, his eyes fixed on Raymond Carrou, who said, "I still say why, but I know. She's white. I'm black."

"If she goes down with you, it kills my brother and his wife. Raymond, you owe me one."

"How do you figure that?" Raymond asked through chattering teeth.

"You murdered my nephew," Lieberman reminded him. "This morning you . . ."

"The baby," said Raymond. "Hey, tell them to stop inching over here."

Lieberman turned. El Perro, Jorge, and Piedras had moved forward. El Perro's eyes met Lieberman's and the young man held up his hands to show he was stopping. Lieberman turned back to Raymond, who had moved even closer to the edge of the roof.

"All I wanted here was to take the baby back home to my family when it was born," Raymond sobbed. "She would have killed it. You guarantee she won't hurt my baby."

"I've already talked to her. She won't hurt the

baby. The baby will be fine. You give me the name of whoever you want to have the baby and I'll get in touch with them."

"If I don't involve her," said Raymond.

"Whether you do or don't," said Lieberman.

"I didn't come here tonight to hurt her," said Raymond. "I wanted to see how she was, be sure the baby was all right. Maybe find a way for her to get me some money so I could stay around till he was born."

"I believe you," Lieberman said as a wave of wind pushed him back.

"Viejo," El Perro called. "What the fuck you two talkin' about?"

"Go wait in the stairwell, Emiliano," Lieberman said without turning around. "Three more minutes, tops."

"I hate the cold," Raymond said, hugging himself.

"You learn to live with it."

"I don't know if I can keep up my end of the deal," Raymond said, gulping in chill air. "I can try, but . . . You promise you take care of my baby no matter what?"

"I promise," said Lieberman.

"Damn problem is I can't promise," Raymond said, pounding his chest with his right hand.

"Then just do your best," said Lieberman. "What can I tell you?"

"Goodbye," said Raymond. Then he turned, let out a howling scream, and leaped over the edge of the building.

Lieberman took an involuntary step forward.

"All right," El Perro said gleefully. "Now we can get the fuck out of here."

Eleven-Thirty P.M.

When he walked through the front door of his house, Bill Hanrahan expected to be standing in the wreckage of what he had done. Instead, he found a clean, vaguely familiar room and Jeanine Kraylaw in a green robe putting a broken vase in one of two large cardboard boxes.

She looked up at him and got up.

"Charlie's upstairs sleepin'. Been cleanin' up," she said, brushing her long yellow hair back. "I didn't want to push us on Iris and her father. Charlie and I can handle stayin' here."

Hanrahan looking around.

Even the door had been scrubbed. Only the scoured-away layer of paint indicated that it had been marred a few hours earlier. Hanrahan imagined the young woman scrubbing away at the blood of her dead husband.

"I can't let you and Charlie lie for me," Hanrahan said.

Jeanine stood facing him now across the room.

"Wasn't for you," she said. "For him, me. Well, for you, too. You're all the time givin' to us. You even did what you did to Frankie for us.

275

We've got nothing to give but the lie we told. We'd appreciate your taking it."

Hanrahan nodded.

"Didn't think of it that way," he said.

"Put all your things in those boxes," she said, turning away. "Iris helped me. She had to go home to her father. Said she'd call you in the morning. Said to tell you she'd come back tonight if you want her to."

"Thanks," said Hanrahan, looking at the boxes.

They were filled with things he and Maureen had bought for the room. It was as if the moment of violence had wiped away from the room every trace of his wife, including the family photographs.

"Almost done," Jeanine said, looking at the boxes. "I'm sorry about all those things. Some in there you can save."

"I'll throw them all out in the morning," said Hanrahan, moving to his favorite chair and sitting heavily. "Probably spend the weekend going through the whole house throwing things away or packing them up for Goodwill. Maybe my son, maybe Michael will want some if it."

Jeanine stood puzzled.

"She's not coming back, Jeanine," he said, looking around the room.

"Iris?"

"Maureen, my wife. I've . . . Doesn't matter. She's not coming back," he said again.

"I'm sorry," said Jeanine.

"I'm not sure how I feel about it," he said. "You'd better get some sleep."

"Not sleepy," Jeanine said with a shrug. "Tired, but not sleepy. I gotta tell you something horrible. I'm afraid to go to sleep. Afraid I'll wake up and I've been dreamin', that Frankie's still alive. That's a sinful truth."

"It's just a truth, Jeanine."

"Can I sleep next to you tonight?" she asked, hugging herself. "I don't mean . . ."

"I know what you mean," Hanrahan said. "How about moving Charlie into my bed and you sleep with him."

"O.K.," she said with a forced smile.

"Leave the rest till tomorrow," he said. "Goodnight, Jeanine. Thanks."

"Goodnight, Mr. Hanrahan."

He had long given up trying to get her to call him Bill. She turned and went through the dining room door, and he listened to her footsteps go up the stairs.

Hanrahan kicked his shoes off. They were wet with melting snow, but he hadn't taken them off at the door as he usually did. He would sleep there, right there. He wouldn't move from the chair until morning. But first he had something to do. He reached over for the phone on the table near the door and dialed Lieberman's number.

As the call went through, Hanrahan sensed something new in him, and when he heard Lieberman's voice, he knew what it was. If there was ever a moment when he might need a drink, this was it, but Bill Hanrahan knew he neither needed nor wanted a drink.

Fiona Connery sat cross-legged on her bed wearing a flimsy nightgown and watching a rerun of *Cheers* with a bowl of Orville Redenbacher buttery popcorn at her side.

Paul Nathan, physician-in-residence at Glenbrook Hospital, had stood her up. Well, he had called with the excuse of emergency surgery and a schedule shift about two minutes after she had finished showering, dressing, brushing her hair, putting on makeup, and putting in her contact lenses.

"I understand," she had said cheerfully. "Happens to me all the time. In fact, I've got a case I really should be working on."

If she had been a drinker, the case would have been of vodka, the only alcoholic drink that didn't make her retch.

So she had watched television, had not answered a call from her mother on her answering machine, and had put on the diaphanous night-gown to show herself what Paul Nathan had missed. Or might have missed if they went to a third or fourth date.

Then Fiona had made the mistake of answering a call from Don Fredericks, her boss, a call she would have missed had she been out with the definitely bald Paul Nathan. Had she been out, Don would have found Carrie Traub, Daniel Meinike, someone else who would have been given the case. Now, with the snow threatening again, she would have to get up early in the morning, very early in the morning because she had a court date at noon. She would drive to La Grange to interview her newest client, a George DuPelee, who was being charged with the attempted murder of a pregnant woman during a holdup and of being accessory to her husband's murder.

Fiona gobbled popcorn a handful at a time, cheeks full, finding that, for some reason she could not yet identify, she hated Jean Tortereli, not the man who had shot the pregnant woman, not Paul Nathan, not Don Fredericks. Occasionally, Fiona had a distinct distaste for the murderers, child molesters, muggers, and maimers she was called upon to represent, but this was the first time Fiona could remember having *hated* a client.

But hate her she did, and while she watched Cliff try to explain a lunar eclipse to Woody she considered the ways she might withdraw the pending offer of her client's testimony against Lester Alan Wiggs. She considered the ways, knowing deep inside that she would execute none of thcm.

But hating Jean Tortereli was a lot better than facing what she would not admit to herself, that if bald Dr. Paul Nathan called again and asked for a date, she would say yes. And if he bailed out of it, she would probably even give him a third chance.

Fiona would keep a mental notebook and pay back every time he stood her up by doing the same thing to him on the truth or pretext of a legal emergency.

Only by staying even could she keep her respect for Paul Nathan and for herself.

She searched the bottom of the bowl for a few crunchy kernels, letting them cling to the moist tip of her finger and dropping them on her tongue.

All this she would do if Paul Nathan ever called again.

Meanwhile, she would watch *Cheers* reruns, eat popcorn, and create plots against her own client. It had been one rotten day.

When he entered his house, Lieberman could hear the faint sound of the television in his and Bess's room. He removed his rubbers and shoes with a grunt, put them in the closet with his coat, hat, and scarf, and padded across the living room, through the dining room, past the kitchen and bathroom to his room, where Bess lay in bed watching *Nightline*.

"How's Yetta?" he asked, removing his gun and holster and placing them in the night table.

"Lisa's staying with her tonight," Bess said, looking up at him. "Abe, you look terrible, what's wrong?"

"Catching a cold, tired. A long day. We got the guy who shot Carol. He's in a hospital in La Grange. The one who shot David tried to get to

Carol. We were watching. He ran up to the roof and jumped. He's dead."

Lieberman locked the drawer with the key at the end of the chain around his neck.

"Do Maish and Yetta know?" she asked.

"I called from the station."

"You're not looking me in the eyes, Avrum," Bess said.

Lieberman looked down at his wife. She wore a pink and white robe he had given her for a birthday, Valentine's Day, Hanukkah, something. She had removed her makeup but her hair was still in place.

"You are beautiful," he said.

"You are not telling me something," she answered.

Behind him Ted Koppel was correcting someone or trying to keep him on the subject.

"Tell me about the funeral," he said, taking off his pants.

"So, we're not confessing," she said.

"We've got nothing to confess," he said, unbuttoning his shirt. "I've got nothing to confess. I'm tired. I confess I'm tired."

"Look at you," Bess said.

Lieberman looked down at his pale body, his slight potbelly, his blue boxer shorts.

"A sight to melt the heart of every woman in Troy," he said, sitting on the edge of the bed and looking at Ted Koppel.

"You'll tell me, Avrum," Bess said.

281

"Eventually. Tomorrow. Next week. You'll tell me."

"Probably," he agreed.

"Hungry?" asked Bess.

"I don't know," he said.

"We'll watch *Nightline* and then I'll make you something with no fat or cholesterol," she said. "Now, go shave."

Lieberman got up and had taken a step toward the bathroom when the phone rang. He turned toward Bess, who had reached over to pick it up.

"Hello," she said. "William? What . . . Yes, he is. Thank you. Maish and Yetta are all right."

She put her hand over the receiver and said, "He sounds like he's been drinking again, Abe."

Lieberman took the phone and sat again. A commercial darted before his eyes: Michael Jordan and Bugs Bunny.

"Father Murphy, you all right?"

"Frankie Kraylaw's dead, Rabbi," Hanrahan said.

It wasn't alcohol in Bill Hanrahan's voice. Lieberman knew that sound too well.

"What happened, Bill?"

"I shot him. He broke into my house looking for Jeanine and the boy. Had a shotgun."

"You want me to come over? Or you come over here? Lisa's staying at Maish and Yetta's and the kids are with their father. Bring Jeanine and Charlie."

"I'm O.K., Rabbi. Jeanine and Charlie seem

O.K. too. I went to church. Just sitting here now."

"Get some sleep, Father Murphy," Lieberman said. "We got the guys who shot David and Carol. I'll tell you the rest tomorrow. Now get some sleep."

"You, too," said Hanrahan. "It's been a hell of a day."

"Hell of a day," Lieberman agreed. He handed his wife the phone and she hung it up.

"What happened?" asked Bess.

"He shot Frankie Kraylaw," said Lieberman.

"The one whose wife . . ."

"The one," said Lieberman, lying back.

"Shot?"

"Killed him," said Lieberman, covering his eyes with his left arm.

"God help me for saying this," Bess said. "But there may be times when it's best for everyone when someone really bad dies."

Bess looked at her husband, who was lying there in his boxer shorts and white cotton socks, face covered by his arm.

"I'll make you a snack," she said, leaning over to kiss his gray-stubbled cheek and starting to get out of bed.

"No," said Lieberman, holding out his right hand. "Just turn out the lights and come into my arms."

"Promise not to snore," she said.

"I'll promise not to sleep."

"Sleep, snore," she said. "I'll get the lights and turn off the television."

"That will do it for tonight," Ted Koppel said. "For all of us at *Nightline*, goodnight."

The television clicked off followed by the lights. And in no more than the beat of a heart or the tick of a clock, Bess was back in bed and cradling her husband's head against her breasts.

Abe Lieberman was asleep almost instantly and dreaming a short time after that, a dream he would not remember when he woke up, a dream in which he sat in a box seat right behind first base with Barry and Melisa on one side of him and Lisa and David as they were as children on the other.

It was opening day and the sun was hot. Rick Suttcliffe was warming up right in front of them. It felt good. It felt right.

Warm-up finished, Rick Suttcliffe, his red beard catching the light, lobbed the ball into the air. It came spinning in slow motion toward Lieberman, who raised his right hand and plucked it out of the sky. The crowd cheered and Barry, Melisa, and Lisa clapped as Abe handed the ball to David, who took it gently in two hands as if it were a fragile treasure. Lieberman heard the umpire shout, "Play ball."

Dr. J.W.R. Ranpur put on his neatly ironed sleeping gown, turned off the lights, turned on the burglar alarm, and went into his bedroom where he turned on the television set and watched and listened to Ted Koppel talk about terrorists for a few minutes.

Then he turned off the television, got into bed, and turned off the lights. He slept with no pillow and no blankets on a queen-size bed with an extra-firm mattress. He always slept on his back, turning seldom to right or left and never onto his stomach.

He reached over and pushed the power button and play button on the remote control that rested on the nightstand.

The scratch of the old 78 record that he had transferred to tape came through like radio static, and then the plaintive voice of Bert Williams singing, "Good Lord, I thought I was prepared, but I wasn't prepared for that. It seems my theory of success was only idle chat."

Yes, thought Dr. Ranpur. Yes and many yeses again. He would hear this tale and the following song, the Preservation Hall Jazz Band's simultaneously happy and sad rendition of "Maple Leaf Rag." His hands would move in the darkness trying to mime the slide of the trombone. His lips would pucker and his cheeks fill with air and he would fall gently asleep as the song finished and the machine clicked off. When the weather changed, perhaps he would make a pilgrimage to New Orleans, perhaps he would even push himself to sit it on a session in Preservation Hall or one of the other places he had heard allowed musicians to sit in.

He did not deny himself thoughts of the man

who was murdered on his lawn this morning. Nor did he deny himself concern for the woman and her unborn child. His thoughts, however, paused on the sad face of the policeman named Lieberman, the one who looked a little like Harry James.

In the morning, he would call the policeman, ask him what had been discovered, perhaps suggest that the policeman stop by for a bottle of green life-herb tablets.

And then, through the sound of Bert Williams saying, ". . . ace of spades," Dr. Ranpur heard another voice in the darkness, the voice of a woman.

For an instant it seemed to be coming from outside and then he knew it was the voice of memory, the voice of the woman who had been shot saying, "Raymond, why?" over the crying wind. He had forgotten this or masked its sad memory, but now it was vivid, clear. It had happened. He had heard these words. But what they might mean he did not know.

In the morning, he would tell this to the policeman with the sad eyes. But for now, he thought, closing his eyes and letting the Preservation Hall Jazz Band carry him away, for now I rest.

It had been a long day.

IF YOU HAVE ENJOYED READING THIS
LARGE PRINT BOOK AND YOU WOULD
LIKE MORE INFORMATION ON HOW
TO ORDER A WHEELER LARGE PRINT
BOOK, PLEASE WRITE TO:

WHEELER PUBLISHING, INC.
P.O. BOX 531-ACCORD STATION
HINGHAM, MA 02018-0531